"I have a few ideas on to loosen you up…"

Luke smiled.

Ignoring the way her knees wobbled at the offer, Kennedy told herself she didn't need his kind of help. She didn't need a man at all. Just because she'd bought a shop whose success relied on free apples didn't mean Kennedy couldn't make a go of it. On her own terms. "If they're anything like your previous ideas, then I'm good."

His grin turned wicked. "I'm better."

Maybe he was, but she was scrappy. And she wasn't about to let some smooth talker with a sexy smile and apple envy steal it. "Doesn't matter since I have the apples. And flexing those big muscles and that golden boy smile won't charm me into handing them over."

"Sweetness, I'm not flexing. This is all natural. And I haven't even tried to charm you," he said lowly.

"Well, don't waste your breath, I'm not charmable."

Luke released both dimples her way, in addition to a determined look that had her stomach fluttering. "Challenge accepted, sweetness."

last kiss of SUMMER

A DESTINY BAY NOVEL

MARINA ADAIR

FOREVER

NEW YORK   BOSTON

Copyright © 2016 by Marina Chappie
Excerpt from *Feels Like the First Time* copyright © 2016 by Marina Chappie

Cover design by Louisa Maggio
Cover image © Masterfile
Cover copyright © 2016 by Hachette Book Group, Inc.

Forever
Hachette Book Group
1290 Avenue of the Americas
New York, NY 10104
forever-romance.com
twitter.com/foreverromance

First Edition: August 2016

Forever is an imprint of Grand Central Publishing.
The Forever name and logo are trademarks of Hachette Book Group, Inc.

The publisher is not responsible for websites (or their content) that are not owned by the publisher.

The Hachette Speakers Bureau provides a wide range of authors for speaking events. To find out more, go to www.hachettespeakersbureau.com or call (866) 376-6591.

ISBNs: 978-1-4555-6227-5 (mass market), 978-1-4555-6226-8 (ebook)

Printed in the United States of America

OPM

10 9 8 7 6 5 4 3 2 1

To Barnaby Dallas.
For teaching me that writers write.
Every day.

Acknowledgments

To my editor, Michele Bidelspach, for believing in my work and pushing me on each book to grow and evolve as a writer. Also for loving *West Wing* as much as I do! To the rest of the team at Forever, thank you for making each and every book sing.

A special thanks to my super-agent, Jill Marsal, for the advice, the guidance, and, most important, the friendship. I couldn't have asked for a better partner to take this journey with. I treasure your expertise and your friendship.

Finally, to my husband, Rocco, and my daughter, Thuy. You are my reason. First, last, and always.

last kiss of
SUMMER

Chapter 1

Kennedy Sinclair had taken only two steps toward her new life and already her toes were beginning to pinch.

"I don't think I have what it takes," she admitted, plopping down on the changing room bench to loosen the buckles on her new *Comme Il Faut* ballroom dance shoes, sighing as the blood rushed back to her feet. The red satin straps were trouble enough—looping tightly around the ankle and pulling across the tops of her toes, pinching off all circulation—but the heels were the real problem. Staggering toothpicks that added enough height to cause lightheadedness and excessive teetering. A result, no doubt, of attempting to perform aerobic activity in depleted oxygen zones.

Or her body's preference for practical.

Too bad for her feet, she was done with practical. At least for the summer, she thought, taking in her matching cardigan set, glasses, and hair secured with a pencil at the back of her neck. Sure, right then, she supposed she resembled the bookkeeper that she was. But in a week's time, the summer semester at the culinary school she did bookkeeping for would end and she would be in Argentina—spending the next few months in the most exciting way possible.

Getting engaged.

"Engaged," she whispered to herself. A warm bubble of giddiness bounced around her stomach and tickled her heart.

Her boyfriend of four years, Philip, had been selected for an educational exchange program, teaching elevated Southern cuisine for the fall semester at one of the top culinary schools in South America. Not that anyone was surprised by the honor. Philip was handsome, charismatic, and the youngest master chef at Le Cordon Bleu School in Atlanta. In addition to being the perfect boyfriend—he scored a solid 9.9 on the compatibility test she gave him on their first date—he was so dedicated to his career that he'd elevated the school to worldwide acclaim.

Sometimes he was almost too dedicated. Not that there was anything wrong with that. Dedicated people tended to be reliable and stable. They had the ability to see things through—something her perpetually unemployed mother could benefit from. But lately Philip had spent so much time heating up his teaching kitchen, he couldn't even manage a simple tangled-sheets stir-fry when he got home.

So when he asked Kennedy to go with him to Argentina, days after she'd found a sizing slip to her favorite vintage jewelry shop, she'd nearly exploded into tears. And had been walking around in a bliss-induced haze ever since.

She'd once read that traveling together ignites romance and intimacy between couples, opens the lines of communication, and builds healthy relationships. So it was the perfect time for them to reconnect, to take their relationship to that next level in an exotic land—to make that commitment into forever.

For her to have a long-overdue orgasm.

What better way to embrace what was to come, than with a new pair of shoes that made her feel sexy, spontaneous, and exotic. Daring even. There hadn't been a lot of opportunity for that in her life. She'd been too busy trying to find a safe harbor in an unpredictable childhood, which left her a little uptight. Okay, she was obsessed with organization and order, but now that she had a secure future ahead of her, and a stable man by her side, it was time to push the comfort of their relationship a little and experiment with new things.

Standing again, precariously balanced on her heels, she looked at her toes in the changing room mirror, then to the sensible cream flats she'd been dancing in for the past few months they'd been taking lessons. The flats matched her outfit—and her future if she didn't do something now to spice it up.

A loud thump sounded from the changing room beside her, followed by a low moan. Thinking someone had teetered right out of their heels, Kennedy pressed her ear to the wall.

"Is everything okay in there?" she asked, dropping to her knees when the only response was another thump, this one vibrating the wall between them.

A similar pair of mile-high red heels stood on the other side of the divider, fastened around a set of gorgeous tanned legs, which had a little gold anklet with an orchid charm dangling.

Oh my God! It was their tango teacher, Gloria. The woman who had inspired Kennedy to come to class early and try on the red shoes in the first place. The twenty-two-year-old Latin ballroom champion had legs to her neck, enough hip action to tempt the pope, and wore raw sex appeal like most women wore perfume.

And speaking of hip action!

Kennedy covered her eyes, then peeked through the cracks of her fingers to watch as a pair of black and white, very classy, very masculine, wing-tipped shoes stepped toe to toe with the red heels, one of which lifted off the ground to lightly trace up the outside edge of her partner's leg and wrap around in a perfect *caricia*.

The wing tips stepped even closer, another thump ensued, then Kennedy heard the telltale sound of a zipper lowering.

Frozen, Kennedy watched as the wing tips started rocking in a perfect T-A-N-G-O rhythm, working toward, what Kennedy *knew*, would be a standing O. Back and forth, they swayed as the soft moans turned louder and the panting drifted under the dressing room door.

Kennedy found her hands were a little sweaty because for the first time in her life, she didn't have the right answer. Should she sneak out of the room and run for it?

A good choice, except she'd never been all that graceful and didn't have a sneaky bone in her body. Even worse, the hinges on the changing room door squeaked when she had come in, and getting caught would make for an awkward class. And she really loved their class.

It was the one hour a week when she had Philip all to

herself, his undivided attention as he'd swept her across the floor, making her feel elegant and feminine. For a woman born with the coordination of a gazelle in snowshoes, it was something of a feat—something she wasn't willing to lose.

Which left hiding until they finished. An option that rather intrigued her. In fact, Kennedy felt embarrassed, intrigued, and a little bit naughty all at the same time. She also felt a tinge of disappointment, which started in her chest and moved up into her throat, because leaving the lights on was as kinky as Philip got. So this might be as close as Kennedy would ever be to a standing-O-Tango.

With that sobering realization, she took a seat, pulled her knees to her chest, and stared at the wall. Which was all kinds of ridiculous.

It wasn't as if she could see anything through the wood divider, but sitting there in her red shoes gave her the courage to imagine. Only she didn't have to imagine much since the thumping got louder—and so did the dancing duo next door.

"Ai, papi," Gloria said, her accent making every vowel sound like a promise. "You are such a good lo-bar."

"Uh," was all Mr. Lo-bar said. A single release of air that was neither sexy nor expected from an experienced Latin Lover. It was more of an admission that he'd had all he could handle. Not that Kennedy was judging—she had crested her comfort level about two moans back.

"Yes! Yes, papi," Gloria mewed and Kennedy closed her eyes. She had to. She was a private person by nature and tried her best to respect others' privacy, so the guilt began to build low in her belly. But before it could settle, Gloria cried out. "Just like zat, Phil-ep."

Kennedy's eyes flew open and the guilt quickly faded to confusion and finally shock. She climbed on the bench to get a look at this Latin lover *Phil-ep* who uttered a simple "Uh" in the throes of passion.

Breath left her body as her heart tried to adjust, to make room for the familiar ache of disappointment pressing in. Because there on the other side of the divider, with his pants around his ankles and another woman around his waist, was the man she lived with, the man she'd planned to spend the rest of her life with, executing moves with Gloria that told Kennedy this wasn't their first tango.

No, it appeared that *Phil-ep* was just exotic people's talk for a cheating, rat bastard of a boyfriend, and suddenly the past few months made sense. His shift in schedule, his sudden interest in "extra" dance classes, the way he pretended to be asleep when Kennedy would snuggle up behind him at night.

She didn't remember making a sound, or maybe the blood rushing through her ears made it hard to hear, but suddenly Philip looked up—and froze. At least she thought it was Philip. Right height, right build, right piercing blue eyes behind wire-rimmed glasses, but he looked different somehow.

"What are you doing here," was all he said. No "I'm sorry," or "Whoops, I tripped and accidentally ended up having sex with another woman," or "Please forgive me." Just "What are you doing here," as though this were somehow her fault.

Maybe it was. What kind of woman didn't know when her boyfriend was sleeping with someone else?

The kind who puts all her eggs in the wrong basket. A trait that had been passed down from Sinclair mother to

Sinclair daughter for five generations. A trait that Kennedy had spent a lifetime trying to overcome, without much luck.

Until today.

"You know what, *Phil-ep?* I have no idea what I'm doing here," she said then stepped off the bench.

Grabbing her purse, she walked out of the changing room, proud that she wasn't toppling over in the heels.

"Wait," Philip said and she heard a lot of rustling of fabric from his stall, but she didn't stop, refused to wait. She'd waited four years for him to pop the question, four years for him to take her on a vacation, to show her the world like he'd promised, and now she was tired of waiting.

Only Philip had always been an efficient dresser and incredibly quick, as Gloria must already know, so he was out of his stall and in front of her before she could make her escape.

"Let's talk about this."

"I am a visual learner, Philip, I think I understand. Tab A, slot B, no further explanation needed." Plus, there was nothing he could say that could make this any less painful—or more humiliating.

"I didn't mean for it to end this way."

Except that, she thought, her heart beating so fast she was afraid it would pop right out of her chest. He'd just broken up with her, in a public dressing room, with his fly down and his mistress listening to every word.

Part of her wanted to ask *why?* Why did everyone else always seem to move on before she got the memo that it was over?

"Well, it didn't end 'this way,'" she said. "Because I reject your pathetic breakup since I broke up with you the second you became *Mr. Lo-bar*."

He stuffed his hands in his pockets, only to remove them when he realized his fly parted. "I never meant to hurt you, Kennedy. It's just that we're so"—he looked at her starched pants and shirt and sighed—"solid."

"Most people would think that solid was a good thing." It was one of her biggest strengths, right along with reliable, steady, accountable.

The look he gave her said that he wasn't most people; that he was no longer looking for solid. Maybe he never had been. Maybe she'd been nothing more than someone to fill the gap between life's high points. A position Kennedy knew well.

"It is, but we've become so predictable"—he shrugged—"boring."

"Excuse me?" she said, the words getting caught on the humiliation that was clogging her throat.

"There is a color-coded, itemized itinerary for our Argentina trip on the fridge." He said it like that was a bad thing. "With Gloria, everything is fun and unexpected and new. Exciting."

Kennedy wanted to argue that she could be fun and exciting, too, try new things. *She* was the one who submitted his application for Argentina—not that *she* was going anymore. *She* had signed them up for dance classes. But then she thought of Gloria and her Latin moves and impulsive tendencies, and figured Philip wasn't willing to settle for classes anymore when he could have the real thing.

"With her, *I'm* exciting," he added.

"Exciting?" she asked, heavy on the sarcasm. The man

thought golfing without a caddy was living on the edge. "You need a humidifier to sleep at night."

At one time Kennedy had thought he'd needed her, too. Just last semester he told her how he slept better, breathed easier, had less stress in his day knowing that she had his back at work and she'd be there when he got home.

Every cell of Kennedy froze in sheer horror because— *oh my God*—she was his humidifier. Kennedy Sinclair, winner of Berkeley's esteemed THE WORLD'S YOUR ABA-CUS award, was a certified life humidifier. Ironic because in that moment, with her whole *solid* world crashing down around her, she found it hard to breathe.

* * *

Whoever said one could never really go home obviously wasn't a Sinclair, because later that night, with all of her worldly possessions in the trunk, a bag of mostly eaten cookies in her lap, and a light dusting of powdered sugar everywhere in between, Kennedy pulled into her grandmother's drive. She'd made this journey a thousand times as a kid, the inevitable walk of shame to Grandma's house whenever her mother's world fell apart.

Only now that she was an adult, making the same pilgrimage felt so much worse. Maybe because it was *her* world falling apart or maybe because instead of packing for her first big adventure—which didn't come from a book or movie—she was once again packing up her entire life, forced to start over.

It was as if Sinclair women were destined to wind up alone and displaced. A disturbing thought, since Kennedy had done everything right, everything in her power to avoid ending up like her mother. The right school, right profession, right man. Yet there she was, single, homeless, and as of tomorrow, unemployed.

From a job she really loved. Balancing books at a culinary institute was the only way to blend her profession and her hobby—baking sweets.

Shoving another cookie in her mouth, Kennedy bent down to pop the trunk, crumbs falling out of God knew where and littering the floorboard. Wiping her mouth on the sleeve of her hoodie, she stepped out of the car, grabbed her suitcase, and walked up the brick pathway to the modest-sized Queen Anne–style house.

Even before her feet hit the landing, she knew Grandma Edna had stayed up and was waiting for her arrival. The "dreaming swing," which hung in the corner of the porch, was moving idly. Perched happily inside with Amos and Andy, her two cats, was Edna Sinclair.

All soft curves and frosted tips, she wore a teal house robe, matching crocheted slippers, and a warm smile. She also had a single strip of toilet paper wrapped around her curlers and secured with bobby pins.

"I'm home," Kennedy said, dropping her suitcase on the welcome mat, which read, WENT BIG AND CAME HOME.

"Figured it was either that or I was about to be robbed." Edna glanced at Kennedy's black hoodie pulled over her head and yoga pants. "Glad it's you, seeing as I made cookies and the boys don't like to share none."

The "boys" sent her their best *disrupt our pet time and we will pee on your bed* glare.

"I made cookies, too." She held up the bag, which was surprisingly light, and joined her grandmother on the swing. They both had to scoot down to accommodate

Andy's swishing tail. "Snacked on them on the way over."

"I can see that," Edna said, brushing at Kennedy's shoulder and unleashing an avalanche of crumbs onto Amos's back. He growled, his little whiskers doing double time.

"Snowball cookies." Kennedy rubbed at a large cluster of crumbs that had collected in her cleavage, but it made only a white smear, so she shrugged and gave up. "They're Philip's favorite. I made a batch while I was packing."

"Did you leave him any?"

Kennedy shook her head. "Just a dirty kitchen. And my resignation."

"That was nice of you." Edna patted her knee and Kennedy's eyes started to burn. "Most women would have assumed letting the air out of his tires was word enough."

Most Sinclair women would have shot first, asked questions second, and then let him pull up his pants after they felt they'd been properly heard. But Kennedy had always been the more reserved one in her family.

"I wrote it in Sharpie across all of his dry cleaning that I had just picked up," she admitted.

"There's that creative, passionate girl I know," Edna said and an unexpected flicker of excitement ignited at her grandmother's words. No one had called her creative and passionate since she was a girl. Instead of being embarrassed by her impulsive behavior, she gave in to it, surprised at how liberating it felt.

Almost as powerful an emotion as the choking fear of not knowing what was next. Of how she was expected to pick up and move on—again.

Torn between laughing and crying, Kennedy settled on

staring out at the Georgia sky and letting the gentle evening breeze be her guide. Like Kennedy, Edna lived in the greater Atlanta area, which meant that the city lights snuffed out most of the stars, leaving an inky blanket over the city. But tonight, there were a few bold ones whose twinkle was bright enough to break through the night and be seen. And for some reason that made Kennedy smile.

"I miss that girl," Edna said, wrapping a pudgy arm around Kennedy's shoulder and pulling her close.

"I do, too." Without hesitation, Kennedy snuggled in deeper, wrapping her arms around Edna's middle and breathing in the familiar scent of cinnamon and vanilla and everything that was safe. One sniff and Kennedy felt her smile crumble and the tears well up.

"They were doing it during the light of day against the wall of a dressing room," she whispered. "With their shoes on. He's never asked me to keep my shoes on."

"Of course he didn't," Edna cooed. "You're a respectable woman who knows the value of a good pair of shoes."

Oh God. Even her grandmother thought she was respectable, and everyone knew that *respectable* was just another word for boring. And boring people wound up living in their childhood bedroom at thirty with the neighborhood crazy cat lady as their roommate. "What if I wanted to keep my shoes on?"

"With what he's been stepping in lately, you should count yourself lucky," her grandma cooed.

"Gloria's the lucky one. He's taking her to Argentina next week." And there went the tears.

She tried to hold them back, but sitting there in her grandmother's arms, once again being the one snuffed out by something—or someone—bigger and brighter, brought back every time her mom had taken off with some guy on some other adventure, leaving Kennedy at home.

"He's the one who cheated, the one who lied, and he still gets to go teach in Argentina, and cross something off his bucket list. And I am stuck in another life time-out." A realization that not only sucked, but also challenged every belief she'd ever held dear. Including the belief in herself.

"That just means you get to check something off your *own* list now."

"That was my list. Argentina was *my* dream." Then it became their dream, and somehow Philip would get to be the one to live it.

"Ah, child, then find a new dream, something fun that doesn't include listening to all that wheezing the jackass does when he gets excited," Edna said, stroking Kennedy's hair.

Kennedy chuckled. "One time he snored so loud, our neighbors thought we were doing it all night."

"Probably thought he'd taken one of those blue pills," Edna said in the same tone she'd read a bedtime story. "Philip doesn't strike me as the most resilient man."

He wasn't, but Kennedy hadn't been interested in sprinters; she was looking for someone who was slow and steady. Only her best chance at going the distance had handed his baton to another woman.

"How can I have any fun when I know he's out there living his life, having shoes on while making whoopee, and tangoing all over my future?"

A future Kennedy had worked so hard to make safe. With a man she thought she could trust.

Edna tsked. "Even as a little bit of a thing, you were so

busy making checks and balances, you let the fun pass you by. Maybe this was God's way of saying you need to let go of the future you planned, and take some time to taste the icing."

The size of a large child, Kennedy still was a little bit of a thing who didn't know the first thing about life's icing. Hadn't had the luxury. Between her unstable childhood then working toward gaining fiscal stability, she hadn't had a lot of time for dreaming, let alone something that whimsical. Sadly, the closest she'd ever come to eating the icing was a fun four years working the morning shifts at a little bakery near campus to put herself through business school.

"I wouldn't even know where to start," she admitted, her voice thick with emotion.

"How about with one of these?" Edna pulled an old journal out from beside her and set it on Kennedy's lap. It was pink, pocket sized, had a well-worn spine and a picture of a cupcake with sprinkles on the cover.

The hurt and disappointment had settled so deep inside, it had turned into aching numbness by the time she'd walked out of her downtown loft for the last time, so she assumed any more pain would be impossible. Yet as she clicked open the gold-plated latch, which was rusty from years of neglect, and saw the swirly handwriting at the top, her chest tightened further.

This disappointment felt different, as though it originated from someplace old and forgotten, and it packed the kind of punch that made speaking impossible.

Kennedy wasn't sure how she managed to let herself stray so far from her life's goal. She hadn't felt the kind of hope and excitement that was apparent in the words she'd written since she discovered that while most people were looking for a copilot to happiness, not everyone had what it took to be more than just a brief stopover. Sadly for Kennedy, she'd figured out early on which category she fell into.

"'Life's short so eat the icing first,'" she read as her finger traced lightly over the words on the first page. Edna had given it to her the summer she'd turned thirteen, when Candice Sinclair had taken off with a truck driver from Ashland, leaving a brokenhearted Kennedy behind with her grandmother.

Kennedy was still naive enough to believe that one day her mother would take her along. That one day the two of them would see the country together like Candice promised. By July, Kennedy had realized that if she were going to live an exciting life, then she'd have to make it happen herself. And she took the *icing first* rule to heart and entered an apple and rhubarb pie in the State Fair. She'd found the recipe in an old cookbook, and Edna had spent hours with her in the kitchen helping her perfect it. Her entry won third place in the junior category, earning her two tickets to the theater in Atlanta. Something she'd always wanted to do, but her grandmother could never afford.

"Look at you, set to take on the world," Edna said, pointing to a photo of Kennedy as a teen. She stood in front of a table filled with winning cakes, lanky and still finding her feet, but the smile she wore was so bright, it burned Kennedy's heart.

She was wearing her favorite blue summer dress that her grandmother had made especially for the fair, and pinned to the front was a third place ribbon.

"I thought I lost this recipe," Kennedy said, looking at the swirly writing on the adjacent page. She'd also forgotten how excited she'd felt when she'd won that ribbon. It was as if she'd finally found some kind of tangible proof that maybe she was special.

Kennedy turned the page and a watery smile spread across her face. There was a photo of her grandma dressed like the queen, wearing pearls, white gloves, and a hat fit for a royal wedding.

"I borrowed the pearls from Pastor Cunningham's wife, and the gloves from Mabel," Edna said, nostalgia lacing her voice.

"You made me that dress," Kennedy said. She'd loved that dress, wore it until it went from midi to mini, and Edna said she was giving too much away for free.

"It's still in the attic."

Beneath each photo was the sweet creation that made that moment possible. A three-tier coconut cake, a recipe straight from her grandmother's Southern roots, that she made the following year. It took second place and she won high tea at the Ritz-Carlton in Atlanta.

It was her fourth attempt, though, a perfect Southern apple and red currant pie with a Georgia pecan crust, that took first place, then took her on a six-week Down Home Sweets journey at the local culinary school, cementing her fascination with small town living, Southern eats, and a deep love for baking.

Kennedy carefully thumbed through the pages of photos capturing some of the most precious moments of her childhood, the respective recipes that made it all possible. Ignoring the photo of her and Edna cooking snowball cookies in their pajamas on Christmas morning, since that recipe would now forever be connected to that rat-fink *lo-bar* and his pathetic "Uh" in the throws of passion, she stopped when she found what she was looking for. At the back of the journal was an extensive and itemized list she'd assembled, her LIFE'S ICING list, which indexed every recipe she wanted to try, every competition she wanted to enter, and every goal she wanted to accomplish, complete with coordinating check boxes.

Not a single one was marked off.

With a shaky breath, Kennedy flipped the page and scanned each item, stopping midway through when her heart gave a little stir.

☐ 39. Make a *Rogel torta* with *dulce de leche*.

She wasn't sure that she had quite mastered the flair for creating the soft, but crumbly texture of that variation of dulce de leche in the Confections of South America class she took over the summer. Let alone something as intricate as the layers of puff pastry required to make one of Argentina's most treasured desserts. But since Philip had robbed her of checking off the first and most important recipe on her list, a *Five-Tiered Wedding Cake*, she was taking what she could get. Because somewhere along the way she'd forgotten that she needed to be in charge of her own destiny.

She remembered it now.

"What I need is a job." One that would allow her to get a new apartment, get back on her feet. Although she had some savings, she needed to make sure her bank account had enough padding so that when she started writing those checks, they didn't bounce.

"Already got you one lined up," Edna said, handing her a printout of a job listing for a pie shop. "It comes with a little frosting, too."

"What's this?"

"Sweetie Pies," Edna said, snatching the paper back and flipping to the next page to display several photos of a quaint brick storefront and their award-winning pies, including the five-pound Deep Dish HumDinger. Between the sixteen Gold Tins hanging in the window and the title of "Best Apple Pie in the Country," the two women in the photo were undoubtedly looking for a true, down-home baker. Kennedy was sadly neither.

"My old friend Fiona owns it with her sister-in-law. She e-mailed me that ad."

"You called her? About me?"

"Of course I did."

"When?" Kennedy's life was still shoved in her trunk.

"The second you said you were heading home," Edna tutted. "Picked up the phone to see if she was looking for some help for the harvest season. Even told her that my granddaughter is a college graduate with a fancy degree from a fancy school, and works at Le Cordon Bleu."

Kennedy was the first Sinclair to finish college, something that gave Edna bragging rights on her side of town. Because people who grew up in this neighborhood seldom got out. But Kennedy had, and there was no way she could go back.

"I worked in an office at Le Cordon Bleu. Writing checks and balancing payroll, not baking pies," Kennedy reminded her grandmother.

"You bake on the weekends, take classes every chance you get," Edna said. "And still manage to win awards."

"I was a teenager, it was the junior category, at the Georgia State Fair." Kennedy looked at the picture of the shop again. It was exactly what she'd dreamed of working in when she'd been a girl. Charming, welcoming, and looked like a mother's kitchen should look—sweet, warm, and a safe place to land. Then she read the address and her head started to pound. "The shop is in Washington State?"

"Destiny Bay. It's a little town on the southern border of Washington, nestled between the Cascades and the Pacific Ocean. Known for apples and, since Fi started baking, pies. It's the perfect place for you to find a new future."

"Destiny Bay?" It sounded perfect. Even the way it rolled off the lips implied it was the kind of place she could go and forget about her problems at home. Create a new life.

Only running away was a classic Candice move, and Kennedy would rather take dance classes from Gloria than be like her mother. Then again, she didn't really have a home any longer, so it wasn't as though she would be technically running away. "Isn't that where you met Grandpa Harvey?"

"I met him in Seattle, near where I grew up, but followed him all the way to Destiny Bay, where he got down on one knee, right there in the middle of town, with a bouquet of spring posies and his mama's ring." Edna sighed dreamily, as if remembering the day, and Kennedy gave in to the romantic nature of her story. "Met Fiona there, too, she was my maid of honor, my best friend, and the person who took me in when Harvey moved to Tuscaloosa, making it clear it was a journey for one. Fi gave me a job selling apples on her family's plantation so I wouldn't starve to death."

Kennedy sat up and shook all that romantic naïveté right off.

She was a finance girl, not a frivolous girl—and baking pies in the meantime to get over a broken heart only prolonged getting her life back on track. And kept the Sinclair curse alive and well. Which was why she refused the urge to make a life-changing decision because of a man.

"I don't want to spend the last few weeks of my summer baking pies. I need to buckle down and find a new job."

"Oh, you wouldn't just be baking, honey." Edna leaned in and lowered her voice as though she was imparting a national secret. "I have it on good word that Fi isn't looking for short-term help, she and her sister-in-law co-own it, and are looking to pass on their legacy. They're looking for a strong-willed, sensible woman, who loves baking and is brave enough to carve out a little slice of life's pie for herself."

"And there aren't any of those in their hometown?"

Edna laughed. "Fi's got herself a slew of nephews, and Paula a son, but not a single female in the family. And Paula's got the arthritis, which is why Fi's still baking pies every day even though she's got more miles on her than my old DeSoto. She's ready to slow down and retire, and Paula needs to give her joints a rest and go on that cruise they've been blabbering on about. They're just waiting for the right owner to come along."

Now it was Kennedy's turn to laugh. "And you think that's me?"

"I think this is one of those opportunities we always talked about, where with a little courage and a lot of hard work, you can change your life."

Kennedy felt her throat tighten. How many times had

she sat right there on the porch swing and wished she could change? Her situation, her options...her life.

And she had.

It'd taken years of hard work and perseverance, but Kennedy had created that new life she dreamed of. A posh downtown apartment, a respectable job, and a man who represented everything her childhood and upbringing lacked.

Only as fate would have it, Philip found her lacking, and Kennedy had lost it all.

Nope. Courage wasn't the problem. Neither was hard work. Kennedy hadn't figured out the difference between an option and an opportunity—between loyalty and love.

"We don't know if it would be a change for the better," Kennedy said.

"That's what's so exciting," Edna said, her eyes lit with excitement. "You can either spend the rest of your life like I did, pushing someone else's pencils and dreams, and end up right here on this front porch, or you could start making some of your own come true."

A strange lightness filled her belly, warming the parts of her soul that had moments ago felt hollow, because suddenly the ridiculous idea didn't seem so ridiculous.

Kennedy had gone into business because she loved the idea of owing her own company, building something of her own that no one could take from her. And this opportunity seemed to combine her two loves with what she was trained to do. But there was one thing Kennedy couldn't seem to get past.

She rested her head on Edna's shoulder and admitted, "I can't even plan my own life, let alone a business." Especially a pie shop in small town Washington.

"Honey, you came out of the womb planning. It's what you do."

A slow panic started to churn in her stomach, moving faster and faster, until she regretted eating three dozen snowballs. Because wasn't that exactly what Philip had said?

"She's willing to sell it to you for a bargain." Edna pulled out a packet from underneath Amos, who let loose a throaty growl, and handed it over. "She almost sold it last year to another buyer, but changed her mind when the woman started talking franchising. Here is the contract she'd had drawn up, told me to have you look it over and give her a call if you were interested."

Kennedy straightened and flipped through the papers. Fi and Edna had both gone through a hassle putting this together so quickly; it was the least she could do.

She took her time, read every word, and decided that it was a standard sales agreement, straightforward and easy to understand. Then she reached the overview of the financials and felt her eyes bulge a little. "Her pie shop made more money last year than Philip did."

"And it was a slow year since they closed up for ten weeks last spring to take one of those senior trips to Alaska," Edna said, sounding wistful.

Kennedy looked over at the woman who had raised her and felt her heart turn over. The dreamy look on her face over the idea of a vacation was a painful reminder of just how much Edna had sacrificed. She'd spent some of her best years raising Kennedy, and most of her retirement savings sending Kennedy to Georgia Tech. Kennedy was diligent about paying her grandmother back, but with her student loans and bills, it was slow coming. Owning this business could change all of that.

"How much is she asking?"

Her grandmother rattled off a number.

"That's it?" Not that it wasn't a lot of money. It was. In fact, it would nearly wipe out Kennedy's entire life savings. But based on the shop's financials, the price seemed extremely low. Which meant either that Edna needed to get her hearing aid checked, or Fi wasn't being honest about the profits.

"Oh, that's the down payment, honey. But since Fi owns the property outright, she's willing to carry the note so you can pay her in monthly installments, with a small balloon payment due at the end of every fiscal year. She also said she'll sell you a few acres' worth of her special apples at cost for the lifetime of the shop and let you stay in her caretaker's house for six months rent-free, so you can get the apartment above the shop cleaned up."

"It comes with an apartment?" This deal couldn't get any sweeter. Having an apartment would allow her to save up enough money for a down payment on her own home someday—one that didn't have a live-in heartbreak waiting to happen.

One that belonged to her.

"The store, the apartment, her recipes, supplies, and name are all yours if you say yes." Edna smiled. "Did I mention Fi's apple pie is a sixteen-time Gold Tin winner?"

Kennedy gasped. Only the highest honor any pie could receive, and it explained the incredible numbers. It was too good to be true, which in Kennedy's world meant it was.

"What's the catch?" Kennedy asked, her eyes narrowing. "And what happens if I can't pull it off? Or I can't make a balloon payment?"

"No catch. But if you default on the payments, the shop

passes back to Fi," Edna said as if the word *default* were
no big deal. As if it didn't cause perspiration to break out
on Kennedy's hands and her stomach to roll with unease.
After a lifetime of being passed back and forth, only to
eventually be passed over by the people who were supposed to love her forever, it was terrifying.

And sure, money would be filtering in for her half of the
condo she and Philip had shared. But she had no idea when
he could make that happen or how much it would even be
worth—details she wasn't ready to face. And money she
couldn't rely on.

"Look at you, already planning yourself right out of an
opportunity," Edna said softly, taking Kennedy's hand in
her frail one, and giving a pat that connected with every
insecurity Kennedy tried so desperately to control. "The
worst that can happen is that it doesn't work out, you check
a few things off your list, get a chance to live in a new and
exciting place, and have memories that will last a lifetime."

In true Sinclair fashion, Edna completely overlooked
that she'd also wind up broke and homeless. Then again,
Kennedy was already the latter, and she'd spent most of her
life being the former. But she'd never been a failure—until
now.

She felt the familiar crushing disappointment close in,
but refused to let it take hold. Because, while the setbacks
caused from her chaotic childhood were out of her control,
she'd chosen the path with Philip.

And she could choose a new path, a path of her own, she
told herself, because more than her fear of failing was the
fear that she'd be sidelined for the rest of her life. Spend
her career behind a desk, managing other people's dreams
and never stepping out to go after something of her own.

Maybe this was her chance. Sure, it didn't come in the package that Kennedy expected, but sometimes the best opportunities presented themselves in the most unexpected ways. And hadn't she just been wishing for some excitement in her simple life?

Kennedy pulled her phone from her sweatshirt pocket, and swallowing down all the *what-if*s that would normally have her wearing out her cream ballet flats, she clicked on the selfie mode of her camera and said, "Smile, Grandma. I need a new photo to go next to my snowball cookies."

"Of you covered in crumbs and crying?"

"Nope, of me going after a little icing." And Kennedy snapped the photo.

Chapter 2

Kennedy was so tired, she wasn't sure what day it was when she finally saw the giant pie-shaped sign that said, SWEETIE PIES. But the second she stepped out onto the cobblestone sidewalk and took in the crisp costal air, all the stress and worry she'd been carrying for the past four days and twenty-five hundred miles vanished.

The daylight was long gone, but a million twinkle lights lit up nearly every storefront on Main Street, while gas lamps lined the sidewalks, casting a warm glow over the town square. Every shop had a brick face, a brightly colored awning, and an array of flowers on the windowsills.

Kennedy closed her eyes, and if she listened hard enough, she could hear seagulls squawking and waves crashing against the rocks in the distance.

"You were right, Grandma," Kennedy whispered under her breath. Destiny Bay was warm and welcoming, and the exact kind of safe landing Kennedy desperately needed. A place she could find her footing, build her business, and plan for a future.

Her future. Her life. The way she imagined it without the restrictions of others.

Feeling courageous and adventurous, two things that had been lacking in years past, Kennedy grabbed her purse and slipped inside the bakery, a warm blast of cinnamon and tart apples greeting her.

Sweetie Pies looked like a turn-of-the-twentieth-century bakery with white iron garden tables, pies stacked in the leaded glass window display, and floor-to-ceiling shelves housing a collection of antique flour tins from around the world. And hanging above the display cases and punch key register were sixteen photos of Fi and her Gold Tin, a snapshot to commemorate each one of her wins.

A reputation of excellence Kennedy vowed to continue.

The bakery was full of customers, some still in their coats waiting to be helped, others relaxing with family or friends at tables while sharing pie and smiling and greeting one another, inquiring about plans for the weekend, how the family was doing, and if they would be in town for the Gold Tin Apple Pie Competition, as though everyone here was one big family.

Kennedy didn't have a lot of experience with family, even little ones, so when the woman next to her smiled and said, "Good evening," then pulled out the chair as if offering to share her table, Kennedy smiled back, then did what any big city girl would do—took a seat at the counter, kept her eyes on the chalkboard menu, and avoided eye contact.

"What can I get you?" a twentysomething co-ed in a

GAMMA GAMMA SIGMA T-shirt asked, holding a pot of coffee. Just watching the steam waft up into the air was enough to make Kennedy yawn.

"I would love a mocha. Double shot with extra whip?"

The woman offered up an amused smile. "We have leaded and unleaded, but I can add a ton of sugar and some whipped cream if that helps."

"Double whip?" Kennedy asked hopefully.

"You bet." The woman grabbed a mug and set it on the counter. "Any pie?"

"Yes." Kennedy looked back at the menu then reminded herself that this trip was all about adventure, being courageous and taking the unknown path. "Surprise me, though. Oh, and I'm here to see Fiona."

A bright smile lit the woman's face, and she patted her hair down. "You must be Kennedy. I'm Lauren, the sometimes baker, sometimes cashier for the shop," she said, sticking out her hand. "Fi told me you'd be stopping by, but I could have sworn she said you'd be here day after tomorrow."

"I got here faster than expected." The moment Kennedy had crossed that Georgia border, she decided there was no going back. She was going to go big or go broke—but there was no going back to her old home. She'd have to find a new one. No matter what.

"I think Fi's already left for the night. It's Channing Tatum Week at the senior center and tonight's showing is *The Vow*. Which is why there is a serious lack of silver hair here." Lauren laughed. "Fi said she was leaving early to get a front row seat. Didn't want to have to use her glasses to see his butt."

"That's a butt not to be missed," Kennedy said with a

wicked grin, then she looked at the unfamiliar inky sky outside and a small chill settled on her shoulders. "She didn't leave a key for me by any chance?"

Lauren glanced around. "I didn't see one, but let me check in the kitchen."

"That would be great."

"I'll be back with your side of whip." Lauren slid a piece of pie across the counter that was nine inches tall and filled the entire plate. "And this is on the house. Fi's HumDinger."

The pie that had started it all.

Mouth watering with anticipation, Kennedy forked off a small slice and lifted it to her nose, impressed with how it held together. She took a sniff, the sweet and tangy scent causing her to sigh. She slid the fork in and—

"Oh my God," she moaned as it melted against her tongue and sent her taste buds into an orgasmic frenzy. "This is better than sex."

"My pie's a prize winner, I'll give you that. But better than sex? Honey, you must be doing it wrong."

Kennedy opened her eyes to find a pistol of a woman in a red SWEETIE PIES apron with spiky white hair, cherry red bifocals, and a name tag identifying her as Fiona. She was squat, floured, and pushing eighty. She took one look at Kennedy and said, "You must be Edna's girl."

Even though the woman seemed as cuddly as a porcupine, Kennedy found herself smiling at the comparison. People were always saying she had her grandmother's baby blues. "Was it my eyes that gave me away?"

"It was your hips." Fi's eyes dropped to Kennedy's backside. "Hope you're not one of those bakers who sample the wears all day long."

"No," Kennedy lied, resisting the urge to peek at her butt.

"Good because I won't have people sampling my product," Fi said. "And why are you so early?"

"I decided not to stop in Montana and drove straight through." A decision she was starting to question.

"That's a long haul," she said suspiciously. "Now, being early is fine, but being late won't fly. Not with me. I run a tight ship. You must have been excited to get here."

"I was." Only now that she was here, little bits of doubt began to creep back in. It started when she realized that half the town was in this bakery, and she didn't know a single soul, and it grew when Fiona pulled out a contract and set it on the counter.

"Now, sign this and I'll take you on a quick tour of the place."

"What's this?" Kennedy asked, still holding to that smile as if her sanity depended on it. Because it wasn't the contract Kennedy had signed; it was an application.

"I need a list of your references," Fi said matter-of-factly. "Need to know who I'm working with. Knowledge is power," she said as if it were a Saturday morning commercial, "plus, it creates positive working conditions."

Kennedy was all for positive conditions, but there was no way she was filling out an application for the business she now owned.

Leaving Georgia to move to Destiny Bay had been impulsive and brave, and she knew there would be consequences. She just didn't expect being steamrolled by a grannie with a 'tude to be one of them.

"I only wanted to have a chance to learn the ropes before you left," Kennedy said diplomatically, even though she wasn't feeling very diplomatic at the moment. "However, if you would prefer, I can come back in two days as expected."

"Leave?" Fi laughed. "Honey, I'm not leaving. Didn't your grandma tell you, me and Paula are staying on. We're going to help you run the bakery. Teach the only other person in the world who has the right to bake my HumDinger what the secret is behind it."

"It must have slipped her mind." Something that she'd take up with Edna later. "But I don't recall it in the contract."

"We can add it if not." The older woman waved a hand as if the contract were an ever-changing agreement. "Right under the part where I agreed to sell you three acres of my best apples at wholesale."

"Plus, Sweetie Pies isn't Sweetie Pies without Fi," a woman two seats down said, gaining her a few nods from the counter, and a "Just ask anyone" from a table by the display. And suddenly Kennedy felt as if she were interviewing—for a place in this town.

She looked out at the customers, chatting like family and bonding over pie and coffee, and that doubt became full-blown panic. The people in this town obviously had decades of shared history, and with history came loyalty.

Kennedy had a history, too. A history that warned her she had nothing but the deed to a pie shop, and if the people of Destiny Bay were forced to choose, that they'd choose their own. Once again leaving Kennedy the odd man out.

A position she'd spent her life trying to escape, and never managing to succeed. Until now. Today marked a new start, her chance to be a part of something larger. And if that meant she had to open herself up to others, even stubborn old ladies, then so be it.

Straightening her shoulders, Kennedy adopted her most professional smile and said, "Of course it isn't, which is why I was hoping you ladies would share your experience with me. I want to be a part of this town, leave my mark, and sharing with me the secrets to your success would help with the transition of ownership. I want to make everything as smooth as possible for the community."

Before Kennedy had even finished, Fi said, "I don't pour coffee, don't work weekends, and I'm not filling out an application."

"Oh," Kennedy said quickly. "I think you misunderstood, I just meant—"

"Did you hear that, Paula? The girl's keeping us on."

"Isn't that just wonderful," Paula said, coming through the swinging kitchen doors. Even though she was at least a decade younger, she walked slower than Fi, leaning heavily on a cane. But she had a smile that warmed the room. "Working with us is going to be as easy as pie. Just you wait."

* * *

Whoever came up with the phrase *easy as pie* obviously never had to shell their own pecans, Kennedy thought as she lifted the side cutter and carefully snipped the pecan hull. The trick was to cut off the ends of the shell and not her fingers—an important lesson she learned yesterday.

The sun was beginning to set over the lush peaks of the Cascade Range, casting a warm glow over Main Street and the historic downtown, when Kennedy flipped the CLOSED sign, ending her first full week as the owner of Sweetie Pies.

She looked around the empty shop, then to the sold-out display case. A strange lightness bubbled up from beneath her chest. She had pie orders up the wazoo, enough dough to cover the Great Smoky Mountains, and hadn't cried over *Phil-ep* once since she'd moved.

She'd been too busy baking her way toward success. Independence. A real life. And it felt good. Liberating even.

So what if she'd gained a few pounds sampling the merchandise? She loved, *loved*, baking. No spreadsheets, no unattainable expectations, and absolutely no one else's agenda to distract her. Nothing but her and a never-ending stream of possibilities in sight. Not to mention sweets.

Pies, turnovers, deep dish, and cobblers; Kennedy was an equal opportunity baker—and taster. Anything that made her shop smell sweet and homey. It didn't take a genius to explain the appeal. Before living with Edna, there hadn't been a lot of sweet and homey in Kennedy's life. And she'd fought tooth and nail for any opportunity that had come her way. Which made her driven and determined.

A good trait to have since business had been going so well she didn't have enough apples or shelled pecans left in the barrel to make a single caramel apple pecan pie— let alone to fill the orders for tomorrow. Which explained the fifty-pound order of pecans and apples she'd had delivered today. Kennedy had no idea how expensive heirloom apples were, or just how difficult pecans were to hull.

So when the mini-apple turnover, sitting all by its lonesome on the top shelf of the display case, started silently calling her name, she ignored it, grabbed the NUT BUSTER apron her grandma had sent with the last shipment of pecans, and got hulling.

Thirty minutes later, the sun had vanished and she sadly had enough pecans to decorate a cupcake. She might love baking, but hulling could suck it. Her fingers were raw, her nails destroyed, and her arm muscles were getting quite the workout. Good thing for her, busting nuts was a skill she was determined to acquire in her new chapter.

A rustle sounded from the back of the kitchen, scaring the life out of her and causing the sliders to jab her palm, slicing the skin. More immediate than the threat of blood was the shadow that could easily belong to Thor coming through her back door.

A big and arrogant shadow because, yeah, it was definitely a man creeping into her shop and stomping all over her fresh start. Although he wasn't creeping so much as smugly moseying—as if *he* owned the place. As if he had every right to help himself to her safe.

Indignant irritation pulsing through her, Kennedy considered saying that she was closed and pointing to the sign on the window, but her burglar obviously knew that since he used the back door. The *locked* back door.

Plus, he was built like one of those MMA fighters with broad shoulders and double-barreled biceps who went by names like The Undertaker or Tank of Terror. In fact, his only hope of sneaking into or out of any place unseen was if it were pitch black and he had a small planet shielding him.

Kennedy grabbed her phone from her apron pocket to dial 911 when Tank bypassed the safe altogether to grab—

Oh, hell no.

Her last six apple pies. Which had been sold, lovingly boxed, and promised to Fi's favorite granddaughter, Elle.

Nothing pissed Kennedy off more than breaking a promise. Nothing except someone playing her for a fool. That the someone in question was a smug man set on burgling away the good in her week only added to her fury.

Acting on pure instinct, Kennedy grabbed the massive rolling pin off the counter. She might not be a trained ninja, but she'd seen *Xena: Warrior Princess* enough times to know how to handle herself. Doing some creeping of her own, she walked right up behind Tank and stuck the handle of the rolling pin in his back—hard.

"Hands off my pies, big guy," she said, then realized he wasn't just big. He was massive. And smelled really good. Like fresh-chopped wood, hot summer nights, and really bad decisions.

She half expected Tank to spin around and do some kind of complicated roundhouse, karate chop to the throat combination to disarm her. Only he kept his hands on her pies and looked over his shoulder, his blue eyes twinkling with confidence as he took in her ponytail to her pink toes, and everything in between.

With his dark wavy hair, the perfect amount of scruff, and a smile that was all swagger and charm, the man didn't need brute strength.

She cleared here throat. "I mean it. One wrong move and I shoot."

"Don't shoot, I'm just trying to figure out what the right moves are, so you wouldn't be so offended by the idea of my hands on your pies." He said it with a grin that was all eye candy and sexy swagger.

It was one of those *Sorry, babe, couldn't help myself* movements that her mom's boyfriends used every time they got caught with someone else's lipstick on their collar.

The same flash of white that Philip gave when he'd come home too tired to tango in the sheets. Only this man knew how to do it right, knew how to do it so that a girl went weak in the knees.

Not that her weak knees had anything to do with *him*. Or that grin. Nope, they were tingling because he had broken into her shop and touched her pies.

Kennedy jabbed him harder with the rolling pin, distracted when it bounced off his muscles. "The right move would be to set my pies on the counter and put your hands in the air."

"Or what?" He turned around, slowly, until her "gun" was pressing into his chest. His eyes dropped to take in her not-so-lethal rolling pin, and when they made their way back up, he didn't look scared at all. He looked amused. "You going to flour me, sweetness?"

"No." She held up her phone, snapped his picture, and waited for his amusement to turn to fear. It didn't. "I'm going to call the cops and report a break-in in process," she said, channeling her inner *NYPD Blue*. "And if you try to run, I will just show them your picture."

"No need," he said, stepping back, not to flee the scene, but to rest a hip against the counter. He casually set her pie boxes down—right beside him. "The nearest *cops* are in Tacoma." He threw up air quotes. "A good couple hours away. Around here, we have a sheriff, and his name is Dudley. He carries a badge and a gun made of metal that shoots bullets, not flour."

"I know Dudley," she said, still holding the rolling pin out, just in case he got any ideas, while she looked for the sheriff's contact info. "He's a good customer. I even have his cell number."

"How about that," Tank said but didn't sound impressed. He reached for the pie boxes again, and without thinking, Kennedy jumped forward and smacked his hand with the rolling pin.

"Ow!" He jerked his hand back and shook out the sting.

Kennedy had the sudden urge to apologize, but swallowed it quickly. She didn't ask him to break in and mess with her day. He did that all on his own. "Keep your hands where I can see them." She waved the pin for emphasis.

"Jesus, I was reaching for the sales slip," he said, snatching it off the box. "Suspicious much?"

With men? Always.

"I don't know. Were you about to walk off with the last six pies and not pay?"

He thought about that for a moment and shrugged. "Fi doesn't charge me."

"Do I look like Fi to you?"

His lips twitched in a way that had her thighs doing some twitching of their own. "Not that I can see. But a quick inspection of your pies will tell me all I need to know." He stuck out his hand with the sales slip. "I'm Luke, by the way."

"I'm not interested." And her pies were taking a permanent vacation from charming men with knee-melting powers. "And I'm still calling the cops, so you can save those disarming dimples for someone who cares." She pointed the rolling pin in the general direction of his dimples.

"Wow, sexy and disarming, huh?" he said as if he wasn't fully aware of their power. "Are you hitting on me, sweetness?"

"You're confusing hitting-on with plain old hitting."

He ran a hand over his jaw; the scruff told Kennedy that his five o'clock was a long time past. "Jenny Miller hit me with a pear in the third grade. The next day she sent me a yes-or-no note." He leaned in and lowered his voice, his breath teasing by her earlobe. "Was all that rolling pin action Southern for flirting? Because up here all you have to do is say, 'Hey, Luke, I think you're sexy.'"

"I'm not flirting with you."

He cocked his head to the side and gave a smile that had her toes curling. "I think you are."

"I think charm clashes with prison orange."

"That might be so, but I bet it goes great with pie."

Warm zings dancing in her chest, Kennedy was too flustered to answer, so she scrolled through her phone to locate Dudley's number. With a grin of her own, she held up the cell so he could see the sheriff's name, put it on speaker, and hit Call.

"Be sure when Dudley answers, you tell him I say hi and that he still owes me a beer," Luke said, crossing one arm over the other. "Then tell him you are interrupting Thursday night poker to report someone touching your pies. I'm sure he'll get right on that call."

"I'm reporting someone *stealing* my pies," she corrected. "And if you'll stop talking, I'll ask him to go easy on you."

"Pe*can*, *pe*can," Luke said in that *tomato, tomah-to* tone, and just the word made her fingers ache. "And if you admit you're hitting me was your way of flirting, I won't press assault charges."

"Press charges?" Kennedy said as the phone rang. "You're the one who broke in, and you're built like a tank. How could I have possibly assaulted you?"

"You look like you went a few rounds in the ring, you're swinging a rolling pin with intent, and your apron says NUT BUSTER. Who do you think Dudley will side with?"

That was when Kennedy noticed her burglar was dressed for the boardroom, not a ventilator shaft. His dark slacks, pressed blue button-up, and silk tie were way too *GQ* for a small town pie shop B and E. Then she looked down at her split knuckles, the smudges of blood on the rolling pin, and saw his point.

The phone stopped ringing and went to voice mail. With a frustrated sigh she dropped her head and silently started counting to ten. She'd made it to three when black dress shoes came into her view. By five, Luke was standing in front of her, his finger gently wrapped around hers—disconnecting the call. And sending one hell of a tingle up her arm. "How about you just admit you like me, and I promise to ask before touching your pies next time, so we can call it a day?"

"I like you almost as much as I like hulling pecans."

"You just haven't spent enough time with me yet." He looked at the cuts on her hands and let out a low, concerned whistle. When he spoke, his voice was soft, full of concern. "Look, I'm sorry about scaring you—"

"You didn't scare me—"

"That wasn't very neighborly of me and I apologize. It's late and you look tired, why don't we pick this up another time. Over drinks."

She must have been exhausted because the idea of a drink didn't seem so crazy. It had been a long week, she was looking at an even longer weekend, and it would be nice to celebrate her small success with someone. Too bad, she still had fifty pounds of pecans to crack, four dozen apple pies to make, and justice to serve. Too many numbers to fit into a single night.

She considered her options. While seeing Luke hauled off in cuffs would make her night, it wasn't worth falling so far behind schedule. Not when she wasn't so certain he'd even be arrested. He hadn't actually *stolen* anything and he might not look the part of a small town hick, but the way he tossed around the sheriff's name told her he was the real small town deal.

Destiny Bay wasn't much bigger than a speck on the map, but it was big on family, apples, and justice. In that order, meaning that having the first sometimes determined follow through on the last. Being a local good ol' boy was nearly as good as being related to the President in these parts.

Knowing that she was going to regret this come tomorrow, she looked at his big, strong hands and said, "I'll make you a deal. If you help me shell that bag of pecans and promise to never come back, I won't press charges." When he went to open his mouth, she added, "And any funny business happens and I call the cops."

He closed it. Then with a raised brow, he said, "Define *funny business.*"

She lifted the rolling pin.

"No funny business," he said with a chuckle. "Got it."

"The tools are on the counter, the rolling pin is within reach. Do we have a deal?" He just stared at her a beat as though she were crazy. "Luke?"

"Yeah, we have a deal, but if I shell this whole bag, I want a pie, made special for me. Hand delivered by the baker, which will be you."

"You hull that entire bag tonight, I'll name a pie after you and even feed it to you myself."

"If I hull the entire bag tonight, they won't be fresh come the weekend," he said as if he were a baking god. And maybe he was. The man had a certain Adonis appeal about him. "Proper nut care is important."

Kennedy did her best not to look amused, but then he smiled and damn if she didn't give in. "Fine, half now."

"And half this weekend." He rested his palms flat on the counter and leaned toward her.

His hands were huge. Big and strong and oh so capable. She forced her eyes back to his. "I won't hold my breath."

With a laugh, he walked over to the bags, lifting one as though it weighed nothing. He carried it into the back room and, ignoring her orders to set it back down, poured the entire bag into an ancient-looking machine sitting in the back of the kitchen that Kennedy had been using to hang her aprons on.

"What are you doing?" she demanded.

"Dreaming about what you'll be wearing when you feed me that pie."

She went to say that wasn't part of the deal, but he pushed the big red button and the machine sprang to life. Noisy gears ground back and forth as pecans were sucked into the machine and crunched.

"What's that?"

"Fi's Nut Buster," he said, leaning in to stick the sales slip to the front of her apron, his fingers purposefully grazing the T and B in NUT BUSTER. "By the way, I'm L. Callahan, Fi's nephew." He pointed to the first name on the slip. "And I think she probably meant the letter L when she called in the order, not E-L-L-E." He tugged on her ponytail. "See you around, sweetness."

Maybe it was the boyish smile he added at the end, or the way he smelled the pies as he carried them out the door, but Kennedy did something she hadn't done in weeks.

She smiled back.

Chapter 3

⌒

Pies in hand, Luke Callahan walked toward Main Street and let his gaze drift back to the shop. The sky was fading from pink to orange as the late summer sun dipped behind the Cascades, creating a silhouette of his hometown, but he could still see Shop Girl through the window. All that big city bluster, and a good dose of mistrust, shining though those baby blues.

With his most neighborly grin, Luke lifted his pies in thanks.

Shop Girl's answer was to lock the deadbolt then disappear back into the shop. A smart move on her part.

She might be as tempting as a sexy fall fling in that flirty yellow dress, strappy little heels, and all those tight curves packed into a pint-sized bombshell of a body, but she reminded him of autumn in the Cascades—challenging, exciting, and unpredictable enough to ward off even the bravest of men. She had a toughness that was impressive, a vibrancy that was exciting, and a warm smile that drew him in. The only thing Luke liked more than a sexy fall fling was a challenge. He thrived under pressure. Had to. If picking up the pieces after his father's death hadn't taught him how, then bringing his family's orchard back from near bankruptcy had.

It took concentration, hard work, and an intense focus that didn't leave room for complicated cuties.

Not to mention, this particular complicated cutie happened to be his mom's new baker. A clear reason to keep his distance, since his mom had been trying to pair him up since he grew facial hair. It had only gotten worse after he father passed away, and Luke had officially become the leading force behind Callahan Orchards.

A strangling sense of regret and obligation knotted in his stomach at the reminder that the greatest man he'd ever known was gone, and it was up to Luke to cement his dad's legacy. To make sure his family was taken care of. Which was why he was ignoring the bright blue eyes and mouthwatering curves in the shop, and heading toward the bar at the end of town.

The Penalty Box was a from-the-tap or straight-up kind of place that was as famous for its handcrafted hard cider as it was for its co-owner, former NHL superstar Bradley Hawk, who had more than one Stanley Cup to his name. Hawk also happened to be Luke's best friend and business partner.

"Hope you're hungry," Luke called out over the crowd as he moved behind the bar to pour himself a cold one.

The place was packed. Not surprising since it was Throw One Back Thursday and the Seahawks were playing football on the big screen. But Luke hadn't come to throw one back or catch the game.

"Jesus, man, what took you so long?" Hawk asked, coming over. He leaned over the bar and gave Luke a hard smack to the back.

"I just landed a few hours ago."

Hawk tugged at Luke's tie. "What's up with the monkey suit? Looking to get lucky, because I haven't seen your pants that pressed since my wedding."

"Funny, since I was the only one that night to get lucky," Luke said with a grin.

Hawk grimaced. "Yeah, well, I rectified that bad decision, and luck is now shining down." Hawk's eyes went the length of the room, focusing on a couple of puck bunnies on the far side. "See that honey sitting over there? She wants to see my championship stick."

"You mean, the blond one wearing the wedding ring?"

Hawk snorted in disgust. He might be the NHL's favorite bad boy, and the town's favorite playboy, but like Luke, he didn't get messed up in marriages. His own or someone else's.

"Nope, the redhead wearing double D's like they're a weapon." Hawk lowered his voice and grinned. "Promised me a Russian if I let her touch the handle. I don't know what the hell a Russian is, but since she has a sweet drawl and is wearing cowgirl boots, I don't think she was talking about her heritage."

"Well, don't get your passport out yet. I said I was stopping by to drop off your pie, not cover the bar."

Hawk's mouth fell open. "Are you serious, bro? A Russian. How many guys get a shot at a redhead pulling a Russian?"

Luke patted Hawk's shoulder in solitude. "A guy who isn't working tonight."

Pouting like a girl, Hawk grabbed a towel and started wiping down the bar. "What kind of wingman are you?"

"The kind who has to get the rest of these pies to the Book Nook before seven." He set the pies on the counter. "My aunt is hosting the Destiny Bay Book Club meeting this month."

Hawk rolled his eyes. "Book club, my ass. There's more illegal gambling going on there than in this bar during the Stanley Cup."

"Even the sheriff is afraid to intervene, which tells you something." When Hawk eventually nodded, Luke added, "Plus, I wanted to drop these by for you to look at." Luke pulled a packet of legal papers from his suit pocket and handed it to Hawk. "Matt Rogers expects our answer by Monday."

Hawk's interest went from the honey at the end of the bar to the packet of papers—and he gave an impressed shake of the head, the weight of the moment not lost. With a single signature, they were both going to take their families' businesses to the next level.

"Matt Rogers wants to offer us an exclusive contract." Just saying the words brought a giddy smile to his face. "If we agree, Two Bad Apples Hard Cider will be served in all of his locations."

"No shit," Hawk said and let out a chuckle. It was gravelly and deep, and full of relief. Luke could relate. This kind of opportunity had been a long time coming. He only wished his dad were still around to see it happen.

Matt Rogers was one of the top restaurateurs in the country. A few months ago, he approached Luke about making a high-end, hand-crafted hard cider for his chain of upscale sports bars.

Hawk was the sports legend. Luke had the apples. And Rogers had the capital to pay in advance. With his dad's secret cider recipe, it was a perfect fit.

"Only, he isn't just looking at Washington and Oregon," Luke said. "He wants to do a complete West Coast rollout before the end of the year."

Hawk met Luke's eyes over the top of the contract. "The entire West Coast would mean supplying thirty-plus bars, in addition to our existing customer base."

"Which was the ultimate plan."

"You mean our *five*-year plan?" Hawk wasn't the kind of guy to show fear, mainly because he had skin as thick as steel, and after a lifetime of facing down the biggest bully in town, then in the NHL, nothing much got to him. But he was as rattled at the proposition as he was excited. Luke could see the sweat beading on his forehead. "We don't have enough apples to fill that kind of order."

They both had a lot tied up in this deal. A lot of money, a lot of time—and a lot of dreams. They were running short on the first two, and Luke refused to give up on the last one.

There were too many people counting on him to even consider passing on this opportunity.

"We don't have five years," Luke said with quiet intensity. "If we tell him we need more time to build to that level of output, he is going to go with another company."

"Problem there is, we need more time to grow to that level of output."

There was that. Even with his dad's winning recipe, it had taken Two Bad Apples a long while to get to where they were. And now they needed to double their business by the end of the year.

Would it be difficult? Sure.

Impossible? Nah, Luke had done the impossible and survived. This would be nothing.

"I think I can convince him to roll out Washington and Oregon in November, and save California for December." Luke pulled a spreadsheet from the packet, one he'd spent the past few days, and plane ride home, working and re-working until it was right.

"You made a spreadsheet?" Hawk said, not impressed.

"It might not have all the color-coded girly shit you do, but it makes sense, and the numbers are right."

While Luke handled the production and partnership, his friend was the numbers guy. Hawk was shrewd, discerning, and so tight his shoes squeaked when he walked. A side effect of living with a father who blew rent and groceries at the track. Not that Luke was complaining. Hawk's penny-pinching ways had allowed them to turn a barn-house hobby into a verifiable business.

"Apple supply will be tight, but we have just enough produce hanging on the trees to fill the first order." Luke pointed to the bottom column. "Then we use the money from that to buy more apples for the California rollout in December."

Hawk studied the numbers, and when he came to the same conclusion as Luke had, he gave a big sigh. "I see how this can work, I do." Hawk looked up and Luke could sense the big *but* that was coming. It was in his friend's eyes. "But I don't see where these apples are that you plan on buying for the second shipment. Every hard cider company in the country is scrambling to find enough apples to keep up with the sudden upward demand."

Heirloom apple shortage was the biggest concern facing the cider industry. There just weren't enough cider apples to keep up with the new consumer trend. With four hundred percent growth over the past five years, the few apples that weren't spoken for were selling for double their value. Which made expanding expensive.

Luke pulled out a stool and sat down. "I put in a call last week to Bay View Orchards. I knew that the father passed away over the summer, and it turns out his family is looking to sell the property before harvest ends."

Hawk let out a low whistle. "Fifty acres of Yarlington Mill and Kingston Black apples would be a game changer for us."

It was also the key to fulfilling a promise Luke made to his dad right before he passed.

Bay View Orchards wasn't just home to some of the most sought-after apples in the country; it had once belonged to Paula and Orin Callahan. His mom used to say that she could spend a lifetime sitting on the front porch swing, looking out at the bay, and sipping cider with Luke's dad. Although the latter part was impossible, Luke was determined to grant her the first wish.

"The family doesn't want to deal with the harvest, which makes them motivated sellers." Luke rattled off the price the family was asking and Hawk laughed in disbelief.

"The bidding might start there, but once word gets out about that many heirloom apples coming on the market, a war will start and drive the price way up."

Luke rested his elbows on the bar top. "Good thing I have a first right of refusal."

"Go on."

"When we originally sold the property to Old Man Stark, I insisted that one be put in. He knew how hard it was for me to sell, how much this property meant to my family, and agreed to a sixty-day period. After that, the Starks are free to put it on the market."

Luke knew enough about contract law from his time in corporate development to ensure that if there ever was a chance to get his mom's home back, then he would work the contract in their favor.

"And you're okay with Two Bad Apples owning the property?" Hawk asked, but Luke knew he was really asking if Luke wanted him to be a part of the deal.

It was his dad's dream to make a high-end cider that could rival reserve wines. He'd perfected his recipe, too. Then cancer struck, and struck hard, robbing Orin of his dream, his family of their legacy, and Luke of his father.

The loss in itself was almost unbearable. That Luke had been living in Seattle, pursuing a career and life as far away from the farm as he could be, and not there for his dad when he needed him most still burned. The memory alone brought that deep, dull ache of regret back, as fresh as if the funeral had been yesterday. He remembered the call, how frantic his mom had sounded, but by the time Luke made it home, his dad was gone and the family business nearly bankrupt.

Luke made a vow that night never to let his family down again. "That's how my dad would have wanted it," Luke said to the man who had been more like a brother to him than a friend. "You are as much a part of the Callahan family as anyone."

Emotion thick in the air, Hawk gave a tight nod, then

took a moment to study the numbers a second time. Even though he took another pass, Luke knew his friend was in. Knew the moment Hawk saw the same promise Luke did, saw what this deal could mean for their company, and what this land could mean for his family.

Hawk cleared his throat. "So you think Rogers will go for a later release in the California market?"

"I know he will." Luke smiled—he knew it was smug, but he didn't care. His trip had been enormously successful, and it felt good to see how the end would play out. "I told him it would be a reserve label hard cider, specially crafted from some of the most sought-after apples. Nothing but the best for his premiere locations in San Francisco, Beverly Hills, Hollywood, and Tahoe. It was what he needed to hear."

"You're a cocky bastard, you know that?"

"When you have the skills to back it up, it's called confidence. And with the money that we get from the first rollout, we can buy Bay View."

Hawk filled up two frosted mugs and handed one to Luke. "To that one stupid decision that changes everything." It was the same thing Hawk had said that fateful day after school when they'd broken into Old Man Whittaker's garage to steal his vintage *Playboy* collection. They managed to find a copy that was post-1969 when Old Man Whittaker surprised them. Whittaker had been looking for his December 1953 issue, Luke wound up grounded for the rest of the semester, and Hawk showed up for school the next day with a black eye.

But their friendship had been cemented.

Luke lifted his mug. "No regrets. Just forward movement."

They both took a hearty drink.

Hawk laughed and shook his head. "Man, I wish I could have seen the look on your mom's face when you told her she was getting Bay View back. I guess that's why she and Fi sold the shop."

Confusion hit hard, followed by an uncomfortable twisting in his gut that left Luke slightly off balance. "My mom's on a cruise and I've only been gone a few weeks. When the hell did they have the time to sell the shop?"

"The new owner moved to town a few days after you left," Hawk said, his smile missing as well. "They sold it to some big city cutie with a sweet little smile. I thought you knew."

Oh, Luke knew exactly the cutie in question. Understood now why she'd been so skeptical.

What he didn't understand was why his aunt had sold Sweetie Pies. To an outsider. Without consulting him first.

"Jesus," he said, the knot in his gut tightening to the point of suffocation. He didn't have a clue as to the nature of the contract, which, if created by Fi, was probably written on a pie tin in lipstick. What if she granted the new owner the accompanying three acres of apples to go with it?

Three acres that could cost him his mom's land.

Chapter 4

⌐

Saturday morning, Kennedy flipped the sign to OPEN and walked behind the counter. The sun had yet to show itself, but a soft yellow glow touched the rooftops of Main Street, illuminating the historic clock tower that sat in the middle of the town square and reflecting off the light dusting of frost that had settled throughout the night.

She had already been awake for over four hours, baking for the past three, yet she was vibrating with energy.

Today marked the official first day of the apple harvest in Washington. Come lunchtime, the downtown area would be buzzing with tourists and locals alike, all seeking out the best apple products in town. Kennedy was certain her pies would top people's MUST BUY list. She'd even baked double the quantity, throwing in a delicious pecan pie recipe she had picked up when her grandmother had taken her to Magnolia Falls for the Miss Pecan Parade.

With crust under her nails, flour on her apron, and

enough cinnamon and nutmeg to pass for a Thanksgiving dessert buffet, she was ready for harvest to begin. Her shop looked amazing and smelled even better—thanks to Paula and Lauren, who had braved the early morning to help her prepare.

Placing an old-fashioned lace-top apple pie on the antique platter in the window, Kennedy added a vase with apple blossom branches to the side. She was arranging a small basket of Sweetie Pies' famous apple turnovers to complete her display when the front door jangled, then opened.

"I'll be right with you," she said brightly.

"No rush, I'm just admiring the display," a husky and amused voice said from behind.

A warm sensation spread through her body and Kennedy convinced herself it was irritation and not attraction she was feeling. Because being attracted to a man who used charm as a weapon, even if his smile had enough punch to make her nipples sigh, was just irresponsible.

And Kennedy hated irresponsible.

According to her results, she needed someone who was loyal, understanding, intellectual, and excelled at verbal communication. A nice guy. Not someone who stole pies, spoke in bro-bonics, and relied on his charm to get ahead.

Adopting her most professional look, Kennedy turned around, and *sweet baby Jesus*, *punch* wasn't the right word. The man was packing enough alpha swagger and testosterone to obliterate all the oxygen in the room. Even worse, Luke was hot.

She hadn't seen it the other day because she'd been thrown off by his smart-ass smile and starched entitlement. But towering there in the doorway, looking cocky and mouthwateringly irritating in a ball cap pulled low and a pair of aviator glasses, she couldn't deny it.

Gone were the suit and tie. Today Mr. *GQ* had put on his Rugged Rancher uniform of worn work boots, faded jeans, and a soft cotton tee that stretched across his chest— highlighting muscles that Kennedy didn't even know existed.

His biceps flexed.

"Good morning, sweetness." The way he said *sweetness* had something entirely inappropriate pulsing below her belly button. And as if she didn't already have enough to deal with, it wasn't purely irritation.

"I didn't expect you to show." She looked at the time on her phone. "Especially this early."

His grin was slow coming, but mesmerizing. "If you didn't expect me to show, it means you were thinking about me."

She ignored this. "Well, you could've slept in, I already hulled the nuts."

Luke didn't look impressed. In fact, he looked confused by the idea of not being needed. To prove her statement, Kennedy pointed to the pecan pies in the window and smiled. It had taken her more than a simple Captain America maneuver of the other bag to get the nuts into the machine, but she had managed.

He paused for a long moment, then that grin grew. "Since you're so capable, maybe you can help me with mine." His eyes fell to her NUT BUSTER apron and lit with amusement. "I prefer a soft touch, though."

He said it as though she were actually interested in his preferences. Which she wasn't. Not one bit.

Kennedy had a business to run, a life to fix—things to

accomplish. And nowhere in that list did it include knowing a man's preferences. Or caring. So with a deliberate eye roll, she wisely went back to her display.

"Okay, seriously, I promised you I'd hull the whole bag," he said. "And I always come through on my promises."

"Yes, well you're a man, which means everything you say is up for interpretation."

"Then you've been spending time with the wrong kind of men," he said quietly.

Damn, that was a good answer. Sweet and completely endearing. A trait she hadn't noticed when he was stealing her pies.

Maybe she'd missed more, something deeper, because what kind of man showed up at 8 a.m. on his day off to help someone hull nuts? Not any kind of man Kennedy had ever met.

Then again, Kennedy wasn't looking to meet a man; she was looking to build herself a future. Find her happy place.

"Thank you, but your help is not needed."

With a parting smile, Kennedy headed toward the counter, giving him a clear sign that this conversation was over. In typical male fashion, he did the exact opposite of what she wanted. He followed her.

"Have a nice day and come again," she deadpanned.

Unsure what to do when he didn't head toward the door and instead came even closer, Kennedy picked up the stack of autumn-themed pie boxes she'd ordered last week, and started assembling them.

"You have to serve me before you can tell me to come again," he said lowly.

A ripple of heat pricked her skin. Blaming it on the turn-of-the-twentieth-century wood oven in the back, Kennedy looked up and smiled her most professional smile. "What can I get you, sir?"

"Hmmm, there are so many options," Luke said, taking his time to catalog each and every option. Too bad he wasn't looking at the display case. He was looking right at her, his gaze laser focused, so intense and full of male appreciation, she began to squirm. And heat. "But today, I'd settle on sharing a piece of pie. With you."

Kennedy swallowed hard, partly because she was flustered. No man had ever looked at her like he wanted to savor her slowly. But mostly she swallowed because there was something about this man that made her wonder what it would feel like to be savored slowly. By him.

"And by *pie*, you mean *sex?*"

"Aw, sweetness, is that big city for you want to have a sleepover? With me?"

Luke flashed her one of those grins that were full of promise and short on accountability. The kind that charmed women out of their panties and into bad decisions. The kind that guaranteed an epically amazing night and an even more epically lonely morning. It was the kind of grin to which smart women were immune.

And enduring or not, Kennedy was always smart. Sure she'd had a lapse in judgment with Philip, and was a glutton for heartache when it came to her mom, but she was past that now. She was moving into the icing phase of her life. And nowhere in that recipe was there room for someone like Luke.

"You are so predictable." She picked up a bag. "Now point to the item in the case that you want, I will put it in this bag here, then you can go back to your day, and I can go back to mine."

"Can't do that. Not until we have a little chat." Luke pulled out a chair and sat down, sprawling his legs out and making himself right at home. "Recently, your days and mine have somehow become intertwined."

He kicked out the chair across from him. When she stared warily at the chair, like if she were to take a seat, it would be agreeing to dessert sex, he added, "Strictly professional. I promise."

He held up the Scout's honor sign and Kennedy regretted snorting earlier, as doing it again now would only be repeating herself.

She looked at the time and, with a resigned sigh, grabbed one of her caramel apple breakfast cakes, two forks, and took a seat. "You have ten minutes until my next batch of pies are ready."

She handed him a fork, which he took with a victorious grin. After savoring his first bite, that grin of his turned to pleasant surprise, and finally blissful pleasure. Kennedy knew her cake was going to be a hit—it was too good not to—but it still gave her a small burst of pleasure to see someone taking joy from one of her creations.

"Oh my God. This is incredible. It tastes like..." He trailed off, unsure of how to finish the sentence. Luke took another bite, savoring it. "Halloween." He took another bite. "Yeah, a Halloween party."

"It's my caramel apple breakfast cake," Kennedy said, remembering the first time she'd tasted it. "My grandma took me to a Halloween fair in town and we saw all these kids walking around with giant caramel apples. The woman selling them was a friend of Gram's, and offered me one for free, but I had just gotten braces."

Luke grimaced. "I tried taffy and braces once. Not good.

Managed to rip out every bracket in one chew. Ended up picking apples for three months solid just to pay my parents back. I imagine caramel would have the same outcome."

"That's what I told the lady." Kennedy had been devastated, not because she couldn't eat the apple, but because her mother had been a no-show that Halloween. Leaving Kennedy nothing more than a giant green pea without a farmer.

Momentary sadness swept over her but she shook it off, reminding herself that it was in the past, and her present and future were up to her.

"The next morning when I woke up, Gram was in the kitchen, and a warm caramel apple breakfast cake was cooling on the counter." Kennedy smiled at the memory, at how once again her grandma had made something sweet out of a bitter moment. "She wanted me to have the same experience as everyone else."

Wanted her to know she was loved and didn't have to miss out on the sweet moments of life just because she'd been dealt a sad hand.

Kennedy looked up and found Luke staring at her with warmth, and maybe something as horrifying as concern. That's when she realized that her eyes were a bit misty.

Startled, and a little embarrassed that she'd shared so much of herself with a practical stranger who made a habit of breaking into ladies' shops, Kennedy reached for her fork. At the same time Luke reached for his. Their fingers brushed and a zap of awareness danced up her arms and Kennedy finally knew where that happy place had been hiding all these years.

Stupid happy place.

"What did you want to talk about?"

"Well, there's the obvious," he said, looking at her hands, which she had crossed over her chest in a defensive stance.

"Strictly business, remember."

"If you say so." When she said nothing, Luke sat forward. "Then let's move on to my apples."

Kennedy didn't know if she was more shocked or disappointed. Of all the possible reasons she could have imagined he had for stopping by, pitching her on his apples was not one of them. She may have been caught off guard at their first meeting, a situation she wanted to avoid happening again, so she'd taken it upon herself to do her homework.

Not that she'd had to dig deep. It seemed news of Luke's homecoming was the talk of the town. According to Proud Auntie Fi, Luke ran one of the largest apple orchards in the state and was co-owner of a hard cider company. According to everyone else, Luke was successful, secure, sexy, and the best catch in nine counties.

"I have more apples than I know what to do with." And she could barely afford those.

That seemed to please Luke, since his shoulders relaxed a little and that grin grew. "Well, that's great news, since I want to buy back your apples."

"This is pleasantly unexpected," she said, sitting back in the chair. "When Fi agreed to sell me the acres of apples at cost, I had no idea how I was going to use them all. I mean, that's like—"

"Forty-eight thousand pounds of apples."

"Wow, I knew it was a lot, but...forty-eight thousand pounds?"

"Approximately."

"Wow," she said again, wondering how many pies she'd have to make to use up all those apples. "So it got me thinking, what happens to the remainder of the apples that are left over at the end of the harvest? Do I pay for them, or is it a wash? The contract didn't stipulate, and I didn't think to ask about it at the time." She'd been too swept away by the thought of owning her own bakery—a good twenty-five hundred miles from Philip and all the disappointments of her past.

"Well, wonder no more," Luke said as if he were the genie, and all she had to do was rub his bottle. "I am willing to offer you ten percent over your cost."

"Really?" That was beyond generous. And a life saver. She didn't want Luke to know, but she had been running the first week's numbers and something wasn't adding up. Her revenue rivaled Fi's, but her profit wasn't anywhere near what she'd expected. In fact, Kennedy was doing little more than breaking even on anything apple-related—which was ninety-nine percent of her merchandise. She needed to offload some of her apples or add some non-apple items to her menu. Maybe she needed to do both. "I can work with that. After I prep and freeze the apples I'll need to carry me through until next season, the rest are yours."

The corners of his mouth twitched, as if her statement amused him. "I was talking about buying all of your apples."

"All of them?"

"All three acres."

Kennedy choked on a laugh, because surely he must be joking. She was the owner of Sweetie Pies, a bakery specializing in apple delectables. She needed apples in order to make pies. And not just any apples, the famous Sweetie Pies' recipe called for specific apples—Callahan apples. "Yeah, that's not going to happen."

Without even blinking, he said, "I'll pay you double your cost. That's doubling your investment in just two weeks of being in business."

A familiar prickle of irritation pulsed behind her right eye. "I have a degree in finance, I can do the math."

"Then you know this is a great deal for you."

He was offering her a ton of money, but something about the way he was posturing himself had warning bells blaring. He'd purposefully worded his offer so that she could either accept or look stupid.

"It's not a great deal for someone who owns a bakery with a big neon apple hanging over the door."

"Listen, sweetness," he drawled, but this time it came off as bad as calling her "little lady." "I will give you enough money to buy an entire orchard of apples. Then you'd never have to pay for apples again."

"I don't need an orchard, I just need those apples. The ones I already have. Because you and I both know that the secret ingredient is Callahan apples, and not those delicious reds that you grow, the special ones," she said, making sure *he* knew that *she* knew her business. "Mixed in with the typical baking apples every baker in America uses, the special ones add a tartness that can't be duplicated. And there aren't many orchards growing this kind of heirloom apple."

Luke's smile faded. Right along with that easygoing charm he normally wielded. In fact, it was the first time Kennedy had seen him look frustrated. His brows puckered and his face kind of folded in on itself, as if he were pouting.

"It's because they're cider apples," he said sharply, and Kennedy could hear the soul-deep frustration in his voice, but it was the desperation she saw in his eyes that got to her. He needed those apples for some dream just like she did. "No one but my aunt would be crazy enough to mix cider apples in with Granny Smiths or Honeycrisps. But one year the frost killed our entire Granny Smith crop and she went rogue."

"Well, it's brilliant." Kennedy leveled with Luke. "And I can't keep Sweetie Pies open without them. So I'm sorry if you were counting on them for your cider, but I use them in some way in nearly everything that's on my fall and winter menu."

They were too bitter and tart to be the main ingredient, but used correctly, they gave a depth to all of her recipes that she'd never been able to reach before.

Luke signed, long and tired, and she almost felt bad for him. Almost. Then he said, "I'll buy you out of the shop. What you paid plus twenty percent. You walk with a nice nest egg and away from all of the risk attached to owning a small business. It's a win-win."

"For who?" Certainly not for her. That kind of money could be a life changer, but she liked the life she was creating. A lot. "Do you think it's as easy as throwing some money my way and I'll just happily up and relocate?"

Luke looked at her as if that was exactly what he thought. And something about that rubbed her the wrong way. The way he casually offered to buy her out of her future, putting a price tag on her dreams, had frustration coursing through her body.

Philip had done the same thing. Buying her out of their condo as if with the exchange of a few bills they were good—and he was forgiven. And she would be just fine.

And why not? It had worked for her mother. And her father.

"What is it with people?" she mumbled, realizing the old Kennedy would have packed up without complaint. Taken the hollow gesture and moved on.

Well, not the new Kennedy. If she was going to pack it in, start over again, it would be on her own terms. Not because someone was paying her to go away. She was ready for some of life's icing, and Sweetie Pies was her best chance to make something for herself.

"I guess I like the risk, because this woman isn't for sale. And neither is her shop." Kennedy stood, but Luke remained in his seat.

She watched him school his features, any hint of softness gone. "Look, I didn't want it to go down this way, but there's no way that contract will stand up in court." He forked off a piece of tart and savored it as if he didn't have a care in the world.

"What does that even mean?"

"I'm trying to be a good guy here." Luke pulled out a corporate check, from Callahan Orchards made out to her, Kennedy Sinclair, with a blank line in the amount section. "Take the money."

"And what? Leave town?" *Find a new place to start over?*

He shrugged. "If that's what you want."

After a lifetime of rejection, Kennedy was good at masking her emotions. A master at ignoring the sting that came with being tossed aside like yesterday's garbage. Any ounce of compassion he'd earned evaporated.

Quick.

Kennedy couldn't believe she'd been so easily hood-winked. A crooked smile, a touching moment over her grandma, and just like that, she'd forgotten that she was done being charmed. Done with men. "You didn't come here to help with the nuts. You came here to take my apples."

"I promised to help, and like I said, I always keep my word." He sounded sincere and genuine all at the same time, and Kennedy felt some of that anger turn to confusion. "And I promise that this is the best offer you're going to get, so I suggest you take it. Everyone knows my aunt wasn't in her right mind when she sold the shop."

"The hell I wasn't!" The door opened and there—with her flapping apron, rolling pin, and a tray full of cooled pies—stood one of Kennedy's helpers. And the crazy aunt in question.

Today her hair was silver spikes, her lips coral and puckered in outrage, and her attitude was as warm and fuzzy as a hornet.

"Not right in the head," she mumbled, setting the trays down. "Been running this town for nearly a century and no one's ever dared to question my sanity."

Kennedy had a sneaking suspicion that their silence on the matter had more to do with fear of retaliation than opinion, but she wisely kept quiet.

"Aunt Fi." Luke stood and took off his ball cap, as if he were twelve and caught tracking mud through the house. "What are you doing here?"

"Helping out our new friend," Fi chided. "Didn't think she could run this on her own right out the gates, now did you?"

"I didn't think she'd be running it at all, especially since you and Mom have turned down every offer I brought your way over the years."

"Unless you're dealing with apples, your pickers always led you astray."

Luke ran a hand through his hair, leaving it in complete disarray, but there was a teasing, a lightness to his voice when he spoke. "Just make sure you explain that to Mom when she comes home from her cruise and discovers that you sold her shop."

"Mom's home," Paula Callahan said, trailing out of the kitchen with a display tray of cookies in one hand and her cane in the other. "And she knows all about the sale."

"What are you doing?" Luke said, his anger about the sale replaced with concern. He easily plucked the tray from his mom's clutches as if it didn't have six five-pound HumDingers on it. "Holding the tray like that is bad for your hands."

"Well, I can't carry it on my head."

"You shouldn't be carrying it at all." Luke set the tray on the counter and took his mom's frail hands in his larger ones. Gently, as if she were the most precious thing on the planet, he massaged her wrists. "That's why you hired Lauren."

"Lauren's in class," Paula said, waving him off as if she didn't love the doting. "And this morning I woke up and thought, I need some time in the kitchen, so I called Kennedy, who was nice enough to put up with two old coots, and keep us on part time."

A decision that in hindsight wasn't so bad, since Lauren was a student at the local university and could only work early mornings before class, and help with the occasional prep in the evenings.

"Now before you go saying things you'll regret, or misquoting facts, come give your mom a hug and tell her about your trip." Paula held out her arms, and Kennedy found herself wanting to walk into them.

An unfamiliar urge that shocked Kennedy to the core since she'd stopped needing hugs a long time ago. She remembered the first time she'd come home from school to find their apartment completely empty. She'd been seven, and her mom's boyfriend decided he wanted to move to Florida—with everything but Kennedy.

Kennedy sat on the porch all night smelling like peanut butter cookies and gardening soil, waiting for her mom to come home and sweep her up in her arms like other moms did with their kids and tell her everything would be okay. That she wasn't losing her home and her school and her friends. Promise her that Daryl was wrong, and Kennedy wouldn't be left behind. But when her mom pulled up after collecting her last paycheck, there were no hugs, no words of comfort, just a story about wanting to see the ocean and how it was a trip for two.

It was a year before she'd see her mom again, a year of wishing for her love and that hug she'd dreamed about but never received. Even after that year came to an end, and Daryl turned out to be Mr. Wrong, there were no hugs. So Kennedy worked hard to keep herself guarded, to keep an emotional distance from anything that could leave her vulnerable.

But there was something so comforting about Paula. A warmth and security radiated from her that drew Kennedy in.

"Only if you promise to stop carrying things that heavy." Luke gave a final rub to the middle of Paula's palm, then clutched both of her hands. "It was good. Better than good."

"I never had any doubt, which is why I made your favorite cookies."

Luke smiled, boyish and a bit embarrassed. It was the first honest smile Kennedy had ever seen from him. It took him from handsome to lethal.

Luke's concern softened and he leaned down and gave Paula a kiss on the cheek, pulling her in for a hug. Kennedy felt a strange tug of longing watching the obvious flow of affection between the two. The way that Paula pulled Luke in as though he were still her precious baby, and how Luke wrapped his body protectively around hers.

It was so intimate, so warm, Kennedy felt as if she were intruding on a private family moment.

She'd witnessed them before, but never having experienced one herself, she was always unsure of what to do. Stay? Leave? Insert herself into the moment?

The first sounded awkward, the last humiliating, so as ridiculous as it seemed, Kennedy was leaning toward leaving—her own shop. On the busiest day of the year.

Thankfully, a buzzer went off in the kitchen, paving the way to a graceful exit.

"I'll get that. It's my pecan pies," Kennedy said, her feet already in motion.

"Pecan?" Fi said, her words puckered like she'd just sucked on a lemon. "Who sells pecans at the Apple Festival?"

"I was just changing things up a little," Kennedy said over her shoulder. "Adding a few new items to spice up the menu."

"The menu is spicy enough," Fi snapped, clearly offended. "And this here is apple country, not pecan country. People around here know that."

"Fi," Paula chided in a sweet voice. "We use pecans all the time."

"As decoration or for texture, not as the star. The apples are always the star!"

"You always know how to balance texture and heart," Paula said, gently taking Fi's hands. "It's what makes your pies so special. Everyone know that."

Kennedy watched as Fi's stance softened, her defensiveness disappeared, and she became warm, even a bit shy at the compliment. Paula took the time to validate Fi's concerns and offer her comfort without caving. It was impressive, and Kennedy wondered how it felt to have a support system like that. Someone who knew your deepest fears, your biggest weaknesses, and loved you through it all.

Her heart a little raw, Kennedy turned to face the older woman. "I'm not taking away any items, Fi, just adding a few."

"You can do what you feel is right," Paula said with a motherly smile that Kennedy was helpless to return. Then to Luke, "She's a smart one, very creative. Pretty, too."

Luke didn't comment one way or the other. Just sent Kennedy an unamused glance.

Off balance by the whole family reunion, and feeling unsure of where she fit into the mix, Kennedy said, "I have pies needing me in the kitchen. You guys have fun catching up."

*   *   *

It was well after closing when Kennedy dropped a ball of dough back onto the cutting board and continued to knead.

One look at the mangled ball of flour and shortening told her she wasn't over Philip's betrayal as she'd originally thought.

Or nearly being chased out of her own place.

By Luke.

It wasn't bad enough that he'd shit all over her morning, a morning that was shaping up to be a pretty spectacular day. He'd gone and made her feel out of place. In her own home.

Okay, so she technically resided in Fi's guest cottage since the apartment above the shop needed more than a little TLC to make it inhabitable. But this shop, the menu, the customers...

They were slowly starting to feel like hers.

After the success she'd had today, another complete sellout with orders already placed for tomorrow's Apple Festival, she knew that she could make it here.

Yet she couldn't get past Luke's offer. How he thought she was the kind of person who would give it all up for money. For a moment, a brief moment of weakness when she'd watched him and his family reunite, she considered it. Considered what it would be like if she never found that for herself, and considered taking the money. Then she realized that this was her best shot at making a home.

Sadly, two weeks into becoming a resident and Kennedy had managed to make an enemy out of the town's golden boy. But that wasn't going to stop her.

With a heavy sigh, she dusted some more flour over the top. Realizing it was hopeless, that even Betty Crocker couldn't save this batch, she tossed it in the garbage and grabbed another ball of dough.

That's when she noticed Paula standing in the doorway.

Luke's mom was wearing the same cream-colored pants and coral-colored knit sweater from earlier, but the weariness that had grown as the day had progressed was gone. Paula looked refreshed—younger.

Free of pain.

"What are you doing back?"

"Saving that dough from a senseless beating." Paula laughed. "Unless you're looking to start selling Play-Doh, why don't you give it a rest?"

Kennedy relaxed her hands. "I'm prepping them for the Apple Festival tomorrow and I have two dozen more pecan pies to go." That wasn't counting the Dutch apple pies and Granny Smith pinwheel biscuits she had left on her to-do list. Kennedy decided after a long day, she'd rather prep everything tonight and get an extra few hours of sleep, then have to be back here at four.

"Honey, no one's going to buy pies missing the magic ingredient."

Kennedy stilled, mid-knead. Had Luke convinced his mom to renege on the sale? "You mean apples?"

"No, dear," Paula mused as if Kennedy were the funniest thing in the world. "People can taste the difference between a pie made out of obligation, and one made from the heart."

Kennedy was short on heart at the moment, but she had spunk. "How about one made from determination?"

Paula gave Kennedy one of those motherly smiles that seemed to warm the whole room. "I guess that works, too."

Kennedy watched as the older woman hobbled over to the little table at the back of the kitchen, and that was when Kennedy noticed the small basket the woman was carrying. Without explanation, she pulled out and placed an array of storage containers on the table that were steaming and smelled incredible. Then from her Mary Poppins basket, she took out two plates, some silverware, matching mugs, and a bottle of wine.

Kennedy's mouth was watering from the heavenly aroma, reminding her that she hadn't eaten since lunch. It was one of the downfalls, she was learning, to being a baker. With all their time spent baking and tasting, there wasn't a moment to actually eat.

"What's all of that?"

"Dinner," Paula said. "I've got twice-baked chicken, sautéed green beans, and a nice salad, all made from my garden. Plus a four-cheese potato torte, which is just fancy talk for potato and cheese casserole." Paula sat down and patted the chair next to her. "Might as well eat it while it's hot."

An unfamiliar sense of warmth rolled through Kennedy at the unexpected gesture. "You didn't have to bring me dinner."

"I wanted to," Paula said, serving up both plates. "You worked all day baking up treats for everyone else, making their day sweeter. Giving of yourself all day like that is gratifying, but taxing." Paula placed her napkin in her lap, but didn't touch her food, as if waiting for the entire table to be seated first. "You need a little pampering and care of your own."

Not wanting to disappoint the woman, Kennedy took her seat and awkwardly placed her napkin in her lap. Once upon a time, she'd dreamed of having her mom cook a dinner for her exactly like this. Until the day her mom had called and said that she'd enrolled Kennedy in the school across the street from Edna's. After that, Kennedy had been content eating with her grandma while they watched *Wheel of Fortune* in the front room.

"Thank you," she said, her throat tight with gratitude. "I don't know what to say."

Paula laughed. "Start with telling me how wonderful the chicken is, so I can pass it along to Fi. Sometimes I think she cooks just to one-up the rest of us."

Kennedy took a bite of the chicken and moaned. "Well, bragging rights are more than deserved. This is fantastic."

"She'll be delighted."

Kennedy took a bite of the fancy cheese and potato casserole. It was rich and creamy, with a kick of spice and a texture that was so unexpected, her eyes slid shut in ecstasy. "Is that nutmeg?"

Paula leaned in to whisper, "Among other spices. I sprinkle my apple pie spice over cauliflower, roast it, then puree it in the cheese sauce."

"Cauliflower?"

"When Luke was six, he got the chicken pox and decided that it was a reaction to the vegetables he'd eaten at dinner. The boy's so hardheaded, he convinced himself of it, so if he sees anything remotely vegetable shaped on his plate, he starts scratching. Instead of arguing with the mule, I got creative, pureeing every vegetable I could find and hiding it in things."

Kennedy pictured a defiant mini-Luke, and imagined it was similar to the way he looked earlier—when she refused to sell her apples. "What did he do when he found out?"

"I still put carrots in my marinara sauce and cabbage in the mashed potatoes. Never once has he come down with even a touch of a hive."

With a mischievous smile, Paula opened the bottle and poured them both a glass. She lifted her glass in a toast, and Kennedy, touched by this moment of sharing, did the same. "To another successful National Apple Day."

Kennedy went to take a sip and the warmth from their earlier moment faded a bit. It wasn't wine at all. It was a family-size bottle of Two Bad Apples Hard Cider. "So do we toast and then you tell me that you made a mistake, and Luke needs his apples back?"

Paula's eyes went round with surprise. "No, dear, giving Luke his apples back would be the worst possible thing for him."

"How is that?"

"For most of his life, things came too easy to him. Then his father passed." Paula stopped to take a shaky breath, and patted her chest. "Sorry, no matter how many years pass, it still makes my heart ache. I lost my best friend that day. But Luke, my poor boy, he lost so much more. He lost his direction, and before he can find his way back to us, he needs to remember that, just like cauliflower doesn't cause him hives, happiness doesn't rest in a company or a silly few acres of apples."

Kennedy wanted to ask where happiness did come from then, because Paula seemed to have found hers. For a woman who'd lost her husband and lived with debilitating pain, she was one of the most joyful people Kennedy had ever met. Happiness radiated from her.

Kennedy had been looking for that kind of happiness for as long as she could remember. Only, just like Luke, she was relying on a shop and those apples to see her through. But what if after everything, she didn't find it here?

There wouldn't be anyone to blame. Not her mother.

And certainly not a man. If Kennedy couldn't find that kind of peaceful existence she was searching for, then maybe she never would. And she'd have to admit that it wasn't the situation lacking—it was her.

Kennedy took a sip of the cider and her head nearly spun right off. It was crisp, tart, and unlike anything she'd ever tasted. "Is this Luke's?"

"No, that bottle is from his father's collection. My Orin had a magic hand when it came to apples." Paula gave a sly wink. "And the ladies."

Kennedy ignored that image, and asked, "This was made from the apples in the orchard, I assume. Wow, now I know why Luke wanted them."

"Like I told you before, it isn't the apples that are so remarkable."

"Then what is it?" Based on the way Luke all but snuck into the orchard and stole her apples, he seemed to agree.

Paula rested her hand on Kennedy's in a maternal gesture that had Kennedy leaning closer. "It's love, dear."

Chapter 5

Early Sunday morning, Luke was at the Penalty Box helping Hawk set up for the Apple Festival. This year, the bar was hosting the second annual Bob for Cider booth, where anyone over the age of twenty-one who still maintained the majority of their original teeth could bob for a Bad Apple bottle koozie, redeemable for a complimentary cider. It was a fun way to give back to the community that had been a big part of their success, while bringing attention to their new autumn brew.

"You hear back from Matt Rogers?" Hawk asked, setting a massive metal basin on the hay strewn under their festival tent.

"Yeah, talked to him late last night." Luke had called him the second he'd left Sweetie Pies. No sense pissing off the new pie shop owner if Rogers wasn't onboard with the updated delivery dates. "He's willing to give us until December for the California rollout, but that was his hard limit because he has the new Hollywood location opening New Year's Eve."

Hawk looked up from the bin, clearly impressed. "This shit is really going to happen, isn't it?"

"It is," Luke said, feeling a little impressed with himself as well.

Five years ago, Luke had lost his father to cancer, Hawk his hockey career to a shattered kneecap. Floundering, disillusioned, and angry with the world, they'd both found themselves back in Destiny Bay, looking for an outlet. So when the old lumber yard in town went up for sale, Hawk approached Luke about opening a bar. At first he'd been hesitant, still dealing with his dad being gone and the financial shit storm he'd left behind.

Between saving the family business and taking care of his mom, Luke didn't have the time, or the energy, to take on a new project.

Unless he could merge the two.

He'd crunched some numbers, researched different markets, and the dream bar became a brew and cider house, serving over a hundred local ciders and beers on tap. Within a year Hawk had the Penalty Box open and turning a profit.

The next step was to make a hard cider that was rugged enough to take on beer, but had enough finesse to appeal to the wine crowd. Even though Orin couldn't balance a spreadsheet to save the farm, literally, the man knew his ciders. And Two Bad Apples brew was one of the best.

Now it was all about expansion. Reaching the right markets, a job that fell to Luke. If he could solidify this deal with Rogers, they would shave three years off their time line. And that was damn impressive.

"Did you talk to the cute shop girl about buying back the apples?" Hawk asked, picking up another basin and filling it with koozies.

Irritation pricked Luke's neck as he glanced down the road toward Sweetie Pies, and watched as Cute Shop Girl stepped out onto Main Street in a flimsy little number that was sweet, sophisticated, and sexy in that office girl kind of way. It was blue with little white dots and tiny straps that disappeared beneath her practical cardigan sweater.

That she was smiling as if the day couldn't be better didn't bode well for his offer. That he'd stood there watching her flip the sign to OPEN didn't bode well for his self-control.

"We talked. I made her the offer."

Hawk paused and looked up, all business. "Did she bite?"

Luke was surprised she didn't leave marks. "She pretty much told me to go fuck myself."

"Well, if that's what it takes, then go grab the lotion," Hawk said, zero bullshit in his tone. "Because we need those apples."

"I know, which is why I offered her double for the apples."

Hawk's eyes bulged. "Double? Please, God, tell me she took the offer. Wait, no, don't tell me." He held up a hand. "Double?"

"She's thinking about it," Luke said because once Kennedy realized she was being stubborn, she would see what she was actually passing up. A damn good return on investment.

"What do we need to do to get her to think faster?" Hawk asked.

Neither of them were all that practiced with patience

when it came to the business, which was why they'd accomplished so much in such a short amount of time. But Luke had a bad feeling that if they pushed Kennedy too hard, she'd push back, because it was what came naturally.

"She just needs to be finessed a little," Luke said. "I need a few days to watch her, see what it is she really needs, then close the deal."

Years in corporate development had taught Luke that everyone had a need that drove them, an emotional desire that the physical goal represented. Kennedy wasn't holding on to the apples; she was fighting for what those apples meant to her. The key to closing a deal was pinpointing what she needed, then delivering before she realized what had happened.

"Amateur," Hawk scoffed. "I could go over there right now, sweet talk her a little, soften her up with a few choice words, maybe dinner, maybe more, then show her how accommodating we can be."

"Sleeping with her won't work," Luke said, so sharp, Hawk held up a hand.

"Jesus, man, I was kidding. Not that I'd be opposed to sharing a pie in her kitchen. She's sexy in that uptight teacher kind of way, and I've always had a thing for sexy schoolteachers."

"She was an accountant."

"Accountants work, too, as long as she wears one of those buttoned-up sweaters and a tight little bun when she talks about taxing me," Hawk said with a grin that got him laid regularly, which faded the second he saw Luke's look. "Oh, you meant *me* sleeping with her isn't going to happen because *you* want to sleep with her."

Luke wasn't warning Hawk off just because he wanted

Kennedy to himself. Although he absolutely did—in a skip the dinner, definitely more, red dress optional kind of weekend.

Nope, Luke didn't want Hawk, the legendary hockey and hookup bad boy, anywhere near Kennedy because there had been a moment when she was talking about her grandmother that he'd seen a hint of vulnerability. A brief flash of someone who'd had a rough go of it, knew deep disappointment and loss, but wasn't willing to give in.

And that was as sexy as it was impressive.

She was rallying, but still tender around the heart. Kennedy talked a big game, but she wasn't as tough as she wanted everyone to believe. And that, he feared, was what got to him more than the red dress. He knew all too well what it was like to keep going even when everything seemed hopeless.

"What I want is her apples."

Hawk snorted. "Apples, peaches, call it what you want, you're hot for her pies."

As true as that was, what drove Luke was the overwhelming need to fulfill his promise to his dad.

* * *

Kennedy wasn't one to dwell on the past. If she allowed herself to give in to regrets, she'd be too busy crying to get anything accomplished. So worrying over her decision to buy a pie shop on the other side of the country without clarifying that she had been given the complete financial accounting was pointless.

What she needed was a plan—and she'd come up with a great one.

Armed with her sunniest dress and the official DESTINY BAY APPLE FESTIVAL SHOP STOP sign in her window— letting the crowd know that she was a proud participant and local apple supporter—Kennedy opened her shop door with a smile, and stepped out into the morning sun.

It was a perfect fall day. Main Street was brimming with apple enthusiasts, the sky was clear, and clusters of red and yellow leaves danced down the cobblestone side- walks. The crispness in the air was a reminder that the holidays were almost here. A sentiment that had inspired her latest creation.

Fall had officially arrived, and so had Kennedy.

Deciding that the Apple Festival was the perfect oppor- tunity to see what non-apple items she should add to her menu, Kennedy had stayed up all night baking new treats. And she had come up with a winner—she knew it.

Now, she just needed to convince the town's people of it.

She was clear out of apple pies—traditional, deep dish, old-fashioned lace, HumDingers, even the turnovers—yet not a single pumpkin tart or pecan pie had been purchased. So she'd locked up her shop, tossed on her tennies, and grabbed a wicker basket she'd found in the storage room, deciding to take her tarts to the people. She walked them up and down, along the cobblestone sidewalk of Main Street, talking to every person she came into contact with.

"Would you like a pumpkin spice pecan tart?" she asked the friendliest face she saw.

Ms. Collins, head of the Destiny Bay Welcome Com- mittee as well as the Sunshine Girl for the senior center, looked into the basket and gave Kennedy a disappointed look. "Is there apple in that?"

Kennedy briefly considered lying, because she knew that look. In the South, it was usually accompanied by the phrase *Bless your heart* or *Isn't that the sweetest*, which was just a polite way of saying someone was slow in the head. But Kennedy didn't believe in lying, especially when it came to grannies with rosy cheeks and silvered haloes. She believed in her tarts, so she smiled and said, "This tart is made of slowly roasted pumpkins and Georgia state pecans."

Ms. Collins didn't look impressed. "So no apples?"

"No," Kennedy said, the first signs of doubt creeping in. "But it tastes like a little slice of the holidays. Who doesn't love the holidays?"

Ms. Collins took a second look in the basket and Kennedy held her breath, because she didn't care if other people loved the holidays like she did. She cared if people liked her pies. And embarrassingly enough, if they liked her.

"It's September," the older woman said with a warm confusion in her tone. "Apple season."

Kennedy glanced down at her basket full of golden browned tarts, flaky on the outside and soft and creamy on the inside, with just enough pecans for a nice crunch. Each was hand wrapped and tied with a yellow ribbon and a matching new item coupon, which advertised twenty percent off their next order.

Telling herself there wouldn't be a next order if she couldn't get a first, and putting that belief she talked about into action, she said, "Actually, for today only, they're free."

"Well, if they're free." Ms. Collins snatched not one, but two, and quickly shoved them in her canvas shopping bag, then saw the coupon. "That twenty percent you're toot-ing. It's good on Sweetie Pies apple pies, too, not just the pumpkin, right?"

A thin sheen of perspiration broke out on Kennedy's forehead. She hadn't taken into account that people would read the coupon that way. She had intended it to be applied to the new menu items, to encourage people to branch out from their favorites and perhaps find a few new fa-vorites to add to their list, but she hadn't exactly specified that. But twenty percent off her apple pies? Her bestselling HumDinger used over five pounds of apples—half of them heirloom.

She'd lose money on each sale for sure. But if she didn't accept the coupon after passing out over a hundred, she'd lose loyal customers.

"If you don't love those tarts, then I will apply it toward a treat of your choosing."

"Well, aren't you sweet," the older woman said as if the entire thing had been Kennedy's idea to begin with. She gave Kennedy's hand a parting squeeze. "I'll be sure to let the ladies at the bobbing apples booth know."

"You mean bobbing for apples?" Kennedy asked, but Ms. Collins was already making a beeline for the candy ap-ples booth.

"Nope, bobbing apples," a woman about Kennedy's age said from behind a festival booth. "Two Bad Apples spon-sors the booth every year. They bus in some co-eds from the local university, put them in white T-shirts, and then send them bobbing."

The woman was petite with piercing green eyes and chin-length dark, curly hair that had a mind of its own, and somehow she managed to look feminine while rocking a pair of coveralls and a beat-up ball cap—both boasting STEEL MAGNOLIAS FLOWER AND GARDEN ART. The flower part in her title explained the soil marks on her knees and thighs. The soldering iron and lethal-looking cutters told Kennedy that the garden art was most likely made of steel.

"Of course they do," Kennedy said, glancing at the growing crowd amassing at the end of Main Street, rolling her eyes when she spotted two blond Barbies in cowgirl boots, denim shorts, and Bad Apple mini-tees, which showed off their enhanced apples.

"People put their money on who they think will pull the most apples. Winners each get a VIP pass to next week's VIP Cider Tasting, and a photo with the biggest apple bob. All the proceeds go toward helping needy families in the area. Mostly farmers."

"Let me guess, the owners pay the girls with cider and charm?"

The woman laughed. "Oh, not girls."

Confused, Kennedy gave a second, more thorough look, and *holy hotness*—

Beneath the LOOK AT THEM APPLES banner and behind the Barbies, surrounded by a swarm of single ladies flapping their bills, stood what appeared to be the cast from *Magic Mike* dressed in low-slung jeans and tissue-thin BAD APPLE T-shirts.

"What's that?"

"That," the woman sighed dreamily, "is the University of Washington hockey team. And behind them is their revered coach and honored leader."

Forget Magic Mike, Kennedy thought, taking in the underwear model in a coach's cap with enough biceps for the entire hockey league. The man was big, beautiful, but not the badass that had Kennedy's insides cooking.

That honor went to Luke, in dark jeans, a dark T-shirt, and a dark ball cap pulled low. In case that wasn't mysterious enough, he had on a pair of aviators—mirrored. He was a sexy corporate hottie lurking around in secret agent attire.

"They know their demographic," Kennedy said, a little impressed, because as the women flocked to the players, the men in town flocked toward the women. It was brilliant really. "Smart and charming."

"Is that a bad thing?" the woman asked with a smile.

"It is if you're allergic to charm."

"It's the sweet part that always gets me," she said in a way that had Kennedy wanting to take back her comment. Destiny Bay was a small town where everyone knew everyone, and it was obvious by the woman's expression she knew one of them intimately.

Kennedy grimaced. "Oh, are you and Thor dating?"

"Thor? Oh, you mean Hawk? God no," she said as if she'd rather swallow glass. Or maybe she was trying to convince herself of that. Either way, it seemed Kennedy had found common ground. "He was married to my sister."

"Was?" Kennedy asked.

"Yeah, Hawk was her dream man until he busted his shoulder and a knee and it ended his career a few years back. She filed for divorce shortly after and then traded up for a newer model."

"Ouch."

"Massive ouch on the whole family," she said. "I tried to lose both of them in the divorce, but Hawk decided to move back home, and resume his role as my keeper." The woman held up a blowtorch. "Like I can't take care of myself."

She not only looked like she could take care of herself, she was an honest-to-God Nut Buster. Two things Kennedy could learn from. "Hi, I'm Kennedy, want a tart?"

"I don't do handouts." The woman set down her torch and extended a gloved hand, holding a twenty. "I'm Ali, your neighbor." She pointed to a brick-faced storefront directly across Main Street from Sweetie Pies. "I am just out showcasing some of my new sculptures for the Apple Festival."

Kennedy held up her basket of tarts. "Me, too."

"Why didn't you get a booth?"

Kennedy looked up and down the street at all the booths, lining both sides of the road. Her shop was one of the few that hadn't taken their wares outside. "I figured that the shop is right there, people would come in."

"And how did that work out?" Ali asked.

"Great," Kennedy said, suddenly feeling the weight of burning the midnight oil settle down on her shoulders. "Until I sold out of Gold Tin apple pies, then the store was a ghost town."

"Your luck will change as soon as word spreads about that coupon." The way Ali said it made it clear that wasn't a good thing. "I don't think a Sweetie Pies apple pie has ever been discounted."

"Because there is no need to discount perfection," Fi said, storming over. She was wearing a bright floral top, mauve pants with an elastic waistband, sparkly silver Converse, and a look of extreme outrage. "Something you'd know if you weren't so busy making those tarts. Tarts in

LAST KISS OF SUMMER   87

a pie shop, who'd ever heard of such a thing? Next thing you'll want to start selling crumbles."

"It isn't all that far of a leap," Kennedy defended, because that was exactly what she was thinking. Running a bakery that sold only five items was hurting the bottom line.

"You going to make those out of squash, too? Because you're in apple country, child. Around here, people are purists—they want two layers of crust with apples in the middle."

"Around here, people are also neighborly, Ms. Fi," Ali said with so much sugar the older woman lost a little of her bluster. "Now, you trusted Kennedy enough to sell her the shop, right?"

"That was before she ran short on HumDingers on the most important day of the year and started disrespecting the apples."

"I'm not disrespecting them," Kennedy said gently. "Just sharing some of my other sweets." She pulled out her tart and handed it to the older woman as a peace offering. "This pumpkin tart won a blue ribbon," Kennedy said, leaving out the part that it was a Sunny Side Senior Shake While You Bake blue ribbon—amateur division.

"Well, Sweetie Pies is a *Gold* Tin winner, voted on by the National Apple Council," Fi said, referring to one of the most respected organizations in baking. But she took the tart, smelled it, gave a shrug, and then stuck it in the seat compartment of her walker.

"All I'm trying to do is keep the business profitable," Kennedy explained. "But I have gone over the books so many times, and can't seem to figure out how you managed to make money selling pies so cheap. The price of the heirloom apples is eating up nearly all my profit."

"Our pies always made a profit," Fi said, one hand on her heart, the other in the air as if swearing under oath. "They sell good, too—we couldn't make them fast enough."

"Moving pies isn't the problem," Kennedy explained. "It's the cost of the heirloom apples, they are so expensive. One solution is to change out the apples."

"Those apples are the heart of Sweetie Pies. It is what makes us stand out."

"I know." Just like she knew that those apples were what gave Sweetie Pies its reputation and name in the industry. "Which leaves adding other, high-margin, apple-free items to the menu." Fi gasped as if Kennedy had just announced she hated kittens. "Or we can increase the price of the pies?"

"Sweetie Pies has always been affordable. It's one of the reasons people keep coming back," Fi said, her voice solemn, as if taking the situation seriously. She shook her head. "Honest to God, child, we've never had a problem with the cost of the apples."

"You don't know what a barrel of Mutsu apples go for," the last person in town she wanted to see right then said.

Kennedy told herself to ignore the way her body responded. Ignore how the throaty timbre of his voice had her temperature rising and her thighs quivering. Then she turned to face him and—big mistake! One glance at the six-feet-plus of solid muscle and alpha male swagger, and every happy place known to womankind went spiraling into a frenzy.

That he was looking over the rim of his mirrored glasses at her and appeared a little sweaty only added to the effect.

"It doesn't matter if I know what a bushel goes for or not. I know pies, and I know this town," Fi defended.

Luke's face softened. "It matters if you're doling out advice on pricing for pies when you've never paid for an apple in your life."

"What?" Kennedy said, a hot rush of panic settling in her stomach and lighting her dreams on fire. "The shop never paid for the apples you used?"

"Why would it?" Fi asked. "I owned the orchard and the shop."

Of course she did. A fact Kennedy knew going in. A fact she'd chosen to overlook even when the numbers were saying it was too good to be true. Because just like her mama, Kennedy had led with her heart instead of logic. Sure, she'd bought the shop, but it hadn't come with the orchard. Just the apples at a discounted price. A price that was expected to be paid upon delivery.

She took a deep breath to keep her thoughts from spiraling into doomsville, and her tears in check. When that didn't work, she called on every ounce of restraint she owned, reminded herself there would be time for tears later, and asked, "That wasn't something you thought to mention before now, seeing that it is the shop's biggest expense?"

Fi looked around the group as if asking them for the answer. "You never asked. And when the signed contract came in, I assumed you had all the answers you needed."

Right. There was that, because when you focused on greener pastures, it was hard to see the potholes in front of you. Kennedy closed her eyes against the threatening tears.

"But now that you bring it up, those apples we grow *are* expensive."

"So I've been told," she whispered, well aware that the

person who told her was standing right there, so close she could smell the smugness rolling off him.

"Don't look so serious," Fi said, giving her an awkward pat on the hand. "You'll attract more flies with honey, and more customers with apples."

"I've always been partial to honey," Luke said silkily, and Kennedy did her best to ignore him. Hard to do when he seemed to be taking up all the space in the area.

"Then we are in agreement!" Fi clapped her hands as if the cost of apples, and her lack of disclosure, was no longer an issue. "All you need is honey, apples, and a little creativity to loosen up that frown of yours so you can explore the possibilities. I'll go spread the word."

"Creativity is my middle name," Kennedy defended, but Fi was already toddling her way over to the apple butter booth.

Kennedy wanted to toddle away, too—all the way back to her cottage, where she could process what had happened and lick her wounds. But she had a business to resurrect.

"Creativity is always a good skill," Luke agreed, his voice like honey and proving Fi's earlier point. His attractiveness was impossible to ignore. "I have a few ideas on how to loosen you up, though. Want to hear them?"

"I don't need your kind of help." She didn't need a man at all. Just because she'd bought a shop whose success relied on free apples didn't mean Kennedy couldn't make a success of it. On her own terms. "As for your ideas, if they're anything like your previous ones, then I'm good."

His grin turned wicked, and those zings turned heated. "I'm better."

Maybe he was, but she was scrappy. Something that came with having no backup, no plan B. Heck, this was her plan B—C, D, and E if she were being honest. And she wasn't about to let some smooth talker with a sexy smile and apple envy steal it. "Doesn't matter since I have the apples. And flexing those big muscles and that golden boy smile won't charm me into handing them over."

"Sweetness, I'm not flexing. This is all natural. And I haven't even tried to charm you," he said lowly, a ripple of tingles sliding down her back.

"Well, don't waste your breath, I'm not charmable."

Luke released both dimples her way, in addition to a determined look that had her stomach fluttering. "Challenge accepted."

*   *   *

After the festival, Luke packed up the booth and headed toward the orchard. No matter how many times he drove down this same stretch of road, as he got closer to his folks' place, the memories always returned. Some were good, but most were the ones he wished he could go back and change.

He'd once hated the idea of working on the orchard, but that had been before he understood just how much he could have learned from his dad. Growing up with his future laid out in front of him had been like a noose, every year cinching tighter and tighter, until he felt as if he was going to drown in expectations. But as time went on, and Luke matured, he realized that he was the only one who'd placed those limits on himself.

Sure his dad wanted their legacy to continue, wanted his son to take over the family business, but he'd also wanted

Luke to be happy. What Luke hadn't seen was that he would have been happier staying right here by his family's side—he might have felt suffocated, but at least there wouldn't have been the paralyzing guilt.

An emotion that seemed to get heavier every day.

Where had today's dose of guilt come from, though? That honor went to Kennedy in her little yellow dress with a matching cardigan sweater. Her hair had been loose, falling in long blond waves, and her boots had been high, hugging her legs all the way up to the hem of her dress— only leaving a sliver of skin visible. What had sucked him in, however, were those big blue eyes, so determined yet so damn uncertain.

A paradox—just like the woman herself.

Which was part of the reason he'd come to the orchard. If he was going to figure out a solution to this situation, he needed to understand why she'd uprooted her life to come to Destiny Bay. Surely there were a thousand and one bakeries she could have bought between here and there. So why this one?

"Because she's smart," he told himself as he pulled up to the Callahan farmhouse. "And it was an amazing deal."

Throwing his truck in Park, he grabbed the take-out he'd picked up on his way out of town so that his mom wouldn't be tempted to cook, and he headed up the front porch steps. Paula worked hard not to let her arthritis take over, but some days were harder than others. Today was one of those days. He'd seen it in the way her smile hadn't reached her eyes.

The door was unlocked, but that didn't mean she was home. Paula and Fi had an open door policy that drove

Luke nuts, because they'd open their door to Ted Bundy if they thought he was in need of a good home-cooked meal.

"Anyone home?" he called out.

When there was no answer, he hung his coat on the rack and went into the kitchen to put dinner in the oven to keep warm.

"Ding dong."

Luke didn't bother answering the door, since the bell sound came from his aunt's pet cockatiel, who was perched on top of one of the cabinets, fanning out his coral tail feathers and bobbing his head.

Lola had the beak of a pterodactyl, the feathers of a Vegas showgirl, and an affinity for imitating smoke alarms and machine guns while dive-bombing people's heads. He also fancied himself a pickpocket, collecting everything from bottle caps to ball caps.

So when the bird whistled and said, "Nice hat. Nice hat," Luke held up a single finger.

"Don't even think about it. One peck and you'll end up pillow stuffing."

Lola's eyes went huge, zeroing in on Luke's hat, and the rest of his body remained motionless, except his tail feathers, which fanned all the way out, as if in challenge.

With a stern glare, Luke grabbed a cider from the fridge, popped the top, and headed into the other room.

Mine. Mine-mine-mine.

Ignoring the fluster of feathers and kamikaze-inspired dive-bomb, which resulted in Luke losing yet another ball cap, Luke sat down in the big recliner in the corner of the family room. Before he could lean back, an opened folder caught his eye.

His body went on high alert when he saw Kennedy's

name at the top. His throat tightened with guilt when a quick glance revealed it contained all the financial documents relating to the sale of the bakery. Documents that would tell him the exact terms of the deal, and give him a better understanding of how things stood or, more important, how things could stand to change.

Documents he had no business riffling through.

A frustrated moan rumbled in his chest, followed by a defeated sigh. He knew what he was about to do was wrong—it was an invasion on so many levels. But Luke had broken his back the past five years, clawing Callahan Orchards back from near-bankruptcy, and he wasn't about to go back there.

A lot of folks believed Luke had inherited a legacy, when in fact he'd inherited a sinking ship. Between college loans, past-due property taxes, and his dad's medical bills, he'd been forced to do the one thing he'd promised his dad would never happen. He sold the weekend home on the bay in order to keep the other, more profitable, Callahan properties afloat. Something that logically couldn't have been avoided, but emotionally Luke could never get past it.

Now he had a chance to right that wrong *and* grow his company. A chance to get his mom back in her Bay View Orchards house, and make his and his dad's dream of a successful hard cider company a reality.

First, though, he needed to assess the seriousness of the situation with the three acres of apples, then make his move, which would hopefully be nothing more than making the right offer. Which meant he needed to understand Kennedy's financial standing.

Luke casually shifted the papers around until he found

what he needed—a copy of the loan, which told him that Callahan Orchards was carrying the note on Sweetie Pies. But the further he read, the bigger the pulsing behind his right eye became. And then he reached the actual bill of sale and Luke nearly lost his shit.

"You've got to be kidding me!"

His mom, bless her generous bleeding heart, had not only promised a *lifetime* of the Mutsu apples he needed for his cider at wholesale, she'd also financed the woman who could take their entire expansion down in one harvest.

Luke flipped the pages and the pulsing became a loud, steady thumping. It was Kennedy's personal financial statements. She would feel personally betrayed if he read any further, which should have been enough to force him to put them down and walk away.

He already knew she was struggling with the business, and that she hadn't anticipated the high cost of apples. If he were just patient, in time she'd run herself out of business and he could sweep in and buy her out for a fraction of the cost.

Too bad time was the only thing Luke didn't have. Well, besides the apples. So instead of leaving her private matters private, Luke called himself a dozen kinds of asshole, then took a quick peek.

Only the numbers caught his eye before his time was up, and the next thing he knew, he was studying her bank statements, accessing the information as if he were a corporate raider looking for her vulnerable spots. And there were many.

To damn many for her to make it.

For starters, there was enough in her savings account to last her no more than a few months unless she managed to find a cheaper supplier of apples—which was about as likely as Luke getting his hat back from Feather Head. Then there was a huge deposit, followed by an immediate withdrawal.

Sure, her file was nothing more than a bunch of numbers and balances, but to a guy like Luke, who made his money reading between the decimals, he could easily put together a story. One that started with a chunk of cash that landed in her account then quickly left it the week she purchased his mom's shop, and ended with her moving across the country. He wasn't sure what she was running from, but this was clearly a fresh start for her.

There were no loans reported, no co-signers to the business, no previous businesses, which left only one answer.

Kennedy had sold an asset. Most likely her home.

Something in Luke's chest shifted painfully. It took guts and a whole lot of determination to start over in a town where she didn't know a soul—didn't have a support system. But that's exactly what she'd done, uprooted her entire life to make pies—here in Destiny Bay.

That had to mean something. What, Luke didn't know. But he was going to find out.

He just wasn't sure he'd like the answer.

* * *

Word that there were free Sweetie Pies samples spread like wildfire, cleaning Kennedy out of her entire stock in less than an hour. She wasn't sure if it was the free tarts or the twenty percent off coupons that brought the crowd, but once they tasted her roasted pumpkin treats, people weren't just asking about next week's apple pies. Ms. Collins even

placed a standing order for a dozen pies—and two tarts—
for her monthly Welcome Meeting at the senior center.

Kennedy knew that the distance between a single standing order and running a successful shop was enormous, but
she was determined to win over the entire town by Thanksgiving. Even if it was one tart at a time. With how hard
this town clung to tradition, it just might be. A daunting
thought that had Kennedy sighing as she drove down the
cobblestone road that led toward her cottage.

The daylight was long gone, but a million stars twinkled
over the apple trees that lined either side of her driveway,
casting a glow over the nineteen-twenties carriage house
that had been converted into a quaint one-bedroom cottage.

The one-story dwelling boasted a wide wraparound
porch, complete with a wooden swing and a lovely chef's
garden off the back. It was warm and welcoming, and Edna
was right—Callahan Cottage was the exact kind of safe
harbor Kennedy had desperately needed. And after pulling
another sixteen-hour day, she couldn't wait to sink into a
hot bath and soak away every worry and ache.

Kennedy grabbed her purse off the passenger seat, her
bra off the floorboard, and dinner out of the truck—the last
remaining pumpkin tart and a bottle of local wine.

She was celebrating making it through her first Apple
Festival and, regardless of her run-in with Fi, being one
step closer to happiness, finding a home—and baking six
hundred pies and tarts without sampling the product more
than twice.

Okay, three times, but she'd made six complete passes
of Main Street carrying that basket, the equivalent of a
marathon, she was sure.

Kennedy reached for her keys and pulled out her cell

instead, because the door was open—and someone was inside.

Reminding herself she was in the middle of a dark and desolate apple orchard, with the nearest neighbors owning a cane and dentures, Kennedy grabbed the wooden umbrella from the copper can next to the door.

"Unless your name is Paula or Fi, you might want to leave now," she hollered down the hallway. "I've called the sheriff and he is on his way."

"You might want to call him back, I didn't make enough for company, and Dudley's a sensitive guy when it comes to being included. Doesn't do well with rejection."

It wasn't fear that coursed through her body at the confirmation that someone was indeed inside her house. It was growing irritation—brought on by the man in her kitchen.

Luke.

Dropping her cell back in her purse, she choked up on the umbrella and stormed into the kitchen.

Luke stood at the stove. His hair was wet and finger combed, as if he'd just swum the length of the bay. He was in jeans—no shirt, no shoes—just damp skin and soft, well-worn denim, which hung dangerously low on his hips.

"Get out," Kennedy demanded and, *great*, he looked up to find her staring at the impressive set of hard-cut abs.

"Can you hand me the chili powder." He wasn't even looking at her, but using a wooden spoon to stir something in a giant copper pot—the scent surprisingly delicious. "It's in the pantry to your right. Top shelf."

Her answer was to set the bag on the counter and raise the umbrella.

"Right." He grinned sympathetically. "You're a little on

the short side, would probably need the step stool. No problem, I'll get it."

Kennedy didn't know what bothered her more, the way her breath caught and her eyes zeroed in as all that naked, tan skin brushed past her, his back muscles bunching and coiling as he reached up to grab several spice bottles. Or that he tapped the tip of her umbrella on his way back and said, "You may want to set that down. You know what they say about seven years' bad sex and all."

She forced her gaze to meet his, which was the color of whiskey and twinkling with humor. She'd never been able to handle her whiskey. "Opening an umbrella in the house is seven years' bad *luck*."

"Imagine what swinging it will cost you." With a pinch of this and a dash of that, he went back to stirring. He lifted the spoon, cupping his hand beneath it, took a taste, and offered her one. "You think it needs a tad more cayenne?"

Kennedy ignored this. "What are you doing?"

"Making dinner. My dad's favorite chili, best in town." He glanced at the bag. "Oh, good, you brought dessert."

He reached for the box and she swung purposefully low. "Get your hands off my tarts."

He lifted his hands in surrender. "Don't worry, sweetness, I wasn't going to touch...Just wanted a little peek at what was to come."

She swung again, this time getting closer. "Get out of my house."

"About that," he said, ducking down and around her, so fast and fluid that when he stopped, he had the umbrella in his hand—and hers were shockingly empty. He stuck a wineglass in it, uncorked the bottle, and was pouring before she could throw it at him. "This dwelling is an asset of Callahan Orchards, used to house employees during the harvest. And since the harvest officially started yesterday, and I am Callahan Orchards' top employee, that makes you my guest." He poured himself a glass and held it to hers. "Welcome to my cottage."

"Sorry, buddy, I'm renting the cottage from your mom, and she said I can stay here for as long as I need."

He took a sip. "She told me."

"And I need more time."

"Take all the time you need. I mean, what kind of man would I be to deny a lady of her needs." He smiled behind his wineglass, but didn't move toward the exit. Kennedy got the distinct impression he had no intention of leaving anytime soon. Which irritated her as much as it turned her on.

She didn't want to want someone as pigheaded and smug as Luke, but the truth was, she did. And not just in a sexual way; she wanted to flirt and laugh and be challenged. Three things that happened when he was near.

And the top three ingredients in a recipe for disaster, she told herself. She'd only recently lost one home to a man; she wasn't about to lose another.

Deciding to be proactive instead of reactive, she set the glass down, picked up her phone, and dialed. Two seconds later it was ringing.

"Well, isn't this a surprise," Paula said into the phone, but didn't sound surprised at all. In fact, she sounded hopeful. "How was your day?"

The question caught Kennedy off guard. She couldn't remember the last time someone had asked her that, and sounded genuinely interested. "It was great. Once I cleared up the misconception about pumpkin being nature's Ex-lax, I cleared out all the day's inventory."

"That's lovely, dear," Paula said, and Kennedy could hear the older woman beaming through the phone. "And don't worry about Fi, she means well. But don't fret, she has been spoken to. You shouldn't have any more problems with misconceptions running about town."

Kennedy looked at Luke, moving around her kitchen as if he owned the place. "About that, I came home to find a visitor in my kitchen."

"Oh, is Luke there?" Paula asked, all innocence and sugary surprise. "I was wondering if he would come. Every harvest he comes, but a few years ago he bought a house in town, and his time at the cottage has been unpredictable. I wasn't sure if he'd move in this year."

"Move in?" The words stuck in her throat. "But this harvest you said I could move in. For as long as I needed." Kennedy repeated the woman's promise verbatim, working hard to keep the panic at bay.

"No one uses the cottage, dear, so you take as long as you need."

"But you just said Luke uses the cottage."

"Just for harvest, and don't mind him, he's always tidy, cleans up after himself, good in the kitchen, too. You won't even know he's there," she said as if this were the perfect arrangement, but somehow Kennedy doubted that. Luke was one of those guys who took up too much space. "But if it's a problem, you could come sleep at the farmhouse with Fi and me. We can make up the sofa bed."

And be kicked out of her own house by a man—again? Not going to happen.

Plus, after her day, the thought of trading one Callahan in for two made her eye twitch. She was already spending nearly every morning in the kitchen with them and their well-intended suggestions. Nope, what Kennedy needed was a little peace, a lot of quiet, and a space all her own. "That's okay, I'm good down here, but I am sure Luke wouldn't mind visiting. Say the word, and I'll send him right up."

"Oh." Paula sounded concerned. "That's wouldn't work. Lola just loves Luke, but he's allergic to her dander."

"Allergic?" Kennedy narrowed her eyes.

Unconcerned about how unmanly being allergic to dander was, Luke gave a pathetic sniff of the nose, then grinned—and flexed his pecks.

Rolling her eyes, Kennedy picked up a T-shirt off the back of the chair and tossed it. The man had amazing reflexes, because he managed to catch it without dropping the spoon.

"It's why he bought his own place. Poor guy can't stay in the house for more than two minutes before Lola starts in on her kisses, and Luke begins to break out in these awful hives."

Two minutes with Lola and Kennedy would get hives.

"Plus, Luke being there during harvest, right down the road, really warms my heart," the older woman said. Kennedy's heart warmed at the thought, too—from irritation. "Luke and his daddy used to spend harvest in the cottage when he was growing up. After my Orin passed, Luke stopped going, chose instead to commute in from his house in town. Maybe this is his way of coping, finally finding some sense of closure," Paula said quietly. "I thought I told you he might come by, must have slipped my mind."

"Must have," Kennedy said, wondering how she was supposed to kick him out now. Paula had shared something so personal and touching she actually felt for the man.

Kennedy had never buried anyone close to her, but she knew the power of loss—understood how it could reshape a person's life.

Her life had been reshaped so many times, Kennedy often wondered what she would have turned out like had she been born into a different family. One that had staying power.

"Thanks for understanding," Paula said. "And tell my boy I love him."

There was a gentle quality to Paula's voice that had Kennedy ready to pass along the message. She looked at Luke, who smiled back. It was warm and genuine, similar to the one he'd given his mom the other day at the shop. Unfortunately, it created a similar reaction in Kennedy's chest. Which was also warm and way too genuine for her comfort.

Because that one smile transformed him from ruggedly handsome to insanely.

"Tell her I love her, too," he said, not even trying to hide the fact that he was eavesdropping.

"To the moon and back," Paula said as an alarm sounded in the background. "Gotta go, dinner's ready."

Kennedy didn't have the energy to point out it was Lola, or the heart to admit that Paula knew that. She ended the call and glared at Luke. "Well, we can't both stay here, if that was your big grand plan, and I'm not leaving, which means you can see your way out."

"After dinner," he said as if she hadn't just kicked him out. "Do you want to eat at the table or the counter?" he asked.

"Cut the crap, Luke," she said indignantly. Whatever his game was, she wasn't about to play. "What are you up to?"

Chapter 6

Luke was up to nothing good, that was for sure, he thought, looking at the storm brewing in Kennedy's blue eyes while she glared at him from across the kitchen counter.

Unafraid of the weighted silence, Luke took the time to study his hostile houseguest, trying to get a handle on what had inspired Kennedy to buy a pie shop on the other side of the country. If he could figure that out, then maybe he could pinpoint what she needed to feel comfortable saying yes to his offer. If he had learned anything about Kennedy Sinclair, it was that she couldn't be persuaded by money, wasn't afraid of his aunt, and knew how to swing when she got cornered.

Three things that meant he'd have to be extra diligent about staying focused.

Focus that evaporated the second she crossed her arms and sent him a look that was irritated, tired, and sexy as hell.

Her blond hair was spilling out of its clip, her eyes were dialed to bedroom, and she had a smudge of flour on her right cheek. She was still wearing that dress, although the practical shoes and prim sweater were MIA. Tonight, her feet were naked and her shoulders impossibly bare. But what had his mind scrambled was what she had on beneath.

Or what she didn't have on.

One of the straps had slipped down her shoulder, showing off more cleavage than lace, and leaving Luke ninety-nine percent certain that she wasn't wearing a bra. As for the panties, he could only hope she was into coordinating, because commando would suit her well right then.

"Cooking dinner. Glad I made enough for guests." He leaned against the counter and waited for his words to settle. Her eyes went wide, then fuming mad. God, she was hot when she was riled. It was the only reason he could come up with for what he said next. "I wasn't expecting a roomie."

"It's a one-bedroom, Luke. There is no room for a roomie."

"I know. When I used to stay here with my dad, I always got stuck on the sofa. So sleeping in the bed should be a nice change."

Nice change? What the hell was he saying? He hadn't planned on moving in; he'd come here to figure her out, throw her off balance, and find a weakness. But one look at her in her dress and too-much-skin-to-be-strapped-in and his brain had been scrambled.

Then she'd seen right through his BS and called him on it, and damn if that didn't turn him on—and turn him stupid.

The whole point of buying the house across town was

so he'd never have to spend another night here, surrounded by the memories of the last harvest he'd spent with his dad. Never have to smell chili cooking on the stove, the scent of apples on his hands, or the regret in the air.

Angry frustration rose up inside him at the situation, and he felt the walls start to close in, guilt tightening around his neck.

"I'm not sleeping on the couch," she said, steel determination in her voice.

And there it was, his cue to leave. He didn't want to be there. She sure as hell didn't want him there. It was clear by the tug he felt toward Kennedy he had no business staying, but he couldn't find the strength to leave.

"What kind of man would I be to make you sleep on the couch," he said. "I don't mind sharing, but I gotta warn you, wine makes me a cuddler so I'd cut me off after two glasses."

She paused as if trying to figure out if he was being serious or screwing with her. The correct answer would be both.

"There will be no sharing, of the wine or the bed, and I am not your sweetness, your roomie, or your answering service." She plucked his glass from his hand and emptied the contents into hers. When it wouldn't all fit, she tipped it back to down the remainder—handing him back an empty glass.

"Is that a no to the cuddling?"

"I'm also not some naive woman you can charm out of her panties or her home, or apples FYI. So whatever game you're playing, whatever plan you've come up with, like I told you the other night, I'm not interested," she said with a tired sadness that made a direct hit to Luke's chest.

"After today, I figured you'd want to revisit the offer."

"After today, I just want to soak in a hot bath, with a glass of wine, and celebrate having tomorrow off, and the fact that I happen to love pumpkin more than apples, so other people must, too."

Luke scratched his hand. "You brought home a pumpkin tart?"

"What's wrong with a pumpkin tart?" she demanded.

"Nothing," he said brightly, thinking that he'd prefer an apple pie. "And since dinner's not quite ready, you have plenty of time to have a glass and a little soak. But leave the door unlocked and I'll come get you when it's ready."

"So you can see me in nothing but bubbles, maybe accidentally fall the tub, and *whoops*, tomorrow's walk of shame will be too awkward for me to stay and you win."

"Whoa," Luke said quietly, because he had a feeling she had been played. Whatever she'd been through had burned so bad, the scars would never fully heal. "I was really just offering you dinner, a chance for us to talk, revisit things, and get to know each other better."

"I know enough, Luke," she said, and Luke experienced an unfamiliar prick in his chest. "I know how guys like you work, how you see this situation panning out, and I am telling you, I am not interested in anything you have to offer. I'd rather take my chances and work it out alone."

And in that moment he knew he was fucked.

Beneath the frustration and sexual heat that sizzled between them every time they were in fighting distance was a woman with a big heart, a beautiful smile, and the saddest fucking eyes he'd ever seen.

Kennedy wasn't trying to be mean; she was just calling it how she saw it. She chose to go it alone because she'd learned it was less painful. It made him wonder what kind of assholes she'd been exposed to—and how he'd ended up being lumped in the same barrel.

A position he liked about as much as losing those apples.

"I'm tired and sore from a long day," she said. "The last thing I want right now is dinner." The "with you" was implied.

Luke knew that she probably hadn't eaten all day, just like he knew that Kennedy's day was more than long—with his aunt on the warpath, it was a painful experience in perseverance.

Fi Callahan loved fiercely, lived loudly, and was the town's biggest know-it-all. She was always right, never in doubt, and made Gandhi look soft when it came to fighting for what she believed in. And she believed in God, family, the Seattle Seahawks, and Destiny Bay apples.

Not always in that order.

"You just don't think you're hungry because you've been smelling food all day," Luke said, pulling two bowls out of the cupboard. "Which is why I went with savory. Smelling sugar and cinnamon all day used to get to my mom, too. She said good bakers taste every step of the way, so the Apple Festival and harvest time always made for a lot of salads in my house. And after a long day in the orchard, a salad wouldn't cut it for me and my dad."

Kennedy paused to look at him, as if trying to figure out why he was sharing this with her, if this was all a part of his game. *Good luck*, he thought, because he was as confused as she.

Luke never talked about his dad. To anyone. Sure, he

listened when his mom or people in town brought him up, reminisced about what a great guy he was. But Luke never did much more than listen and give the expected smile or solemn nod. Anything else felt like a lie.

He'd made it clear when he left for college after that last harvest that he was moving on to bigger and better. Oh, he found his bigger, working as some starched corporate developer for one of the top tech firms in the state. Had the fancy car, cush corner office, and downtown loft to prove it. As for the better, his world always came up lacking. Karma, he guessed, for walking away from his family when they'd needed him, and being laser focused on the wrong things. Which made seeing what was in front of him impossible.

"So your mom cooked you guys this chili?" she asked, and Luke looked up to find that Kennedy had taken a seat at the counter. The exact place he'd wanted her a moment ago, only now he just wanted air.

"Nah," he said, checking the loaf of sourdough he'd popped in the oven. "Mom was too tired when she came home to cook, so my dad started making dinners. Came up with a bunch of recipes my mom loved, but this chili was her favorite."

Luke remembered how his dad would smile while tinkering with the spices to get it just right. Luke knew he was the kind of bone tired that only picking apples for twelve hours could bring on, because Luke had been, too. But the second his dad got behind the stove, started thinking about his wife coming home to dinner on the table, it was as if he got a second wind.

"No matter how much she'd baked that day, she could never pass up a bowl."

"That's really sweet," Kennedy said, a wistfulness in her voice. "He sounds like a good guy."

"He was the best." Luke cleared his throat and wondered what his dad would think of him now. Of how he was strategizing and sweet-talking a woman right out of her home. Then he thought about what his dad would think if he lost his mom's house. For a second time.

Fuck. Luke didn't do the bad guy—he'd been raised better than that. Problem was, he also didn't do disappointment, not when it came to his family.

Which left him up the creek with Cute Shop Girl swinging the paddle.

On the bright side, it wasn't like he was robbing her of her home. The woman had lived in Destiny Bay for all of two weeks. How settled could she possibly be? Not as settled as the pretty nest egg he'd give her to build a home anywhere she wanted.

Kennedy would get her shop, his mom would get her home, and his dad would get his dying wish. Luke would get the luxury of breathing without the weight of his dad's death pressing down.

It was a win, win, fucking win for all involved. He just needed to show Kennedy that.

Channeling his Callahan charm, he lifted the lid of the bakery box and smiled. Inside was a perfect tart with a flaky top, dusted with sugar, and worthy of Sweetie Pies' name. "He was sweet to my mom, but I am interested in the sweetness of this tart, which no doubt needed a lot of tastings. So I imagine the last thing you want is to stand in front of another stove and make dinner."

She looked at her creation and blinked. Opening her mouth to say something, she glanced up at him and closed it, as if so thrown by his comment she didn't know how to respond.

"So the chili, this whole setup, was just a welcome to the neighborhood gesture?"

"What can I say? I'm a nice guy." When she rolled her eyes, he added, "Ask my mom, she'll vouch for me." A line that always had women smiling.

Kennedy didn't smile. In fact, she yawned, an irritating *I am unimpressed* yawn that had his ego taking cover. "Telling someone you like that they're wrong isn't the way to start a lasting friendship."

He touched the tip of her nose. "I knew you liked me."

"I was talking about your mother."

"Oh, you like me, sweetness." To prove it, he rested his hand flush on the counter, crowding her body with his and leaning in until there was nowhere no run. Nowhere to hide from the obvious chemistry.

He waited, silently watching as she swallowed hard, tried to school her reaction to him. When he was close enough to smell the baked sugar on her skin, he whispered, "You just don't like that you like me."

A feeling Luke knew all too well. There were a dozen women at the bar who wouldn't bat an eyelash at the thought of going home with him. But he wasn't up for the fast and loose lifestyle anymore. Nope, Luke wanted the only woman in town who drove him bat-shit crazy.

Kennedy snorted. "Does that really work with women?"
Always.

And it was working now. The pulse in her neck picked up, her eyes dilated with desire, and he found himself thinking that three weeks was a hell of a long time to keep his hands to himself. Especially if every time they were around each other, all he could think about was kissing her quiet. Or using that temper of hers in a more productive environment.

As if reading his mind, Kennedy shifted in her stool.

Interesting. She was as uncomfortable with the sexual heat that sizzled between them as he was.

"Okay, maybe I did have another reason for coming. Maybe I came to sample your tarts." He let his eyes slowly glide down her neck and lower, and damn, he was good. From this angle, he had a perfect view, and it was a wide expanse of nothing but silky, smooth skin.

Kennedy followed his gaze, then smacked his chest, shoving him back. She grabbed her wine and went to stand, but he captured her hand, halting her. "Seriously, the word around town is they are pretty amazing."

Made from vegetables, which would mean that he'd have to take some allergy meds after, but at this point he wasn't ruling it out.

"*Amazing* is a pretty charming word," she said with a knowing smile. "There's one in that box, help yourself. You can take it with you—to go." She headed toward the hallway with the entire bottle of wine, so she didn't see him cringe. Then she paused at the threshold. "Or you can just call Hawk, the really hot guy who owns the Penalty Box. He came in after closing and cleared me out of the rest of my stock."

Luke frowned. "He bought your tarts?"

"Sampled my pies, too." Her smile grew to release two adorable dimples in a move that she totally stole—from him! "Didn't beat around the bush either. Just came out and told me what he wanted."

Luke swallowed. "And what was that?"

"That's between me and Hawk," she said sweetly with a wink that drove him crazy. "Have a good night, Luke. And be sure to lock up when you leave."

* * *

When Kennedy's alarm went off the next morning, she had a hard time finding it. Partly because she was hungover from her pity party for one, but mostly because it was oh-dark-hundred on her day off.

Her first day off since she'd arrived in town.

Cracking open one eye, she finally located her phone—on the floor next to an empty wine bottle, her dress, and a half-eaten tart—then hit it four times before she realized that it wasn't her alarm at all.

The annoying beeping was coming from outside her window.

"Make it stop," she groaned, pushing a pillow over her face in hopes of snuffing out the awful noise. When that didn't work, she flung the pillow at the window, her days as a high school pitcher coming in handy as it nailed the glass pane. And sure, it grazed the ceiling fan, took out the bedside lamp, and took down the blinds. But the beeping stopped.

And for one incredibly beautiful moment, there was nothing but silence—and the world seemed perfect.

Beep. Beep. Beep.

Kennedy's eyes flew open, and in one fluid motion, she tore off the covers, shoved her feet in her slippers, and was marching out the front door.

Images of Fi circling the house with Lola flashed through her head as she raced down the hall, past the unslept-in sofa bed, snagging a sweater off the coat rack, and out the front door.

By the time Kennedy reached the edge of the porch, pulling her sweater tightly around her to shield against the early morning frost, the beeping had stopped. Too bad the pounding in her head hadn't.

The sun was peeking over the mountains, shining off the bright red and green fruit that hung from the thousands of trees. Beneath each tree in the closest row sat a few dozen white ladders with empty wicker bushels, just waiting to be filled. And ten feet from her bedroom window, going a steady two miles per hour up and down the rows of trees, was a giant green tractor.

And at its helm, dressed in denim and red flannel, with a faded ball cap pulled low, was Luke, looking like a sexy rancher-for-hire.

Kennedy looked at her phone and wanted to cry. It was six-oh-eight. On her only day off. "Surely, there's some kind of noise ordinance you're violating," she hollered over the roar of the engine.

Luke turned to look over his shoulder and, one hand on the steering wheel, the other cupped to his ear, hollered back, "Hang on, can't hear you."

To prove it, he revved the engine a few times, then headed her way—in reverse, with the backup beeper blaring as if announcing the second coming. The tractor reached the edge of her porch and sputtered to a stop. He shut down the tractor and smiled down at her—

"What was that, sweetness?"

Even on the porch, she still had to crane her neck to look up at him. "Aren't you afraid you'll wake the neighborhood this early?"

He looked around, his body language all innocence and concern. "You're up. I'm up. No one else around for miles." He took in her bedhead, her puffy eyes, and grinned—not that she could see his face, the sun was behind him, casting a long shadow, but she knew he was grinning at her. She could feel it. "I'm sorry, didn't I mention that today starts the harvest?"

"And it's tradition to kick off every harvest with a crack-of-dawn tractor pull around my house?" she guessed.

"Nah. Just this year. Thought I'd try something new, give you all the bells and whistles that come with living in the country." He stroked the hood of the tractor with reverence. "Impressive, huh? They call her the Porsche of tractors."

"I dated a guy who drove a Porsche once," she said. "He was quick off the line but a little too compact for my taste."

"Well, no need for worry here. I give you my word that Callahan Orchards is in possession of the biggest tractor in the county. Big, range tough, and overflowing with power. Always up for the task, and gets the job done." He winked. "Want to take it for a spin?"

"I'll pass."

"When you change your mind, let me know."

She noticed he said *when*, not *if*.

In one fluid motion, Luke hopped off the tractor and onto the grass. All those muscles moved with a power and confidence that said he could handle anything that came his way. She also got the impression that he was the kind of man who came through on his word.

"Actually, I am glad you're here. I'm nearly out of apples at the shop and need to schedule a delivery from my orchards," Kennedy said, proud at how professional she sounded.

Luke studied her—all of her—for a long, intense moment, then flipped his cap around in a move that was all male confidence and grinned. "I don't do business deals before I've had my morning cup of coffee."

"I would ask if you prefer cream or sugar, but that would imply I'm willing to make you coffee and invite you in."

"For the record, I'll always take sugar if a lady offers. And while I'd love to see you skirting around the kitchen in nothing but my old shirt and lace, I already made a pot, it's on the counter next to the stove."

Kennedy didn't know if it was seeing him in his element with dirt under his nails and yesterday's scruff, or maybe she was still a little drunk, but the idea of sharing a morning coffee with Luke made her thighs quiver.

"Or we can talk right here," he said. "Your call. Although I'm sure the crew is hoping for front porch negotiations." He looked over his shoulder. "They should be here in about three minutes—all fifty of them are scheduled to show up on the south orchard. Who knows, one look at you in nothing but bedhead, sheet prints, and that old shirt, and I bet a good dozen of them will offer up their services for free."

Kennedy looked down and—

"Ohmigod! You waited to tell me this until now." Her hands tugged at the bottom of what appeared to be an oversized UNIVERSITY OF WASHINGTON tee that she'd pulled from the hall closet last night. The cotton hung long enough to cover all the important parts up front, but she tugged down the back just to be safe.

"Yeah, that isn't much better." His gaze drifted toward

her apples, which were embarrassingly ripe, and there went that smile. "But it sure puts the good in my morning. Apparently in yours, too."

"It's cold," she lied, feeling ridiculously charmed. "And you're just trying to get to me by making me believe you slept over last night. When we both know that you didn't stay the night. I heard you lock up when you left."

"I left to go get some clothes, but then I came back." He took one step, then another, stopping when they were toe to toe, and he let his heated brown eyes travel from her face to her mouth, down her chest, where it hung for a long, intense moment.

Kennedy's mouth? Well, that went dry—the exact opposite of what was happening down south. The look on his face did her in. It was intense, hot, and sheer male appreciation. A look she hadn't been on the receiving end of in far too long.

"Just in time to see your little striptease."

Kennedy poked him in the chest, noticing how firm and sculpted it was. "You are so full of it."

"That shirt and your yellow panties say differently," he said, his lips giving a small curl at the corners. "Didn't take you for a cuddler or a sheet stealer. Gotta' say, you're full of surprises, sweetness."

"I'm not a sheet stealer!" Which was the same thing she'd told Philip when he'd accused her of being a blanket burglar. "And I am not wearing yellow underwear."

"You sure about that?"

"Yes," she said, hating how hard it was to breathe, how one wicked look could derail her entirely.

Carefully, she glanced down the neckline of her shirt to see if—shit!

Yellow panties.

She looked back up, to find Luke rocking victoriously back on his heels, because he'd been checking, too. She shot him her most intimidating glare, only he didn't look intimidated. He looked pleased with himself.

"Admit it, you only knew that because I forgot to put on pants, and you must have seen my reflection in the window." Feeling exposed, and strangely turned on, Kennedy poked his chest again. Only this time he didn't move back.

He moved forward, coming so close he didn't bother to stop until he was all in her space and she could smell the fragrant scent of apples on his clothes. Feel the heat of his body seep through the cotton of her shirt.

She felt herself drawing closer, falling into his vortex of sexy, which made her feel sexy, and feminine—and desired.

He was already a little sweaty from putting in some heavy lifting before the sun was even up. Yup, Luke Callahan was big, badass, and so mouthwateringly male she felt her cheeks heat.

Both sets.

"Wouldn't you like to know?" His breath brushed her lips and she almost moaned yes.

That she did want to know. She wanted to know if he really slept in her bed, and if there was a pot of coffee waiting for her by the stove. And even though she knew it was wrong, she desperately wanted to know what it would feel like to kiss him.

To finally kiss a man who knew what he wanted and took without apology.

"There is nothing I want to do more than take you up on

that offer," he said quietly, his eyes on her mouth. "But a gentleman never kisses on the first date."

"Date?" she said through the sexual haze. "We haven't had a date."

"Not yet." His lips curled up into a grin. "Although I did cook you chili."

"Which I didn't eat."

"Next time," he whispered.

"There won't be a next time."

"Sure there will, and it will end with a kiss that I would put good money on will be instigated by you." He grinned. "Yeah, that's how it will go down, because even though you would rather die than admit it, I get to you. I get to you bad."

"The only thing I get from you is acute irritation."

Luke glanced down at her fingers—which were desperately gripping the loops of his jeans and tugging him closer. Even worse, his hands were nowhere near her, but shoved behind his back—like a damn gentleman. "You sure about that, sweetness?"

Chapter 7

∾

The next afternoon, Kennedy looked out the pass-through window into the front of the shop and felt equal parts excitement and panic bubble up.

The excitement came from the steady cluster of customers, all smiles and all waiting for their turn to sample one of Kennedy's five newest creations—she was sure. She'd spent a good part of yesterday waiting for her apples to arrive, even broke down and texted Luke as to where her apples were. His response was to tell her they could talk about it over dinner—or perhaps during pillow talk.

Kennedy did what any professional businesswoman would do when their apples were being held hostage by a walking fantasy and his big green tractor—she ordered take-out and slept at the bakery. It gave her plenty of time to dream up and execute her new appleless additions to the menu. A smart move on her part, since the apples were a no-show and she was quickly running out.

Only now, it was nearing lunchtime and she was ready for a nap. The twelve-hour, uninterrupted kind. But every time she considered closing her eyes, all she could see was Luke.

In her bed.

And that was where some of the panic set in. She'd spent last night trying not to think about Luke in her bed, and this morning trying not to think about him naked in her bed. Now that Paula and Lauren had showed up to help with the customers, giving Kennedy a little reprieve, she blamed the strange fascination on sleep deprivation and grabbed a slice of pie.

"Thanks for helping me," Kennedy said to Ali as she pushed back through the swinging doors, after delivering yet another tray of Deep Dish HumDingers to the front of the shop.

"You had me at free pie," Ali said, taking her third piece of autumn berry pie that morning. Without bothering to use a plate or utensil, she bit off a piece like it was pizza, then groaned with contentment. "But I would have done it for the sheer fact that helping you will piss off Hawk."

Kennedy didn't like that she'd already made enemies in town, especially with two other businessmen whom people seemed to respect. But the thought of having someone in her corner felt really nice. Even if it was a connection based on a mutual dislike. So when Ali had knocked on the back door about an hour ago, in desperate need of coffee after pulling an all-nighter herself, Kennedy invited her in for a late breakfast—and maybe even a little girl talk.

"Well, thanks. I couldn't have restocked the shop this fast without you."

Kennedy looked at the stacking racks, beautifully

stocked with an array of autumn delights, then to the cooling shelves to the far left, which were nearly empty.

They'd moved a lot of product already that morning, mostly apple pies but some of her newer items as well, and there was still a steady flow of customers—who might be adventurous enough to try her fig cobblers.

Needing two minutes off her feet, and with a warm and delicious-smelling mini pecan pie, Kennedy took her well-deserved break and leaned against the counter.

"So the talk about you and Luke isn't true?" Ali asked.

Kennedy choked on a pecan. "There is talk? About me and Luke?"

"This is Destiny Bay—looking too long at someone who happens to be single is talk-worthy. Having a man's truck parked outside your house?" Ali laughed. "I'm surprised his mom hasn't placed an announcement in *The Acorn*."

"Shhh," Kennedy hissed, checking the pass-through to make sure Paula hadn't heard. Thankfully, Paula was working the cash register and the crowd with equal aplomb. Fi was a no-show, claiming she would never serve customers second-rate produce.

"Wait." Kennedy spun around to face her new friend. "Luke stayed at the cottage again last night?"

Ali paused, then grabbed a mini pie of her own and hopped up on the counter, her feet swinging. "Again, huh? So he *has* been at your place all week?"

Kennedy closed the swinging shutters, shielding them from the front of the shop—and prying eyes. "Two nights doesn't make it all week."

"It does when today is Tuesday. Monday. Tuesday." Ali ticked the days off on her fingers. "Sounds like all week to me."

"The first night he broke in and made me dinner."

"Gawd...what a jerky thing to do." Ali laughed.

"It was," Kennedy defended, knowing how ridiculous that sounded. "He did it to play with me, remind me that I was in his house, his town, and he was just waiting for me to fail so he could swoop in and gobble up my apples."

"Gobble?" Ali took a bite and licked her fingers. "Well, thank God it was all part of his plan to get his hands on your apples. Most women in this town would have taken Luke Callahan making them dinner as a proposal."

Kennedy rolled her eyes. "I'm not most women, so I told him to leave and he did. Although he claims to have come back."

You sure about that, sweetness?

Kennedy had convinced herself that he'd said it just to get to her. Only now she wasn't so sure. What if he had slept there? In her bed?

And watched her strip?

Only to fall right to sleep—like a gentleman.

This was worse than she thought. She had no intentions of encouraging Luke, because she was done with men. But he could have at least made a move and given her the chance to shoot him down.

Gentleman, her ass.

"And last night I was here. All night." She pointed to her pies as proof. "Nothing to talk about."

Ali looked disappointed. "So the bloodshot eyes and dreamy expression aren't from a night being charmed to heaven and back?"

"No," Kennedy said, taking a big bite of pie. "The only thing getting heated in my life is pies."

As it should be, she reminded herself.

The shutters swung back and Paula's round face appeared in the opening. "We need a few more HumDingers." She gave a panicked glance over her shoulder. "Make that all of the HumDingers."

Appetite gone, Kennedy put her cobbler aside and rushed to see what was going on.

One look and panic didn't even begin to convey what she felt. In the past two minutes the cluster had become a never-ending line.

No, not a line—more like a mob of customers waving twenty percent coupons in the air. Some of them were double fisting the discounts, which if applied solely to the HumDingers, would create a problem of gigantic proportions.

"Where did they all come from?" Kennedy asked, understanding how Walmart employees felt on Black Friday. "I didn't print that many coupons!"

"I saw Margret Collins using the copy machine at the senior center this morning. I didn't think much of it," Paula said, her brow covered in a thin sheen of sweat. "I should have made the connection. Today is coupon bingo, and Margret's been telling folks since Sunday that she was tired of losing to Louise Ferndale, said it was time to put up or shut up." Paula lowered her voice. "And by the looks of things, bingo just let out."

"And she went big with my coupons?"

"It's her way of showing you support, dear," Paula said. "Helping you succeed."

Kennedy looked back at the crowd, which had multiplied in the past ten seconds, and wondered if it was too late to close up shop. She could already tell by a quick glance that she didn't make enough pies. Not for this kind of crowd. "How many of those people do you think are open to trying something new?"

"I think a lot of folks will be open to tasting some new items," Paula said, doing her best to look encouraging, then disappeared with the pies back behind the counter to help with crowd control.

"I agree, folks will try it. After all, it's the neighborly thing to do. And I know they'll like it, but what if they like apples more?"

"I should call Dudley just in case," Kennedy said, hating that it sounded as if she lacked faith in her pies. "Have him bring out the riot squad."

"Destiny Bay doesn't have a riot squad. They have a sheriff, three deputies, and a K-9 Unit, which is just what Dudley calls his basset hound so he can bring him to work," Ali said, coming up beside her. "Plus he's three people back on the right in the orange jacket and camo hat, holding"—she squinted against the sun beaming through the large front windows—"six coupons."

Ali grabbed one of the last few trays of deep dish and slid it through the window. "Please tell me you limited it to one HumDinger per customer."

"No limits." Kennedy closed her eyes. She was doomed.

"You're not doomed, you have me," Ali said, shoving another bite in her mouth, then hopping off the counter to grab an apron.

And wasn't that the sweetest thing someone could say to her right then. Kennedy felt as if she were facing a firing squad and a woman she'd met only a few days ago had her back. "Thanks, I'm not used to someone on my side."

"Well, get used to it," Ali said with a bright smile. "Now, go make me some more pies to throw in that oven."

"I can't make more apple pies. Not with those coupons floating around," Kennedy explained, a sense of desperation and deep disappointment filling her chest. "If I were to fulfill every coupon with a HumDinger, which takes five pounds of apples to make, two pounds being heirlooms, I would be in the red by the end of the day."

Out of business by the end of the month.

"How much would you need to sell them for to be in the black?"

"And actually make a profit that I could live off?" Kennedy asked, prepping the mixer for a new batch of dough, hating that Luke's offer was seeming like a sound plan. "Twenty bucks apiece. And that is with a slim margin."

Ali sat down next to her, silent, as though pondering over a solution. Her expression completely serious, she asked, "How bad do you want to make a go at this?"

"Not bad enough to sell my apples to Luke." Not yet at least.

"I only know of one person in town who would spend twenty bucks on a pie that Paula sells for twelve."

"Unless he's ordering fifty a day, it won't help."

"Last offer, he was willing to pay twenty-five per pie, a hundred pies daily," Ali said and Kennedy shook her head, certain she misheard her friend over the growing chaos outside.

"A hundred pies?"

"A day."

A small flame of excitement lit in Kennedy's belly. By the time she did the quick math, figured out the profits on a hundred pies a day, the excitement had warmed into hope. "Do you think he'd meet with me?"

"Are you kidding? One call and you'd have him at your door." Ali leaned across the counter and took a bite of Kennedy's forgotten cobbler. "My Uncle Cosmo owns a number of high-end markets around Seattle, Redmond, and Portland that cater to the technology transplants. They're super posh, super expensive, and he is super serious about selling Sweetie Pies in his stores."

"Why would you do that?" Kennedy asked. "We barely know each other."

"Owning your own business is hard, so us ladies need to stick together. Plus, everyone could use a good friend in their lives. I know I could," Ali said quietly, as if embarrassed by the admission.

There was a loneliness and deep longing in Ali's eyes that Kennedy could relate to, and she began to wonder if she wasn't the only one desperate for connection.

Kennedy looked at the crowd again, then back to her friend, and felt her stomach warm. "I'm surprised he doesn't already have a deal."

"Can't even get a sit-down to discuss it. Even asked me a few years ago to help him out," Ali said around pie crumbs. "Seems him and Fi had a fling back when Christ walked the earth. Didn't end well. She charged at him with her dad's Studebaker, he luckily dodged it in time, and now every time he approaches her about her pies, she threatens to run him down and finish what she started. At this point he's hoping she'll forget about it, because her mind will go long before that woman lets a grudge lie."

And just like that, all the hope disappeared as Kennedy played through each and every possible outcome. None of them good.

"So if I sign with Cosmo, I'm positioning myself against

the Great Oz of Destiny Bay." Frustration had her releasing a
long, tired breath. It also had that little knot that had formed
behind her right eye spreading to encompass her entire head.

"And if you don't?" Ali asked.

"I go out of business." Kennedy said, never one to shy
away from the truth.

After a lifetime of emotional sucker punches, she'd
rather see what was coming—no matter how difficult or
painful the truth was. This time she wasn't looking to duck
or even get out of the way. Nope, Kennedy had sunk her
entire life savings, Philip's buyout of their condo, and every last bit of hope she had into making this shop—and her
life—a success.

If trouble was coming, then she needed time to square
up and take her own swing, because she wasn't going to go
down quietly this time. "Make the call."

*   *   *

"Can I at least go home and shower?" Kennedy asked, taking in her reflection in the windows of the Penalty Box. She
looked like Betty Crocker after a cupcake apocalypse.

Ali snorted. "We both know you weren't going to go
home. You were going to hide out in your shop all night to
avoid running into your bed buddy."

"He isn't my bed buddy." She stopped right outside the
bar. "And I'm not avoiding him. In fact, before you kid-
napped me, I was going to head home."

"Ah-huh," Ali said, calling Kennedy on that lie.

Not that it was a lie, really. She was going to head
back to the cottage. Sometime tonight. After she was certain Luke was asleep and there was no chance for one of

his run-ins. Then she would shower with the door locked, sleep on the couch, and be gone before he awoke.

Keeping her focus was essential—and that meant keeping her distance. When she was around Luke, all logic went out the window. She made impulsive decisions. Stupid impulsive decisions like almost kissing him while wearing nothing but his old T-shirt.

Just thinking about it had her lips tingling.

Kennedy fluffed her hair. When that didn't help, she smoothed it back in a bun. "You could have at least told me I had dough in my hair."

"If you got it out of your hair, people would just look at the pie filling on your right boob," Ali said with a teasing grin, dragging Kennedy through the door and straight for the bar, weaving in and out of the crush of people.

For a Tuesday night, the place was impossibly crowded.

Ali signaled the bartender—who was at the other end, engrossed in a conversation with a couple of patrons. Very female and very giggly patrons. "Two glasses of champagne."

He didn't even move a muscle.

"Champagne?" Not that Kennedy didn't like a glass of bubbly every now and again, but Ali looked more like a Scotch drinker. Straight up and straight from the bottle. Not to mention champagne combined with her new friend's unusually bubbly demeanor had Kennedy feeling a little unsettled.

"Yup." Ali clapped her hands and smiled. "We're celebrating. Cosmo called me back."

Kennedy stopped breathing. "And?"

"He wants to meet."

Kennedy was overcome with emotion. Not only had Ali

already called on her behalf, which was humbling in it-self because their friendship was still so new, but Cosmo wanted to meet Kennedy. To discuss buying her pies in bulk at twenty-five dollars apiece. Never in her life had a Hail Mary worked out.

"He's interested in carrying my pies?"

"Are you kidding? He was so excited when I called, he nearly wet himself," Ali said, her excitement as real as Kennedy's. "He would have asked to meet for a tasting tonight, but he's working at the Portland location this week, so he said Sunday was the soonest he could get back."

"Tasting?" Kennedy asked, trying to stay calm. "But he already loves the pies, why would he need a tasting?"

"Because he wants to partner with you, so of course he'd want a tasting. Him sitting in the shop and eating a Sweetie Pies pie will seal this deal. Why do you look like I just said I hate dessert?" Ali asked as if Kennedy were slow.

She wanted to point out that Luke was the slow one.

For a guy who claimed to corner the market on knowing every woman's needs, he sure was taking his sweet ass time delivering on hers. She barely had enough apples to get through the week, and if Luke didn't drop off her next order by Sunday, she'd be cleared out before Cosmo even showed. No apples meant no tasting and no future orders.

"Hey!" Ali smacked her fist on the cedar top. "Bar-maid!"

Hawk didn't move, except to turn his head and lift a brow in Ali's direction. His expression was one of pure irritation, with enough challenge to intimidate even the toughest of men. Not to mention the scars on his hands said he knew how to use them, and wasn't afraid to get rough if necessary.

"You going to get me my drinks?" Ali asked. "Or is this confirmation that, with you, everything is a serve-yourself kind of experience?"

Hawk straightened to his full height—Thor minus the hammer—and Kennedy was sure he was going to throw them out of the bar—with his own hand—but instead he threw a rag over his shoulder and headed their way.

"Sorry, sunshine, tap only here," he said, resting his palms on the bar top.

"You say that like it somehow makes cider manly," Ali said. "It doesn't, tap or not, it's still the sorority girl drink of choice, Bradley." Ali looked at the giggling co-eds who were sipping from green-tinted martini glasses. "Well, next to appletinis."

Hawk crossed his arms, which had an array of tattoos bulging and rippling under the simple movement. "They aren't co-eds, and trust me, they aren't here for the appletinis."

He was bigger than Kennedy remembered. Better looking, too. With the body of a pro-athlete, the smile of a bad boy, and a swagger that made women want to do crazy things. Looking at the way Fan Girl One and Fan Girl Two were sizing him up, crazy bed things.

Kennedy wanted to do crazy bed things. Only the bad boy thing wasn't doing it for her. Nope, sadly, it was the town's most eligible bachelor who came to mind.

"Good, then you won't mind parting with the bottle you keep stashed behind the bar. The one you use when your cider isn't enough game." Ali leaned over the bar, her head dipping below the lip. She reappeared moments later with a bottle of bubbly and two stemmed glasses.

Ali grinned. Hawk scowled. And Kennedy moved over a chair. The tension between the two was so strong, Kennedy could almost feel it. She wasn't sure if the tension was simple animosity—or something more interesting.

"Didn't know you were paying that much attention to my game, sunshine," Hawk said, his frown fading into a look of sheer amusement, confidence rolling off him like a man whose likeness had been plastered all over Times Square in nothing but his hockey stick and Calvin Klein's. Which he had. "Does that mean you want to play?"

Ali set the glasses on the bar. "My mom warned me about men who carry their stick around in their hand all day."

"Your mom loves me," Hawk pointed out.

"She's also been married six times, so I wouldn't put much weight in that."

Hawk went to say something else, but instead plucked the bottle out of Ali's hand and filled both glasses. Even dropping a raspberry in each before sliding them over.

That was it. Ali had just told the most intimidating man Kennedy had ever seen what she wanted, then demanded that he deliver. To Kennedy's surprise, he did. With a smile on his face.

If she'd known it was that easy, Kennedy might not be closing in on thirty and starting over for the umpteenth time in Nowhere USA. Not that Nowhere USA was a bad place to start over. In fact, Kennedy was beginning to believe that maybe there was something to the town's name. Destiny Bay might be a bit whimsical for her logical brain, but the thirteen-year-old who dreamed of big adventures and life's icing wanted to believe. Believe that there was more out there for her than being a rotating doormat.

But Kennedy wasn't that girl anymore. She was competent, a determined business owner, who was the master of her own destiny. First step was getting her apples delivered. Second step, getting her house back.

Channeling her inner nut buster, she pulled out her cell phone and dashed off a quick text to Luke.

I want my apples.

Happy to be taking action, being pro-active about her future, and making her own destiny, she slid her phone back in her purse and reached for the champagne flute. But before she could take her first celebratory sip, someone scooted in beside her.

Kennedy didn't have to look to see who it was; the scent of fresh apples and wicked promises had her lips tingling.

"I want your apples, too," Luke said.

Kennedy turned, her expression cool and casual, showing not a glimmer of the heat simmering in her belly. She even ignored the melted chocolate eyes and heart-stopping smile—both of which advertised he wasn't talking about the fruit hanging on the trees.

"You got a little something, right there." He pointed to the glob on her top. "Apple?"

"Pear," she said defiantly, resisting the urge to brush at the pie filling.

And it was that, right there, the easy humor that lit his eyes, the way he looked so damn comfortable in his body—in his world. It put Kennedy at ease as much as it put her on edge.

Then there was how close he was standing to her. Their bodies brushing every time he so much as blinked, slowing her mind down to a steady sway as her heart raced at the possibilities. And her mouth tingled, ached with the memory that the last time she'd been this close, she'd nearly kissed him.

"What are you doing here?" she asked, kicking herself because if she knew that he'd be here, then she could have been at home. Showered, clean, and fast asleep.

In the bed.

"I own the place."

"Half the place," Hawk pointed out.

Luke ignored his friend, his eyes trained solely on Kennedy, making her want to smooth down her hair. "Why? Did you come looking for me? Maybe you got lonely at home and need someone to scrub your back?"

"No, I need someone to deliver my apples. You didn't give me a time yesterday, so I waited until well after closing, but they never came," Kennedy said.

"You're delivering her apples?" Hawk asked as if this were an unreasonable request for the owner of the orchard to deliver produce to his customer.

"I was going to discuss delivery options over breakfast, but then you'd have had to actually come home for that to happen." Luke grabbed a frosty bottle from behind the bar and popped the top, then slid onto the stool next to her. "But we can talk now."

"Great," Kennedy said, trying not to watch his throat work as he took a long pull from the bottle. Tried even harder not to notice that he hadn't shaved that morning, which left him looking a little rugged, a little bit dirty, and *holy cow*, every time he smiled, it sent a whole lot of tingles to parts that had no business tingling. "When can you deliver them?"

"I can get them to you tomorrow—"

"Tomorrow we've got to harvest the east sector," Hawk interrupted.

"But it will cost you," Luke finished.

Kennedy rolled her eyes. "Oh, are we back to the kiss?"

"You kissed her?" Hawk said rather loudly.

Eyes on hers, Luke reached across the bar and palmed Hawk's face, squeezing a second before delivering a quick shove. Not that it muffled Hawk's growing concern that this was the worst news he'd heard all year. Maybe ever.

Kennedy felt herself flush. Not from chemistry, but from embarrassment. "I didn't kiss him," she said equally loud in case anyone was listening. Which she feared everyone was.

"But you wanted to." Before Kennedy could argue the point, set the record straight, which would have meant lying, Luke added, "And I meant that the delivery will really cost you. Your deal was for the apples. Nowhere in the contract did it say delivery or the cost of harvesting was included."

An issue Kennedy hadn't run across until now because there'd been enough apples left over in the shop's refrigerator from Fi's last delivery.

"Who delivered them before?" Kennedy asked, her heart pounding so hard she could barely hear herself speak.

Luke set his bottle down. "Me."

"Then you can see how I would have every reason to believe, based on past performance between our companies, that the apples would be delivered as promised." There, that sounded professional.

"I can see how you might have come to that conclusion," he said. "But that arrangement was between Callahan Orchards and the previous owners of Sweetie Pies. Who happened to be my mom and aunt. None of our clients get their apples delivered for free, especially clients who are only paying wholesale. If we did that, we'd lose money."

He didn't say it like she was an idiot. In fact, there was a gentle hint of apology beneath his words that Kennedy wanted to believe was genuine. But she knew better, knew that no matter how sorry he sounded, in the end there would be one winner and one loser, and he was rooting for the home team—and that, more than anything, made her feel like an even bigger idiot.

Of course Luke had harvested and delivered Paula's apples for free. Then again she wasn't just a client; she was family.

Kennedy was an outsider, whom he happened to share some chemistry with, standing in his way. The heat that flickered between them was as intoxicating as it was misleading, a fiery path that would surely lead to immense pleasure and complete disappointment. Because she wanted him as much as she wanted her next breath, but she wanted to make this new chapter a successful one.

And she was determined and a hard worker who didn't mind getting dirty.

"Taking a bigger loss on the apples isn't a smart business move," he said as if he were the Bill Gates of the apple industry. "My crew doesn't work for free. Someone has to pay for the labor."

And Luke seemed to think that someone was her. Too bad for him, she had negotiated with Callahan Orchards. Maybe not with the big, bad CEO of the family, but Paula was an equal owner, had sold her shop and all the assets with it to Kennedy in good faith. Even a first-year business major would know that.

"I can help you out with some comparable apples," Luke offered.

"Nothing compares to the apples I've got," she said, and Luke maintained eye contact, but she got a little thrill when he cracked a smile.

"I have to agree, sweetness," he finally said.

Hawk blew out a long breath, then eyed his partner—who finally eyed him back. Not a word was spoken between the two, but a fair amount of communication happened. A few grunts, a shrug, then a super-secret nod that had Ali snorting.

Luke finally looked back at Kennedy. "I can give you a fair bid." He said it in a way that made Kennedy think he was being genuine in his offer. But who wanted a fair deal when the original deal was for free? It was kind of like promising someone forever, only to cha-cha into the sunset when a slinkier option came along.

"Oh, I know you will because, like you said, any smart businessman would. And as soon as you get over this good-guy act where you have convinced yourself that *you* are doing *me* a favor, you'll realize that while I may not have negotiated with you, I did negotiate with the other owners of Callahan Orchards. And I'm sure Paula will attest that, although not detailed in the contract, your company delivering my apples for free was implied."

Hawk looked at Luke, who wasn't giving away much, but he didn't need to. Hawk's nonverbal communications skills had come to include *Holy Fuck*. Add to that a little sputtering, and it was enough to know that while Luke may have had the advantage, Kennedy had just delivered the winning play.

Kennedy downed her champagne and stood. "Thanks for the drink, Ali."

"That's what friends are for," Ali said, standing, too—as if in support.

The gesture was so unexpected, Kennedy felt her heart smile. Felt some of the growing stress release and give in to the feeling that right now, in this moment, she wasn't taking on the world alone.

Kennedy hadn't just lost her house and her job in the breakup. Since most of her friends were also Philip's friends, and she hadn't wanted them to choose—especially since she was pretty sure they'd choose Philip—she'd lost them as well. But Ali had a lifetime of history with these guys and this town, yet when faced with a choice, she had chosen Kennedy.

"You were right," Kennedy said. "A drink was just what I needed. I feel much better now."

Confidence bubbling, she turned to leave and found Luke was standing—in her way. Sure, to a random on-looker, it would appear as if Luke was living up to his gentleman persona, rising when a lady took her leave. But it was strategic. She was stuck between the bar and his hard, unwavering body.

"You'll feel even better when you crawl into bed," Luke said lowly, leaning in until his lips grazed her ear. "I put fresh sheets on. The silky ones that hug your body like a second skin, hold you just so." His arm tightened around her, not quite touching her but definitely teasing. "They make for one hell of a good night, sweetness."

Kennedy thought about him on her like a second skin, how it would feel to have him hold her just so, and her brain went fuzzy. But when his grin widened, as if that was exactly what he wanted, she placed a hand on each of those impressive pecks and pushed him back, but he didn't move.

Realistically, there was really nowhere for him to go without bumping into another patron. That didn't mean he had to bump closer to her, making her hands slide down onto the top of those gorgeous, flat abs of steel.

"Thanks," she said, refusing to let him know he was getting to her. "That was thoughtful, but my night couldn't possibly get any better."

She had a plan to get back her apples—and her cottage.

* * *

Confused and feeling a bit turned on, like he'd just participated in some kind of twisted public foreplay, Luke watched Kennedy strut out of the bar. His eyes locked on her sweet ass, as it swished back and forth, creating a hypnotic vortex that was impossible to resist.

Oh, she kept her swag light and natural, as if she knew he was watching, but didn't want to appear to care. But she did, because right before she walked out the door, she turned back and caught his gaze and—*Holy Christ*—all sorts of interesting things happened.

Things that made sitting down in his jeans an impossibility. Clearly, she felt it, too, because suddenly she was looking at him as if she couldn't stop thinking about those sheets, a real slip-and-slide event that would end with her moaning and begging for more.

It was that promise of more, he was sure, that had her turning for the door like that ass of hers was on fire. Smart woman, since he wouldn't mind taking her up on that fantasy.

Which would blow the whole *she's an obstacle and nothing more* thing he had going on.

"If you're done eye-fucking the Shop Girl, I'd like to point out that if she gets to your mom first, we're sunk," Hawk said, pulling out his cell and shoving it Luke's way. "Call her."

"My mom is a bleeding heart, but she is also a savvy businesswoman," Luke said but he reached for another drink anyway, bypassing the cider and going for the Scotch. "And she isn't home tonight, she's at her book club."

Hawk put the phone away. "I hope so, because if Kennedy gets your mom to agree, she's here for good."

And if she didn't get her apples, she'd lose the shop and most likely move on. To another town. Which shouldn't matter to him, but it did. Every time he thought about it, this acute pressure started at the back of his shoulders and worked its way through his chest, where it settled—and grew.

"She'll sell—she has to," Luke said, confident that she would. He just hoped that it was in time to deliver on their orders. Hawk didn't look confident or hopeful; he looked stressed out. "When have I ever let you down?" When Hawk didn't answer, Luke poured his buddy two fingers. "I've got this handled."

"You sure?" Hawk gave Luke a long assessing look, which pissed him off. Luke had never not come through— at least for Hawk.

"Yeah. I'm sure."

"Not that I'm one to question your skills with the ladies, but she looked to be handling you. In fact, she just walked out of here with your nuts in her hand, which I have to ad-mit freaks me out as much as it impresses me."

Luke knew exactly what Hawk felt; she impressed him, too. Every time she faced an obstacle that would have most people packing it in, her stubborn chin would shoot up, her determination would increase, and it was the biggest turn-on in the world.

"One tear and Paula will have you out there picking Kennedy's apples and sinking this deal. A deal that I wanted to hold off on signing for this exact reason."

It had taken Luke the better part of the week to get Hawk to sign. Luke knew it was the right move, knew that Rogers wouldn't wait for them to figure out how they were going to deliver. Suits like Rogers didn't give a shit about how people delivered—just that they did.

And he had less than three weeks to make it happen.

"Kennedy isn't a crier," Luke said, finding it hard to imagine a straight-shooter like Kennedy using her emotions to get ahead. "And I'll figure this out."

"Well, I hope so because this is a done deal and there are no more apples in the entire fucking state."

Luke polished off his glass in a single swallow, letting the liquid burn its way down, only to catch fire in his belly. "I saw the financials she sent my mom," Luke admitted, a wave of guilt hitting hard. He had no right to go snooping through his mom's papers. In fact, it bordered on unethical, but he'd done it anyway. "My guess is that she's a few weeks away from going bust."

"She looked pretty damn happy for a woman on the verge of bankruptcy," Hawk pointed out. "What if she doesn't sell?"

"She will," Luke said, pouring himself another glass because a few weeks was a generous estimation.

"I just need a little more time with her."

"We're running out of time," Hawk pointed out. "If we don't harvest those trees by mid-October, we won't get them fermenting in time to make Rogers's timeline. And once the rain starts, we'll lose the rest to rot."

"Which is why I'm meeting Jason Stark from Bay View Orchards in the morning before he heads to Seattle. We need those apples, sooner than later, if we are going to fulfil all of the cider orders. So I want to make an offer to buy his apples early, separate from the offer on the land." Luke knew Hawk wasn't going to close the bar down until one, which would put his friend in bed after two, so he hated what he was about to ask. "Can you run the crew tomorrow morning so I can get to his office in time?"

Hawk rested a hand on Luke's shoulder and gave him a nudge that always managed to lighten Luke's mood, take some of the pressure off so he could breathe easier.

It was Hawk's way of saying he had Luke's back. No matter what. It was that kind of unconditional support that made Hawk such a great business partner—and made Luke even more determined to make this happen. For the both of them.

Partnering with Rogers had been Luke's idea, but Hawk had just as much to lose if it went south—maybe more. Not that he'd ever hold it against Luke if it did. Hawk wasn't the kind of guy to pass the blame; he was too loyal for that.

Hell, he took care of his wife for years after she walked out on him. For another man.

"You think they'll go for it? The Starks?" Hawk asked.

"My option expires at the end of the season. If I end up passing, they will have to move the apples fast. Finding a buyer will be easy; harvesting fifty acres before the rain starts will take a lot of time and energy." Energy that

Stark's kids obviously didn't have. "Plus it will let Kennedy know that she's not the only option in town. That she doesn't have me by the nuts."

She was going to realize soon enough that there was no way she could use all the apples, and her surplus would sink her business. That selling them back to him was the smart choice. He didn't need to tell her that he still needed her apples in order to get the capital to buy Bay View.

Hawk studied Luke for a long, intense minute, then gave a worried shake of the head. "It's not your nuts I'm worried about, bro."

Advice Luke was still considering ten minutes later when he pulled onto the same windy dirt road he'd walked a thousand times every harvest as a kid. If he was going to come through on his word, then he needed to gain the upper hand.

Cutting the engine, he stepped out of the car. The fall night was crisp and the moon was full, casting a soft light over the rolling acres of apple trees. One of Luke's favorite views—a view he'd desperately missed these past few years living in town.

He stood quietly, waiting for the crickets to kick in again, and watched the rocking chair on the front porch of the cottage slowly move in the breeze.

Even though his dad was gone and the cottage had long ago been remodeled into a guest quarters, every memory, every ounce of regret he'd been avoiding for the past ten years, came rushing over him. The familiar scent of tart apples, the dew settling on the leaves, the sounds of the wood creaking under the rocking chair.

That chair had been his dad's favorite. Hand made by some old-timer a county over and bought for him as a gift from Luke's mom for their fifth wedding anniversary. After a long day in the orchard, this was where his dad would come, to smoke his pipe and watch the stars. If Luke closed his eyes, he could probably still smell the cherry tobacco and hear his dad humming his favorite Merle Haggard songs.

A deep longing rolled through Luke. Combined with regret and enough nostalgia to take him out at the knees. Shaking off the memory, he grabbed his keys and headed for the door, sliding the key in the lock, and—

"What the hell?"

He tried again, rechecking his key to be sure, and no luck. That was when he noticed the note nailed to the door.

Bring me my apples and I'll give you a new key.
    Sweet dreams...K

Chapter 8

The sun hadn't even hinted at rising when Kennedy's alarm went off. Promising herself five more minutes, she hit the snooze button, rolled over, and—froze.

Her heart leapt to life, and into her throat, her senses going on high alert. She strained her eyes through the dark, lying stock-still beneath the soft cotton sheets.

Sheets she had begrudgingly changed around 2 a.m. when she'd woken from a steamy dream starring Farmer Luke and his silky sheets. Good night guaranteed was an understatement. Every time she so much as breathed, the deliciously soft fabric felt like foreplay against her skin, leaving her more than hot and bothered—and desperate to take a ride on his big green tractor.

A sad side effect, she was sure, of acute sex deprivation.

After the bar, Kennedy had headed straight to Ali's shop to purchase a new lock. Ali suggested she also get a dead bolt, and a gun, but Kennedy had thought a new door handle was enough. She'd planned on installing it and turning in, but then remembered the back door, to which Luke also had a key. So Kennedy wedged a chair under the handle and piled several pots and lids on top, a makeshift alarm in case of a sneaky and sexy burglar attack. By the time she'd made it to bed, it was well after midnight—but her solitude was secured.

Only the big shape lying next to her, which looked suspiciously human, said her walls of solitude had been breached and she wasn't alone. Nope, the sandman had decided to pay her a visit—and stayed to test out her sheets.

Which apparently weren't too big or too small, but just right. He was taking up more than his fair share of the blanket, too. Burglar turned bed hog.

Ignoring the urge to slip and slide right over to the other side of the bed and wish her burglar a very good morning, she pulled the covers tighter to her, squeezed her eyes shut, and tried to convince herself that she was still dreaming. Only when she reopened her eyes, the outline was even more distinct, and she smelled a lingering scent of fresh apples and sexy farmer.

Kennedy was equally horrified and excited by the possibility of waking her bedmate, but she was also terrified of what the possibilities of having a bedmate meant— like maybe her dreams were more than a dream—so she slipped a hand beneath the sheets and did a quick pat-down.

Top? Check.

Panties? Check.

She even had on her socks—*thank God*.

Reaching over, she grabbed the sheets and yanked them

back, only thinking after that he could very well be buck naked under there. And wouldn't that be wonderfully awkward.

Giddiness mixed with the earlier panic, and quickly became irritation the second the sheets hit the bottom of the bed. Because her guy was clothed, all right, wearing the U of W shirt she'd borrowed—no underwear. Not that it mattered, because her "guy" was a bundle of pillows arranged in a humanlike shape.

And in case that didn't get her panties in a bunch, pinned in the middle of the U of W shirt, right beneath *of*, was a note:

> *In case you missed me and needed a good cuddle ... L*
>   *PS ... Don't worry about getting me a key, the screwdriver worked just fine.*

Kennedy wanted to tell him she didn't do cuddling—it went against her independent nature—but there was no point in yelling at a pillow. Especially since it was clear by the drool marks and indented chest region that she had been spooning Pillow Farmer for most of the night.

Kennedy flicked on the light and inspected each and every window. Completely locked, not a single one messed with. That was when she smelled it. The earthy aroma of fresh-brewed coffee drifting down the hallway and filling the room.

Ignoring her robe and slippers, Kennedy shot down the hallway, flicking on every light as she went. She reached the front door to find it locked and secure. So she followed the scent to the kitchen, which was also surprisingly empty. The chair was in place, the pots and lids still perched to alert her to intruders, everything exactly the way she'd left it.

Except for the big, steaming mug of coffee, which sat on the kitchen table—next to a single cider apple. And another note.

Here's your first delivery. If you want more before next week, I suggest losing your big city shoes and strapping in. It's a long fall.

And that's when Kennedy saw the safety harness hanging over the chair. A big, bright pink, blatant challenge. One that she couldn't resist.

She might be a people pleaser, but she wasn't a pushover. After years of merely surviving, Kennedy was ready to live a life that was full.

* * *

She was upset. Luke could tell.

If the sounds of gravel in his blender weren't enough to have him consider sneaking out of his bedroom window, then the pots and pans slamming around in his kitchen was. Only he wasn't in his bedroom—he was on the couch. And Paula was cooking up a storm in his kitchen.

It wasn't unusual for his mom to let herself into his house, take over the kitchen, and whip up a hearty, home-made breakfast. But the clatter and banging implied she was more interested in whipping up a category five sit-down than pancakes and eggs.

Paula didn't do mad; it was an emotion she couldn't seem to find the energy for after Luke's dad passed away.

But she did guilt like any good Catholic mother—lovingly and with heart.

Luke's dad called it guilt-fueled gluttony. The more upsetting the offense, the more extravagant the meal. One time, when Luke was twelve, he'd been caught kissing Bethany Smart in the confessional booth—by Father Armand. By the time Luke made it home, Paula had cooked enough food to cover Thanksgiving, Christmas, and Easter Sunday—and it was only August.

"What'cha making in there?" Luke asked from the couch.

"Right now?" she said sweetly. Too sweetly. Country-cut bacon and potato casserole kind of sweet. "Eggs Benedict. It seemed fitting."

Luke rolled his eyes but made his way to the kitchen. If he didn't get in there, she'd pull out the roasting pan and he'd never get rid of her.

Passing the bathroom, he glanced at himself in the mirror and groaned. He took in yesterday's work clothes, his hair, which was standing on end, and the time of the day. It was a quarter to eight, which meant even though he'd overslept, he'd achieved less than three hours of sleep.

Between figuring out how to approach the Starks about their apples, and staking out his sexy tenant to make sure she was asleep when he jimmied his way inside, Luke was spent. So finding Paula standing at the counter, elbow deep in dirty pots and pans, and arranging freshly ground hazelnuts on a baking sheet was the last thing he needed.

Luke wasn't sure if the hazelnuts were for the eggs, the potato casserole she had going, or the French toast she was dredging.

"How long have you been here?" he asked.

"Came over right after I saw you sneak out of the guest cottage like some kind of thief in the night," Paula said, dredging the fresh-baked bread over and over again to punctuate her disapproval.

"It's hard to sneak when you own the property." Luke grabbed a mug from the cupboard and lifted the coffeepot. Sadly, the only appliance in the kitchen his mother hadn't used.

A strategic oversight on her part.

With a sigh, he filled it with water, added the grounds, and hit Start.

Paula tutted, then mumbled something about his coffee-for-one lifestyle being a shame. Luke wanted to explain that he liked his coffee-for-one life. Loved it, in fact. He never suffered from a lack of female companionship, but he never took it far enough to warrant handing out his house key. Nope, from the moment he hit the sack until he had to walk out that front door, all he had to think about was himself.

A state Luke rarely had the chance to indulge in. Once he stepped beyond that threshold, and out into town, there were a whole lot of people he was responsible for. He provided paychecks, apples, security, and support. For his mom and aunt, he was tasked with the job of ensuring their happiness. And he was okay with that—most days. But some days he needed space that wasn't heavy with responsibility.

So he'd bought a house across town. Now he needed to invest in some new locks, then he remembered how that had worked out for Kennedy and groaned. Maybe he needed to move to Tacoma.

"This all looks wonderful, but it's Wednesday. Shouldn't you be at the shop?"

"I'm heading there after I finish up here," Paula said, opening the fridge and pulling out eggs, milk, mascarpone cheese, and not two, but three different kinds of apples.

Well, shit. All the ingredients for her famous hazelnut triple-apple sticky buns.

This was worse than he thought. She only made those for Easter Sunday and funerals.

His dad's funeral being the last time.

Momentary sadness slid through him, but since his mom was there, he quickly brushed it off. "What are you really doing here, Mom?"

"I already said, making my son breakfast. He needs more than a bowl of cold cereal to get through a day of harvest."

His mom had two passions in her life: her family and her food. If she could combine the two, all the better. Which was why Luke wasn't sure what had surprised him more, that she had actually sold her shop or how much happier she'd seemed since.

Paula loved her customers—it was the main reason she'd held on for so long—but over the years, baking all day had taken a toll on her arthritis. Luke hadn't realized just how worn down she'd become. Now she had a new spring in her step, a rejuvenated passion for baking.

And life.

Luke hadn't seen her this worked up since before his dad passed. Not that Luke was all that excited about being the center of her newfound passion, because for Paula, passion meant demanding penance, but the warm glow to her cheeks was a nice change.

He hated to admit it, but selling the shop to someone who allowed Paula to still work the occasional shift was perfect. His mom could gab with her friends, catch up on gossip, and even bake a few pies when she felt like it. Then midday would come and she could go home and relax.

Not in her sunroom like she'd dreamed, but looking at her now, even though she was clearly in a mood, she looked lighter. Younger.

Happier.

She dropped three pieces of toast onto the sizzling griddle. After flipping them over, she looked up. She had flour on her cheek and egg dripping all over his counters. "Unless you want me to leave."

Luke walked over to his mom and pulled her in for a big hug, his heart rolling over when she leaned all the way into him, patting his cheek like he was still nine and half her size. "I don't want you to leave, Mom. I just want you to tell me why you're baking Dad's favorite sticky buns."

Paula pulled back with a look of complete innocence. "You say that like they'll bring the second coming. They were your dad's favorite, and I thought they were yours, too."

"They are. It's just you haven't made them since he passed," he said carefully, studying her closely for signs of sadness. Instead of the brittle smile she usually gave when someone brought up her Orin, she gave a genuine smile that was warm and full of nostalgia.

"Well, today's a special day and I think your dad would have insisted." She lifted the French toast off the griddle and, after a good dusting of powdered sugar, placed them on the plate on the counter—then motioned for Luke to sit down.

He inhaled the scene of cinnamon and maple syrup and lifted the first bite to his mouth.

Perfection.

Sweet, rich, and exactly what he needed.

"Plus, I'm not baking them for you,' she said. "I'm baking them for Kennedy. My way of saying welcome to the neighborhood and sorry for my son being a horse's behind."

Luke choked on his French toast. "Did you just call me an ass?"

"I would never say that word." But she was smiling as if she was thinking it. "Even if it did describe someone who would make that poor girl pick her own apples."

"She told you about that?" Maybe Hawk was right, and Kennedy wasn't above using his mom's soft heart to get her way.

Paula snorted. "That girl would never sell out a soul, even one who needs a good confession, like yours. I heard it from Margret, who heard it from her grandson. The one who married that dancer from Vegas, only to find out she was dancing for bills. He was down at the Penalty Box last night and overheard you talking to Hawk."

Luke didn't want to know what else the prick had overheard. He had purposefully kept his mom in the dark about the property. She had lived through enough disappointment for him to get her hopes up, only to have them come crashing down if something went hairy.

Like, say, being short a few acres of produce.

"I told Margret, that doesn't sound like my Lucas," she said in that tone that brought forth equal bouts of pride and guilt. "She was concerned it would affect her standing order for pies, then reminded me how the senior center counts on those pies when welcoming new members. So I reminded her that you have always delivered my apples, and would never put Margret, or any other sweet Destiny Bay resident, in an awkward situation like that."

Luke wanted to point out that the newest resident had many sides, but sweet wasn't one of them. Not when it came to him.

"Her first delivery was handled this morning," he said, leaving out the fact that it had been a cuddle buddy, a single apple, and a little B and E. "I won't be able to complete her order until next week, though."

Paula was back to working the dough for Kennedy's sticky buns. "Well, that explains it. When she called to say she didn't need me at the shop today, I figured it was because she had scheduled someone else to work. Imagine my surprise when Fi said Kennedy went to the shop to bake the day's pies, only to return to the orchard a few hours later in my old picking harness."

Luke dug into the first course of his breakfast. "That is surprising."

Baking a day's worth of pies then working the orchards was tiring work. Not that it couldn't be done. Up until Orin had passed, his mom had done it every harvest.

Paula was the most independent, hardworking woman Luke had ever met. Even though she'd married into the Callahan family, she had worked that orchard, right alongside Luke and his dad. When Orin became ill, she'd stepped in to take over the company until Luke came home from Seattle. To this day, she still helped out in the orchards when her arthritis would allow.

So Kennedy showing up, ready to bring in that harvest,

proved that she was more determined than Luke had originally thought. She wasn't stubborn—she was a fighter.

If delaying her apples wasn't going to slow her down, Luke had bigger problems than he wanted to admit.

Paula mixed the apples, spices, and hazelnuts into a paste, then spread it evenly across the dough, paying extra attention to the edges. "So I called her and said I'd donate my sticky buns to her cause."

Luke lifted a brow. "Her cause?" How was picking some apples a cause?

"Her Big Apple Pie Raising."

Luke choked on some powered sugar. "A big apple, what?"

"Pie raising." Before Paula could explain what the hell a pie raising was, Luke's phone rang. Seeing it was Hawk's number, and that he rarely used the phone, a bad feeling settled in Luke's gut.

"Hey, man," he said into the cell. "What's going on?"

"No apple picking, that's for sure." Hawk's voice was tight with frustration. "I've got the trucks on the way, enough equipment for a whole crew, and only twenty-five guys are here."

Luke straightened. "But I hired fifty guys for today."

"Noted, but it doesn't help me now."

Luke set his fork down. "We have to harvest the north orchard and load the golden delicious today or we'll miss our delivery window for the market. I can't do that with half a crew!"

Doing it with a full crew would be tight. During harvest it always was. From first apple picked until that last truck pulled out, it was a nonstop grind from September through the end of November. Six days a week, twelve hours a day. Missing even a few hours could create a snowball that would affect deliveries, timelines, and even the product.

"I don't know what to tell you. I got on the phone, called everyone who was a no-show to see what was up. Most went to voice mail; a few said they'd be late, personal reasons. And Frank, oh man, Frank." Hawk let out a sigh that was utterly defeated and that bad feeling Luke had went nuclear. "The guy was stupid enough to admit he was helping with the town's pie raising, whatever the hell that is."

Luke ran a hand down his face. "It's code for Let's Fuck with Luke's day." Because although Luke was well liked around town, his mom was as beloved as apple pie. So if she was backing a cause, then people were going to stand in line to help. Even if it meant his life just got a whole lot more complicated.

"Language," Paula whispered as if Jesus himself were coming to breakfast.

But Luke didn't have time even to think about filtering, because Kennedy's plan was working. He had trucks scheduled to pick up last week's harvest of Honeycrisp and Granny Smith, more than an acre yet to harvest, and if he didn't make the meeting with Jason, then he wouldn't know if he even had a valid backup plan.

There wasn't time for another delay.

Missing that appointment with Jason meant there was a good chance he'd have to wait another few days to arrange a meeting. But getting behind on the harvest, leaving long-standing customers hanging, wasn't an option.

He wanted this deal with Rogers to happen, but not at the risk of his existing customer base.

Luke released a breath. "I'll be there in ten minutes."

Standing, he set his plate in the sink and looked at his

mother until she finally faced him. "Want to tell me about the pie raising?"

Paula clapped her hands. "It's genius really. Like a barn raising, only with pies instead of boards. And in the Destiny Bay tradition of bigheartedness, the whole town's turned out in support."

Chapter 9

⟋

It was official: Luke was screwed.

And not in the way he'd first imagined when he'd seen Kennedy skirting around his mom's shop in that apron and challenging smile. She'd been all fire and sass, and now he was seeing how hot she could burn.

The farther down the dirt road he drove and the closer to the south orchard he got, the more his admiration—and irritation—for Kennedy grew. Admiration because the woman was as creative as she was sexy. It was coming on ten in the morning, and there already had to be a few dozen people in the orchards carrying red baskets, courtesy of the home and garden store in town.

Most of the volunteers had on orthopedics and dentures, and came from one of the three senior center buses parked along the road. But they weren't to be underestimated. Destiny Bay was home to more war heroes than the House of Representatives, and held the state record for fastest pickers in the over sixty category. Based on the crowd, which spread from the cottage all the way to the PICK A BASKET WIN A PIE sign hanging from the front porch railing, Kennedy would have a good tenth of her apples harvested by the end of the day.

Prepped and stored by the end of next week.

That was where the irritation came in. Once they were prepped, they were out of play for cider. Not to mention, he had a pickup scheduled for a few thousands pounds of apples later that afternoon, and only half the crew he needed to harvest them. So with every basket for Kennedy picked came the very really possibility that Luke might have to admit failure.

And Luke didn't do failure.

He parked his truck, hopped out, and made his way through the grove, knowing he had about ten seconds to come up with a new plan. One which included getting his guys focused and back to work—on the right side of the orchard.

Only as luck would have it, one glimpse at the event's host and Luke had a hard time deciding which side was right.

Kennedy wasn't only strapped into his mom's old harness, she'd figured out how to use it and was all the way up one of the trees, participating in a picking race against one of his fastest guys. People had gathered around and, based on the cheers, were not rooting for the home team.

Sometime between the Apple Festival and today, Little Miss Big City had become the town's golden child. A title Luke used to hold.

Oh, she wasn't any good at apple picking and she wasn't in the lead, not by a long shot. She was too short to use the ladder, so she'd opted to climb the damn tree, and was struggling to navigate the branches under the weight of the apples and canvas bag. In her defense, the bag was pretty heavy. And half her size. But it didn't matter. She was in nothing more than a harness, a flannel shirt that tied around her curvy waist, and a pair of denim shorts that were soft, snug, and a sight to behold.

And apple red tennies.

Half the guys stood at the bottom of the tree, looking their fill at all that the newest apple picker had to offer The other half were waiting for her to lose her footing so they could catch her—and behold every single inch of her bombshell body. Not that they would get the chance.

Kennedy was wrestling the tree with enough pluck to give his Aunt Fi a run for her money in the stubbornest woman department. She reached out, picked an apple, dropped it in the bag, and moved on to the next. She was quite determined about it, too.

Even though she obviously had an issue with heights. He could tell by the way she avoided looking at the ground and closed her eyes every time she slipped the apple in her bag. But she didn't let it slow her progress.

Nope, Kennedy used her fear to drive her. Which meant, scared or not, she wasn't going to come down until she had won—or the race was over.

Taking a moment to enjoy the view himself, Luke walked over to the baked goods table. Where he found Hawk, dressed in a red apron, passing out pies and manning the booth like this was the annual St. Peter's Christmas Bake Sale and he was Sister Mary Catherine.

Hawk handed a piece of pie to Ms. Sharpe in exchange for a basket of apples. The shit of it was, Ms. Sharpe also handed over a crisp bill and smiled. She'd been the principal at the local school since Destiny Bay was built, and never once had Luke even heard of her smiling.

Hawk took the money, all grins and customer service like he wasn't giving away their future. Then helped the next customer in line.

"What the hell, man?" Luke said when he got to the front of the line.

Hawk picked up the next plate, which was sitting with a few dozen others, gave it a dollop of whipped cream, then took a big bite. "Thank God you're here," he said, licking his fingers.

"Yeah, it seems I came just in time to watch you enjoy your pie," Luke said. "And you said she had *me* by the nuts!"

Hawk looked over Luke's shoulder and gave a respectful wave—at Ms. Sharpe, who was eyeing them suspiciously—then leaned in. "I came down to tell the guys to get back to work and Ms. Sharpe cornered me. Said that stealing a woman's crew was about as low as one could get. Even worse than the time I drew boobies on the cheerleading team's photo in the hallway."

Luke glanced around, feeling like he was twelve again, and hiding behind the trophy cabinet with Hawk, waiting for Ms. Sharpe to go back to her office. "She knows it was us?"

"That woman knows everything. And walker or not, she still scares the shit out of me."

Luke couldn't fault the guy. It didn't matter that he was six-three and two-twenty, Ms. Sharpe had a threat factor that defied size. "Did you explain that Kennedy stole our crew?"

Hawk scoffed. "Yeah, but then she just gave me that look. You know the one she gets?" Luke knew that look well. Had been on the receiving end of it a time or two growing up. "Well, she gave me that look, then said how nice it was that I showed up in support of Destiny Bay's newest resident. And before I knew it, I was wearing this apron and handing out pies."

"You should be in the north orchard, picking the Honey-crisp apples that are being shipped out in"—Luke looked at his watch—"about four hours."

Hawk looked at the crowd by the tree. "Our crew is there, man. All of them came down to see what was going on. We could hear the cheering over the tractors."

Luke watched as Kennedy made it up to a higher branch, her bare legs scraping against the leaves as she went. And he couldn't help admiring her effort—or the way the bottom of her shorts crept up her thighs, in one of those inch for an inch kind of situations that had him matching her inch for inch.

Her face was flushed with the morning chill, her nose a little pink, and her normal sculpted bun was a scattered mess, windblown and attracting more than a few loose twigs and leaves.

She was a mess. A spectacular mess.

"We're totally screwed, aren't we?" Hawk asked.

And because Luke didn't believe in lying, he said, "Yup," then turned and reached for a piece of pie. Ignoring the whipped cream because he liked his deep dish straight up, he forked off a bite and—

"Hey!" a female voice yelled.

Hawk jumped as if Ms. Sharpe was headed their way with the ruler. And Luke, first bite halfway to his mouth, slowly turned to see Kennedy glaring down at him. She was straddling a branch, her hands gripping the trunk so hard he was sure she was going to go home with splinters.

"That pie is for participants only," she hollered, all that earlier nervousness replaced with indignation.

Even though today was shaping up to be complete crap, Luke found himself smiling as he walked slowly over to the tree. He glanced at every guy on his crew, who wisely took a large step back, then he looked up at Kennedy. Who in her current position, directly above him, was giving him a pretty fan-fucking-tastic view. The woman might be petite, but she was all tanned legs and sculpted thighs.

If Luke stepped a little to the left—*yup, just like that*— he had an even better view up her shirt. Though as always, she'd knotted it good and tight. So tight it caused the bottom buttons to pucker, leaving a perfect-sized gap for him to gape his fill.

White lace today.

Nothing overly sexual, but on her it was the sexiest thing he'd ever seen.

"Why don't I participate by helping you down," he offered, and to take her mind off the fact that she was fifteen feet up—in a tree—Luke took a big, heaping bite of her pie, letting the fork glide out extra slow.

As he'd hoped, her gaze went frosty, then she frowned, becoming pissy and irritated, and looking sexier than any woman covered in twigs and tree sap had the right to look.

"I can't afford your help. Plus first up, last down." She let go of the trunk with one hand to point to the sign taped to the front of the booth that said, FIRST UP, LAST DOWN. COME CHALLENGE THE NEWEST APPLE PICKER IN TOWN, and then she lost her grip.

"Whoa," Luke said, his hands going out to catch her.

Only she caught herself. Her eyes wide and dilated, her hands shook with what Luke knew was adrenaline overload and exhaustion, but she managed to save herself from what could have been a pretty spectacular fall. Something he took to heart.

He softened his voice. "You okay?"

"Yup, strapped in." With extreme caution, she tugged her harness. "Thanks for asking."

Now that he was close enough to notice the little lacerations and scratches marring her silky skin, he wished he had asked earlier. Because it wasn't satisfaction he felt seeing her city girl sass up a tree, plucking apples. It was something a whole hell of a lot deeper.

In the short time that he'd known Kennedy, she'd challenged him, frustrated him, annoyed him, turned him on even. Only now she had him concerned—for her.

Luke had enough people to worry about in his life. It was why he always kept things light with women. But this wasn't any woman; this woman drove him insane.

Crazy as that sounded, he found himself growing addicted.

"Plus, I only have my guys for another two hours—"

"My guys," he clarified. "And you don't have them that long—"

"Once the pie runs out, they get to leave. That was the deal."

"Hold up." Luke put his hands on his hips, then took his time eyeballing his crew. "Are you telling me that the crew who charges me a small fortune every day is picking your apples for free?"

A lot of grumbling sounded, followed by twenty very

smart, very wise pickers, depositing their apples at the table and grabbing their tools.

"Hey, where are you going?" When no one answered, just kept walking, she looked at Luke. "Where are they going? They can't leave. There is still pie on the table."

"If they want their jobs come tomorrow, they can. And they will. Heading back to the north orchard, which is where they were supposed to be before someone sweet-talked them into walking off the job," he said, and she had the decency to look a tad bit ashamed.

"I'm sorry I upset your schedule," she said, but he had a hard time hearing the apology through her smiling. "Finding pickers is hard during harvest. Very competitive."

"So I've been told," he mused. "And even though I'd love to stand here and talk shop, I have a rig coming to pick up some apples. Which are still attached to those trees over there. And since they don't pick themselves, my guys need to go back to work."

"But I still have so many apples left," she said, and something about her tone had him shifting in his boots.

"You still have a few dozen volunteers here who can pick the lower-hanging fruit, free of charge." They had usable hands—and canes to bat at the fruit if necessary. "That should get you through next week."

"Nothing is for free," she said with so much acceptance, Luke's heart rolled over and showed its soft underbelly. Because with that one statement, understanding bloomed in his chest, and it added another emotion to the running list—soul-deep compassion.

In Luke's life, there had been some struggle, and even more opportunity, and throughout it all, he'd been given so many things without expectation of a return: amazing memories, friendship, loyalty, laughter—and love.

Luke got the impression that Kennedy hadn't had much of any of that growing up. Which made her determined outlook all the more impressive.

"They're getting paid in pie," she said proudly.

And damn it, she had every right to feel that.

He'd delivered her an obstacle of epic proportions, yet she'd managed to figure out a solution. On her own terms. In no time flat.

Kennedy wasn't looking for a handout, and she certainly wasn't looking to start a war. She just wanted a chance, and Luke couldn't fault her for that.

He also couldn't stand around watching his guys screw off. Not if he wanted to make today's delivery.

He looked at his watch; it was nine forty. With a deep breath, he did something he'd never done before.

He helped the competition.

"I'll give you my crew until the top of the hour, then my guys go back to work, and you figure out the rest of the apples yourself. From the ground," he added.

Kennedy opened her mouth to argue—or maybe to ask what the catch was—then closed it. She eyed her troops, retreating to join the other side, and the remaining apples, and he could almost see her making mental calculations. "Your whole crew?"

"Yup. For twenty minutes."

No doubt, Hawk was calling him all kinds of pussy. But Luke knew a lot about strong, stubborn women. He'd been raised by two. And Kennedy was going to get her apples, even if it meant being carted away in an ambulance for taking an impact from twenty feet up.

"Deal," she said, reaching for an apple.

"Oh, no," Luke said. "You got to come down and shake on it, sweetness."

With a satisfied smile, she slowly began to make her way down the tree, hugging it for dear life a time or two, and giving him a heart attack when she almost slipped. But sexy and capable, the woman used her small size to her benefit and scooted her way down.

When those blinding tennis shoes finally touched the ground, he released a pent-up breath.

"Your whole crew for twenty minutes?" She stuck her hand out.

"And you retire the harness."

She must have liked what he'd come up with, because she accepted way too fast. "Deal."

Those sparkling blue pools zeroed in on Luke, and she released a smile that left him feeling unsettled—in more ways than one. It was determined, calculating, and a hundred percent trouble.

She shook his hand. And while his head was telling him that he was too busy, his dick was too focused on how soft and elegant her fingers were to protest.

Kennedy slipped the bag off her shoulder, the pink harness he'd taken from his mom's garage off her arms, then made a big deal about unhooking it and sliding it all the way down her body.

Placing a steadying hand on his chest, she glided it off one foot, then the next. Finally, she leaned in to whisper, "Strap in, crew leader, it's a long fall."

* * *

The sun was long gone by the time the trucks were loaded and headed toward their respective drop-off points. Luke slowly made his way toward his pickup, the night's dew dampening his boots and the hem of his jeans. He was sore, bone tired, and ready for a hot shower and a cold beer.

The crew managed to fill the orders and harvest an acre of Honeycrisps in the north orchard. It was going to cost Luke a small fortune in overtime, but they were back on schedule and that was what was important. He'd even managed to clear out his in-box, prep for tomorrow's pick, and make a good dent in the mountain of paperwork on his desk.

The late hours had nothing to do with getting ahead, and everything to do with avoiding the spitfire sleeping in his bed across the orchard.

Luke's truck was still parked down by the cottage, making a stealthy exit impossible and an impromptu meet probable. Unless she was soaking in that big claw-footed tub, lying beneath a layer of bubbles and plotting his demise. Or maybe she was already asleep—the woman did rise at the baker's hour. And thanks to him, she'd had one hell of a day

The last thing either of them needed tonight was another run-in. Which was why Luke headed toward his truck with the intention of packing it in and going straight home. Only when he came out from under the last canopy of trees, every good intention he had to keep his distance vanished.

He counted fifteen bushels of apples at the bottom of the porch, five more than when he'd left that morning. More than enough to get her through the week. They were picked, packed, and ready to go—right there out in the open—for anyone with a pickup and strong arms.

Kennedy might be able to muscle one or two on her own, but her little hybrid didn't offer much in terms of trunk space. Or backseat space for that matter.

In fact, the only way she was going to get the apples to Sweetie Pies was a few shopping bags at a time. So unless she was planning on hiring a truck and driver, she'd be smart to conceal her produce a little better.

But what had him stepping past his truck and toward the walkway was Destiny Bay's newest resident apple picker, who sat on the top step of the porch.

She was in leggings and an oversized sweatshirt, surrounded by enough Band-Aid wrappers and half-eaten pies to supply a preschool class, and had a full carton of milk at her feet. Her hair was damp, her face devoid of any makeup, and she looked wiped out.

"The last person I want to talk to tonight is you," she said, and the gravity in her voice had him halting.

Feeling the insane urge to apologize to her, like he had fucked with *her* day and *her* mental state, Luke opened his mouth and went to step from the shadows, but she wasn't anywhere close to done.

"We had an agreement," she said, her tone frosty enough to cryogenically freeze his nuts. "Half when it was signed over, then monthly payments until we are square."

Kennedy turned her head, and that was when he saw the phone—and realized she hadn't seen him. Oblivious to his presence, she continued the heated conversation and, based on the tense way she held herself, lips pursed with an expression of sheer exasperation, it was most likely his aunt. Which meant Luke's nuts were safe.

For the moment.

"That's not what you promised," she said quietly, her

voice so close to cracking, he felt it in his chest. Then she closed her eyes out of raw disappointment and he knew that couldn't be his aunt.

Fi was frustrating as hell, stubborn to a fault, but she'd never purposefully hurt someone's feeling. And Kennedy's feelings were beyond hurt. The little sighs she kept releasing told him as much; they also told him that she was too disappointed for it to be anyone other than family or an ex.

"I'm happy for you that Argentina went better than expected and that they want you to move there, but you still have responsibilities here," she said then paused as if listening to the person on the other end. "No, this isn't me being spiteful. Spiteful would have been demanding that we sell the property since you couldn't buy me out completely."

Kennedy's mouth opened, then closed, and she hung her head, the phone dangling from her fingers. Luke could hear a man huffing and puffing, so indignant he could make out a few words from across the walkway. Jesus, the guy bitched more than Hawk when he lost a bet.

"Again not my problem, because a month ago *you* wanted the condo. So much that you agreed to buy me out. And I agreed to your ridiculous offer, even though we both knew the condo was worth more than that appraisal you got. So either send me a payment before the end of the week, or I will have my own agent appraise the house and we can add the difference to your balance."

Luke could feel the cutting silence from where he was standing. Could feel her anger and frustration; even worse, he could feel her pain. He wanted to tell the idiot to take the deal, but he didn't want Kennedy to know he was there—

listening in on what she had assumed was a private conversation.

"Fine, next Friday, but I'm serious, Philip, if it isn't in my account by the end of the day, I will send my grandma over to collect." She rolled those pretty eyes of hers, but he could tell she was closer to tears than she'd ever admit. "Yeah, well, you also promised not to have sex with other women, so I'm not holding my breath."

Luke winced at the information, but his heart? That did a hell of a lot more. Pinched and ached over the heartache she'd gone through. It wasn't just the disappointment in her tone that called to him; it was the gentle acceptance of the situation, as if she was angry at herself for hoping for more.

Kennedy hung up and he heard the telltale sound of a sniffle, followed by a sharp, shaky breath that had his gut twisting.

Time to peace out. The woman was a few seconds from tears, and the only thing worse for her than crying over some guy would be the knowledge that Luke saw her crying over some guy.

He remembered their first conversation, and what she'd said when he offered to buy her out. *Do you think it's as easy as throwing some money my way and I'll just happily up and relocate my whole life?* The dickwad on the phone had to be the reason she'd moved to Destiny Bay.

Reminding himself of the whole people in glass houses nonsense, he wondered if some other guy down the road would refer to him as the dickwad who had her leaving Destiny Bay. Because now that Luke knew the *why*, he could easily figure out the *what*, and the *how*, to get her apples.

And that made him more than a dickwad. It made him

the kind of person he couldn't look at in the mirror without wanting to punch something.

Figuring that was his cue to head back to the barn, and get some more paperwork done, Luke turned around.

"If you came to steal the apples," she said, her voice disappearing into the breeze. "The bushels are zip-tied together, then attached to buckets hiding on the roof filled with orange icing dye. One tug and you'll look like a giant mango."

"Thanks for the heads-up. Mango clashes with my rugged good looks." Luke walked closer until he could see her face under the moonlight and his stomach tightened. She looked small, and splintered, and torn up. And he wasn't talking about all the Band-Aids on her body. "I didn't come here to take your apples, sweetness. Just picking up my truck so I can go home."

She looked at him long and hard, as if trying to figure out why her bullshit meter was still going off.

"You okay?" he asked.

She wiped at her cheeks and offered up a too bright smile. "You know me."

He did know her, knew that smile was for his benefit, not hers. Just like he knew where her vulnerable buttons were, and up until a second ago had no issues with pushing them. Which was so far from the kind of man he wanted to be—the kind of man Kennedy deserved.

"Night, sweetness." With a parting wave, he headed toward the truck. He reached for the door handle and she called out to him.

"Luke."

He turned around.

"You don't have to run off just yet. You got to see the

fireworks, might as well stay for the pie. I believe that one on the far left is yours."

Right, his prize for picking the most apples in twenty minutes. Little did she know he could have picked three times the number, but he'd told his guys to let him set the pace. He was willing to help out, in order to get his team back and focused on the right job, but he wasn't going to help himself right out of business. Even if it meant sending a woman, who had no business picking apples, up a tree for the day.

A mix of shame and anger washed over him, shame that he'd been a part of the recent struggle, anger that come next week he knew her struggles were going to become worse—and he wasn't in a position to help.

In order to hold strong to his position, he'd have to hinder hers, which would eventually lead to hurting her. And that made him sick. "No worries," he said. "I can pick up my pie tomorrow."

Luke turned to leave.

"No, wait—"

Chapter 10

⌒

T hese won't last until tomorrow," Kennedy said, standing up to hold out his pie.

She told herself there was no logical reason to encourage Luke to stay. Not tonight anyway. Not when she was feeling raw and exposed—and so damn alone she couldn't stomach the thought of being stuck with just her thoughts for the rest of the night.

She needed a distraction—even if only temporarily.

Plus, fair was fair, and he'd won the HumDinger. She still couldn't believe it. Not that he'd won, since the man had outpicked his crew three to one. But that he'd helped.

Instead of yelling at her, which he had every right to do since she'd stolen his crew, he'd pulled everyone together to get the job done. Clapped his hands, gave some curt orders, people got working. Sure, it was only twenty minutes, but his crew accomplished more in that short amount of time than Kennedy and her seniors had over the rest of the afternoon.

She didn't have a game plan ready for when these ran out, but for today she had enough apples—and hope. It wasn't Luke's fault that Philip had decided to crap all over her plans. So she'd offered Luke his pie. No big deal.

Except now that he was coming up the walkway, his boots crunching the gravel beneath, she couldn't help wondering how safe it would feel to be wrapped up in all six-feet-plus of pure unadulterated male.

"You sure?" he asked, his hands shoved in his front pockets and his attitude dialed to *I've got you*. It had been so long since anyone had Kennedy covered, she wanted to pretend, just for a moment or two.

How dangerous could a moment or two be?

She walked down the first step, gasping a little as the cut on her right leg brushed the porch railing. He appeared bigger and stronger with each step he took, until he finally reached out for the pie, their fingers grazing, and she gasped for a whole different reason—one that made it clear that a lot could happen in a single moment.

Really bad decisions could happen in two.

She didn't know whether to be thrilled or terrified when, instead of taking his pie and heading home, Luke sat on the porch. Then pulled not one, but two forks out of the silverware holder and patted the step next to him.

Really bad decisions, Kennedy thought, deciding to remain standing.

"Don't read too much into this, the pie is five pounds. There is no way I can finish it by tomorrow." He offered the fork—and a sly little wink—her way. "Plus, it's the only one you haven't sampled from tonight's spread."

It was true. Kennedy had tried every leftover pie, looking for something to fill her up, to calm that empty ache in her belly. Every pie except for his. She'd come out on the porch with the leftovers to celebrate her good day. But now that the sun was gone, and that awful call over, the adrenaline was beginning to wear off and she started to wonder if she'd come out here for another reason entirely.

Kennedy knew that Luke would have to come back for his truck at some point. Why else would she have brought out his pie and extra forks? Because she wanted to share the excitement of her day with someone. No, not someone—Luke.

She was hoping that she'd get to see Luke, spend time with him, and lose herself in his strength.

Luke was looking up at her like he had the answers to all of her problems, and for a slice of pie he was willing to share. A prospect that was so tempting she miraculously forgot why this was a bad idea. Forgot that *he* was her biggest problem.

"Don't read too much into this," she repeated, taking a seat and snatching the fork. "You helped me out today and won a pie, I'm helping you out by eating the pie, end of story. This isn't me waving a white flag and thinking we have a truce or anything."

"Good to know," was all he said, then forked off a piece of crust—her favorite part—and offered it to her. She ignored it and forked off her own piece. Right next to his.

He gave a loud chuckle, then slid the fork in his mouth, purposefully moaning as he ate.

A few bites in and Kennedy felt her mind slow down, her limbs go heavy with overuse, her body trying to adapt to the rare sensation of stillness.

Luke didn't push. Didn't ask her about the day, or the call he'd overheard, or even bring up her apples. He seemed to appreciate the quiet companionship tonight as much as she did.

Kennedy had no idea how long they sat there, sharing the HumDinger and silently watching the breeze brush past the trees, sending a mosaic of shadows dancing across the grass. It was comfortable, safe, as if the rest of the world had disappeared.

Luke had a way about him, a quiet confidence that set people at ease. Allowed them to hand over their problems and worry without hesitation. She'd seen it before around town, with his family. Now that she was experiencing it firsthand, that same fierce capability directed at her, she wanted to let her worries go.

But no matter how hard she tried, she couldn't seem to relax. Oh, her head cleared, and problems that seemed dire only minutes before lost their urgency, but the lighter her mind felt, the heavier her heart became.

"How much did you hear?" she asked.

"Enough to know that if I were in a bar fight, I'd want you on my side." He offered her another bite and she waved it off.

"And here I thought you'd come to steal my apples in the dark."

He slid her a look. "Sweetness, if I were going to get my hands on your apples, it would be a lights-on affair that involved silk sheets and multiple tastings."

A laugh burst from her lips, only it came out sounding more like a sob, which made her laugh harder until a thin line of water lined her lashes.

"What's wrong?"

She shook her head. "Nothing."

"I've spent my entire life dealing with my mom and aunt. *Nothing* is woman-speak for a whole lot of something. Plus, you look like you're about to cry." He sounded quite calm for a man who was staring down a woman on the verge.

"A real gentleman wouldn't point that out," she said, covering her face with her hands, the movement smarting the cuts on her hands.

"A real man would, though." Luke's fingers traced the Band-Aids littering her hands, then pulled them close to inspect them. His touch was tender and gentle as if her pain were somehow his. "Is this all from today?"

"It looks worse than it is," she said, telling herself that it was true. That her life did look worse than it was. That she was just tired and in desperate need of sleep, and that tomorrow everything would work out. But she knew that it wouldn't.

If Philip was late on his payment, Kennedy would have to work something out with Paula—which required a conversation where she admitted she'd failed and needed more time.

All the stress and worry felt heavy and real, and completely isolating. Kennedy had worked so hard to make the right choices, pick a direction, and determine the way her life would work out. But she was once again waiting for someone who was supposed to be family to deliver on a promise that they'd never come through on.

Luke took the Band-Aid off her most irritating scrape.

"Stop," she said, and he immediately froze, his eyes going to hers.

"Did that hurt?"

So much. But not in the way that he assumed. "No, seriously, it is just a few scrapes, nothing that a few Band-Aids can't fix."

"You forget, I've worked around apples and the harvest my entire life, I know a scrape from a cut."

"Yeah, well, it's my body, so I say they are scrapes." She took her hand back and looked out at the stars overhead. "Plus, you being nice to me is weirding me out."

With a small twitch of the lips, he asked, "Me being nice to you is weird?"

"Kind of," she admitted, leaving out the part that she liked it. Too much. "One more gentlemanly gesture and I'll lose it."

"I think you're sexy when you lose it," he said, his voice a low rumble that had her knees wobbling.

"Seriously? How lucky does that line get you?"

"I don't know. I've never used it before," he said and looked genuinely surprised. "But you're not tearing my head off or telling me what my problem is, so it must be working." He nudged her shoulder with his. "You want to talk about it?"

"About how well your line is working? Or my jerk of an ex?"

"Both. Either. Whatever will make this not weird for you."

"There's nothing to talk about."

"Then why do I feel like I need to pull you into my arms?" His expression went serious, and Kennedy found herself being drawn in by the intensity of his stare. Found her walls lowering and her foundation shifting.

"My ex is a flake who found a more exciting opportunity and went for it. I was slow on the uptake and paid the price."

"I can beat him up." He flexed.

"I'm sure you could," she said, touched by the conviction in his voice. "But looking back, I can see it never would have worked out."

"Why?" Luke asked, and Kennedy got the distinct impression that her answer was important.

"We wanted different things, I guess. The only way I could have made him truly happy was to give up who I was," she whispered. "And I'm tired of giving up things I love."

She watched as Luke focused on the stars, taking in what she said. After a long moment he asked, "What makes you happy?"

"I don't know," she whispered. "But I know I want to build a life for myself, a place that I can call mine." She closed her eyes and let the tranquility of that dream wash over her. It wasn't happiness she felt, but there was the potential. "I was so hurt by Philip's betrayal, and am still so angry that he is flaking out on me, but I'm glad he showed me his true colors when he did."

Luke shifted uncomfortably at her statement. "Any guy who would intentionally ruin your good day sounds like an ass." He slid her a glance—it was kind and gentle, and a little self-deprecating. He was apologizing.

"He does, doesn't he?" Kennedy gave his shoulder a little nudge this time. "Thanks for listening, but can we go back to normal, I'm thrown by you being all sweet and caring."

Luke's good humor died and his expression turned serious, withdrawn, as if her words somehow upset the easy camaraderie they'd formed. In fact, he looked disappointed, but Kennedy had the distinct idea it wasn't in her.

"Don't mistake my ambition for apathy, just like I

would never mistake your tears for weakness. I care," he said as if he needed her to believe him. "So much sometimes it taints every decision, complicates what should be easy solutions." He took off his ball cap and met her gaze, head on. "I'm not a bad guy. Just someone who is trying to do the right thing."

Kennedy looked at him and there was something about the pain she saw in his eyes, the conviction in his words, that called out to her, drew her in. Made her want to believe in good guys.

"I've heard of these good guys," she admitted. "I don't think I've ever met one personally."

He reached out and touched her cheek with so much care, she felt her knees wobble. "Then you've been hanging around the wrong kind of guys." He tilted his head toward her, leaned down, and—

"I don't know if we should, ah...residual weirdness and all," she said, embarrassingly doing nothing to stop their momentum.

"Oh, we really should," he whispered. "No weirdness, I promise."

Kennedy didn't put too much stock in promises, but she was too far into this to resist.

Luke slid his hand down and around to her lower back to pull her close, close enough that all she had to do was move her lips and they'd be kissing.

Only Luke lived up to his promise. He didn't go in for a kiss or a quick grope, but gave her exactly what she needed.

A hug.

The kind of hug that had her heart sighing and her head spinning. It was as if Luke knew what she wanted even before she did, because the second his hands slid around, gently stroking her back, Kennedy realized she needed this more than her next breath.

Clearly suffering from a lack of comfort, the kind one couldn't get from pie alone, Kennedy fell into his strong body, letting her head rest against his chest and telling herself she could be weak for just a moment. For just this moment someone else could carry the weight, hold her world together while she sorted through the emotions she carefully avoided for fear of shattering.

Those big, safe arms of his could right the world, cure acute heartache, and stop a big city girl from giving up on her dream with one squeeze. Of the last she was certain. So she let go of the fear, the *what-if*s, and all the self-doubt she'd collected, and listened to the steady beat of his heart. Matched her breathing to its rhythm and the softness of her body to his touch, until she wasn't feeling anything.

Except Luke. He was everywhere. His scent, his energy, his compassion—his goodness. It was there, in every breath he took, every touch he delivered, creating a whole new set of problems.

Without the fear, there was plenty of room for other emotions. Lust being the most obvious. Closely followed by desire. Warm, luscious, bone-melting desire.

Every time Luke's big hands trailed down her back, they got lower and lower, bringing their bodies closer and closer. Making it more than apparent that her nipples were over the pity part of the night and wanted to get on with the party.

He smelled delicious, like the evening air, apple pie, and tomorrow. He felt even better, pressed up against her, his arms so big that when she tightened her grip around his neck and moved up slightly, they grazed the outsides of her breasts.

"Luke," she whispered, her eyes fluttering closed as he did it again. Just a small shift, but enough to have all of her happy spots smiling, especially when he tightened his grip at the right moment to cause even more delicious friction.

A zing of awareness shot through her and all she could think about was his mouth—on hers. What he would taste like, if his kisses would be as life altering as his hugs. And what it would be like to be on the receiving end of that fierce protectiveness he gave so readily to those in his life.

More than anything, Kennedy wanted to see what it was like to work *with* all of that intense passion, instead of *against* it.

She nuzzled closer, she couldn't help it, and her mouth accidentally grazed the lobe of his ear as she leaned. She heard his breath catch, felt his body tense with what she was pretty sure was desire.

For her.

She knew the intelligent choice was to pull back, thank him for the hug, and scurry inside before they did something that couldn't be undone. Instead she leaned forward, until her lips brushed his ear again, because now that she knew he was feeling it, too, she couldn't think of anything else.

"We have a problem," she whispered.

His hands pulled her closer. "Yes, we do."

"I want to kiss you."

"But if you did, then you'd be admitting that you were wrong?" he guessed and she could hear him smile.

She lifted her head and met his gaze, and *bam*, she was lost. Luke wasn't smiling; there was nothing easygoing about him now. His gaze was hot, heated, and so damn intense, she could feel a pulse start below her belly button.

"I'm more concerned about you being right," she teased. "Which would lead to you being smug, and eventually an argument. And I really don't want to argue right now."

She was enjoying this sweet side of him too much.

"Sweetness," he said, but it wasn't in his usual alpha god tone that implied recreational sex with a guaranteed standing O. This time it felt like an endearment. "The last thing I want to do right now is argue with you."

Man of his word, Luke cupped her by the neck and took any possibility of an argument right out of play when he kissed her. There on her front porch, surrounded by pie and the faint scent of a new beginning, he kissed her as if this was why he'd come here.

Kennedy felt that hopeful beginning bloom into something that had room to grow. Something warm and real, no matter how long it lasted. Because the minute she registered the sensation of his lips on hers, she knew this wasn't a let's-get-to-the-naked-part, prelude-to-sex kind of kiss. It was soft, patient, and controlled, as if it was the main event and he had all night to prove it.

And himself.

Lord help her, when a man like Luke set out to prove himself, women like Kennedy had no choice but to fall. Right into his arms and into that kiss, which was better than amazing.

It was epic. Magical. The main course, dessert, and a dozen apple pies all wrapped up in one fantastic man. His mouth was confident, his hands gentle on her hips, turning her toward him so he could up his game, sliding his tongue along her lower lip.

He held her in a way that was completely unexpected: tender and slightly erotic, and she was pretty sure he could bring the à la mode without even laying a finger on her. But chemistry was only half of the appeal; the rest came from how she felt when she was with him.

Bold, strong, and desirable. Like he was taking the time to show her that she was deserving. And if that wasn't enough to convince her that maybe, just maybe, good ones did exist and he was one of them, Luke brought her hands to his mouth, delivering a kiss to each scrape, giving extra attention to the cut on her palm.

His eyes met hers. "That's going to be a problem."

"Thankfully, I'm a master fixer."

Luke placed her hand on his chest, and held it there. "Remember when I said not to mistake my ambition for apathy. Well, promise me that you won't mistake a good moment for a good guy."

"Because they don't exist?" she whispered, wanting desperately to believe that they did.

"Oh, they exist," he said, "and I'm one of them. But when it comes to you, I don't think I can be good enough."

Chapter 11

✑

S he was late.

With less than two hours before the shop opened, Kennedy parked her car in front of Sweetie Pies, grabbed three of the bags of apples she'd loaded yesterday from her backseat, and hurried toward the shop. Main Street was already a hive of activity, early morning shoppers braving frosted sidewalks to get a jump on their end-of-week shopping.

Kennedy needed to get a jump on her baking if she was going to have anything to sell to her morning customers. After sharing a few "good mornings" with the other shopkeepers, she clutched her coat tightly to her, and made her way toward her shop, her breath catching when she caught a glimpse of the sign hanging from the two marble columns on either side of the clock tower.

Washington State's Sixty-eighth Annual Gold Tin Apple Pie Competition:

*Where harvest and home come together. Entries
Due Friday.*

Kennedy had wanted to enter that contest since she'd
first read about it in *Southern Cooking*, when she was fifteen. Now she lived in the hometown of the competition,
and owned the shop of one of the competition's biggest
winners: Sweetie Pies' HumDinger. Which was automati-
cally entered to defend her title.

A rush of pride washed over her as she unlocked the
door, flipped on the lights, and headed straight to the
coffeemaker.

First order of business: caffeine. Tall, hot, and strong.

After Luke left, Kennedy had told herself that what happened was nothing more than two adults sharing some pie,
casual conversation, and a kiss that was absolutely *not* a
game changer. Then she'd gone straight to bed, pulled out
her journal, and made a list of ways to test the theory—just
to be sure.

By midnight, she had thirty-six different and creative
ways, starting with a private taste-test of her newest
creation—off her lips—and ending with a candlelit dinner
for two at her kitchen table. Which ultimately inspired another list: WHY LIST ONE IS A BAD IDEA: (1) Non-big-deal
issues don't deserve an itemized list, especially one that in-
cludes candles and my grandmother's paprikash; (2) Making
it a list makes it a big deal; (3) Refer back to number one.

When she woke up, face pressed to the pages of her
journal, she compared the two and decided that since list
two was so small in comparison, and lacking in the fun department, she'd spend her morning expanding on list one.

Setting the apples on the counter, she mentally added a

liquor-infused whipped cream to her tasting, and reached for the coffee grinder. Surprised to find that the machine was already percolating, and the first pot of coffee was nearly ready.

Kennedy swallowed past the unexpected lump as a warm rush of gratitude filled her chest. Yesterday, Paula had offered to prep the nonheirloom apples and some of the easier items to bake so Kennedy could finish up her harvest. That she had also come in early this morning to start the coffee was another example of Paula's thoughtfulness—and another reason Kennedy needed this to work.

Paula and Fi had entrusted Kennedy with their legacy, and she wanted to do them proud. She wanted to do herself proud as well. And even though Kennedy was scratched to bits and sore in places she didn't even know had muscles, she was vibrating with all the possibilities this adventure could offer.

Destiny Bay looked out for their own, and yesterday they'd made it clear that Kennedy was included in that group. She didn't think that she'd be invited to the mayor's house anytime soon, but she couldn't walk through town without a half-dozen people stopping her to wish her a good day or ask her about the pie du jour.

Slowly but surely, she was making fans of the locals. And today's specialty was guaranteed to blow their taste buds away: comfort pie.

The toasted graham cracker crust, creamy sweet potato and dark chocolate filling, and marshmallow vodka-infused topping created the perfect treat for a chilly autumn morning. And it was the perfect way to give the town a little of what they'd given her yesterday.

Not having a second to waste, she filled her mug and picked up the heaviest bag so she could peel the apples she needed to get the first batch of HumDingers in the oven. Halfway there, her cell vibrated in her back pocket. It was Ali.

Juggling her bag and coffee mug, she managed to fish it out. "You're up early."

"And you're not here," Ali said, and Kennedy could hear the idling of an engine in the background. "Figured you'd either fallen out of a tree last night or you were stuck under a bushel of apples somewhere unconscious."

Kennedy laughed. "No, I just overslept. You're at my house?"

"Yeah, I called you a few times, and when I didn't see the shop lights on, I came here."

Kennedy looked at her phone, which she must have flipped to silent. "Sorry about that. But I got to the shop a few minutes ago."

She heard Ali release a breath. "Good, because Cosmo called and he is coming today."

"Today?" Kennedy looked around at the empty pie racks, even emptier display case, and felt the first signs of panic set in. "I thought he was in Portland until Sunday."

"He decided that he didn't want to wait. He was afraid that Fi would catch wind of it and try to stop the deal."

Not needing the caffeine, which would be overkill with the amount of adrenaline pumping though her veins, Kennedy ditched the mug for another bag of apples. Her time crunch had just been crunched. "Yeah, well, I understand that he and Fi have a history, but this deal is about new beginnings, a chance at a fresh start. So by definition, no history allowed."

And that included Philip!

"Good to hear," Ali said. "So then you didn't sell the apples to Callahan?"

"No," she said, trying to ignore the pinch in her chest. They both needed those apples, but what if in order to save her business, she hurt his?

Kennedy pushed back her ingrained need to please. She didn't have the luxury of *what-if*s. She couldn't give in. Even a kiss that had enough lasting tingles to power a small country wasn't going to distract her from her goal.

There was a long beat. "And you didn't happen to hire someone else to deliver your apples, did you?"

"No." Kennedy closed her eyes, then offered, "Do you need me to? I know you're super busy, and if you can't do it, I understand."

It would suck, because Kennedy had no idea where she'd find someone else willing to haul fifteen bushels of apples in exchange for a girls' night. But Ali's offer had been beyond generous to begin with, and as Kennedy well knew, life happened.

"I'm still game," Ali said, and Kennedy felt herself relax. "A hot dinner that doesn't come out of a box or the microwave while watching *The Bachelor*? I am so there. But unless you hung your apples back up in the trees, they're gone."

"Gone? How could they be gone?"

"Were they there when you left?" Ali asked.

"Yes. No...I don't know," she admitted. She'd been in a rush when she left; she didn't take the time to check. "But I think I would have noticed if they were gone. Or at least heard whoever took them."

Except that Kennedy hadn't gotten all that much sleep,

but during the few hours she did manage, she'd been dead to the world. Or dreaming about her thief with the mouth of a god.

Kennedy froze. Thought back to last night. Luke appearing out of the shadows, his uncharacteristic compassion, and that sweet side that threw her off balance.

"Is there orange dye all over the grass?" she asked.

"Do pails with orange water lining the porch rail count?"

"Good guy, my ass." Anger, red and hot, had her feet moving toward the kitchen. "What time is Cosmo coming?"

"Around three."

Enough time to get her first few batches in, find Luke, and show him just what a pain in his ass big city heels could be. He played a good game, all right, but she was better. Compared to her turbulent childhood, this would be as easy as pie.

"Thanks, Ali," she said. "I'll call you back when I find out where they are."

Setting her apples on the cutting board, Kennedy grabbed her apron off the hanger, and her sharpest knife out of the cutting block. It wasn't just anger that had her heart pounding; it was confusion and disappointment.

Sure, they'd both made it clear that last night wasn't a truce, but Kennedy had really thought that they'd shared a real connection, one that trumped petty pranks. One that held the potential for a positive relationship of some kind. A relationship that, once again, Kennedy had read far too much into.

Wondering if she'd ever learn her lesson, she washed up at the sink and turned to dry her hands when she froze once again. This time it wasn't panic or anger, but something that went much deeper and warmer.

Lining the back wall of the produce refrigerator were fifteen bushels full of apples. Enough to fill her shop with pies for her big day, and last her for the next two weeks. And on the shelf above them, sitting in the middle, was a single apple—and a note.

With shaky hands, she opened the door and picked up the apple. Unfolding the flap, her breath caught.

The apples are for your pies. The peeler is to make you smile...L

Kennedy choked out a laugh, because next to the apple was a peeler made from a drill, a special bit, and an industrial hand peeler. The drill was electric and bright pink, and the bit was sharp enough to easily slide though the core and spin fast enough to skin an apple in a few seconds. It would cut her prep time in half—and save her fingers from further damage.

But what had her exposing her soft underbelly was the craftsmanship. This wasn't some store-bought device. It was custom made and hand crafted—just for her. Which meant that sometime between leaving her house and this morning Luke had found the time to make it.

For her.

And sometime between last night and this morning Kennedy had started to believe that maybe good guys really did exist.

*   *   *

A warm blast of nutmeg and toasted graham cracker greeted Kennedy as she opened the oven door. She shifted the latest batch of comforter pies around the shelf to make sure they browned evenly.

"Tell me again why you're putting lemon zest in my apple cobbler recipe?" Fi asked from the carry-through window.

"Because a pinch of citrus will elevate the food profile," Kennedy said, even though she had been repeating the same explanation since Fi arrived a few hours ago. It hadn't touched her good mood, though. Kennedy was pretty sure nothing could.

"We don't need any more elevation," Fi explained. "I like my pies at sea level."

"I think the lemon is nice. It adds a fresh surprise to the pie," Paula said, elbow deep in dough. "A little something special for an extra special day maybe?"

Fi took in Kennedy's smile and fancy heels—which she kept in her car for emergencies like this—and frowned. "What makes today so special?"

Kennedy suddenly gave all her attention to cutting the chilled butter in the crust she was making. Paula had shown up ready to help bake, Fi to run the front of the shop—and raise cane—just until Kennedy had caught up with the baking. Then Paula would go home and rest, Fi would meet her speed-walking group for Senior Smoothie Day down at the Juice Barn, and they'd both be long gone before Kennedy's secret meeting with Cosmo.

It wasn't that Kennedy wasn't going to share her good news; she just wanted to make sure that there was good news to share—and that Fi didn't bring stale emotions into Kennedy's fresh start.

That was the plan anyway. Only Paula was grinning as if she were in on the plan. Fi was frowning like she smelled a rotten apple in the shop. And Kennedy started sweating.

"Shouldn't you be out front, helping customers?" Kennedy asked Fi.

"Nah, it's just Lacy from the market, asking for a comfort pie. I told her I don't serve those here."

Kennedy looked up. "Yes, we do. There is an entire display case filled with them, right there, remember?"

Fi looked at the Pie of the Day display. "Of course I remember, I'm old, not senile. And I said *I* don't serve them here. If you want to sell one of those vegetable pies, then wash up, she's been waiting for a few minutes now."

"You finish up here, I'll help Lacy." Paula wiped her hands off on her apron and leaned into Kennedy. "And apologize for the temperamental help."

"Haven't lost my hearing either," Fi interrupted.

"And you still have the best legs in town," a weathered voice said from the front of the shop.

"You," Fi snapped.

"Cosmo," Paula said with genuine welcome as she walked out of the kitchen to give the older man a hug. "It's been ages."

Cosmo was short, round, and dressed in a light gray suit with matching powder blue suspenders and bow tie. He wore a coordinating fedora, a contagious smile, and had a cigar in his breast pocket. He looked like Al Capone on Easter Sunday. He was also early. Very early. "Last time I came here, I was nearly run down in the parking lot."

Fi picked up a wooden spoon and rounded the counter, waving it high for everyone to see. "I'll give you two minutes to hobble out of here, Mo, before I get my keys and finish the job."

"While I'd love to pick up where we left off, Fiona, I'm here on business." But as he said it, he pulled a bouquet of flowers out from behind his back and offered them to Fi.

Her face flushed as she inspected the offering, a cluster of bright daisies held together by rustic twine. They were too perfect to have been purchased. Cosmo had hand picked and selected each stem, in a gesture that was so romantic, Kennedy felt her practical side sigh with defeat.

"Well, take your business elsewhere," Fi said, taking the flowers and bringing them to her nose. "I want you gone."

"While I would love to be the man who delivers on everything you want, it pains me to say today I cannot be that man." Cosmo took off his hat and pressed it over his heart. "After forty years, I am finally about to get a second chance at your pies and, beautiful, forty years is a long time to wait."

The room went quiet at his statement, and the soft steel he put behind it. Mr. Kline wasn't just in love with the HumDinger; he was in love with its creator.

Kennedy watched as his words settled over Fi, watched her eyes soften, and her body sway slightly toward Cosmo as she smelled the flowers once again.

With a slow shake of the head, she said, "You'll have to wait, Mo, because even after forty years, you still wouldn't know what to do with my pies."

"Thankfully, I am here to see Miss Sinclair. Maybe she'll see that I know exactly what your pies need."

Fi didn't yell, didn't even wave the spoon. She turned toward Kennedy, and the expression on her face was devastating. "You made a meeting with him? Here in my shop?"

Although there was anger, it was the hints of betrayal that made swallowing hard. Kennedy hadn't set out to hurt anyone, especially one of the women who had entrusted her with Sweetie Pies. But there would be nothing to argue about if she didn't do something bold.

"I did." Kennedy picked up the tray with the pies she'd set aside for this meeting, and placed them at one of the tables. Then she turned to Fi, and softened her voice. "You told me to get creative, I got creative."

Fi blanched. "First vegetable pies, then you ask me to help bake pies so you can sell them to the enemy?"

"I don't know what happened in the past," Kennedy said, not seeing how the older woman could miss the big picture. Unless Sweetie Pies started getting their supplies for free again, it was going to go under. Taking Kennedy's life savings and, unless they found another buyer, the women's life's work with it. "But it is clear that Mr. Kline is interested in being a partner. A partner who could help this shop get to the next level."

"That's just it," Fi said sadly. "This shop doesn't need to be anything more than it is."

"I bought this shop because it had roots," Kennedy said. "A history that you and Paula made together. And I want to be a part of that, add my own pages and recipes, make something that I can look at someday and see myself in, too. But I would never forget your part of the story."

It was why she'd been open to having the women stay on to help out a few days a week. Why she'd asked over and over again if she was getting their recipe right. Why she never even considered taking down all of the black-and-white photos of the two women that were plastered around the shop. They were family, and this shop was part of their home.

Kennedy just wanted a shot at creating the same kind of legacy.

"The girl isn't switching out flour for gluten-free crust, Fi," Paula said, taking her sister-in-law's hand. "She's just putting icing on what we baked up, bringing a fresh surprise to every pie. We both agreed she was the perfect buyer, so give her a chance to show us what she's got."

"Well, icing has always given me gas. And she hasn't seen what I've got." Fi grabbed her coat and purse and walked straight past Paula, then Cosmo, and out the door.

The bells jingled as the door shut.

"You think she liked the flowers?" Cosmo asked, his eyes never leaving the door.

Paula took his hands in hers. "She loved them."

Cosmo gave a slight nod, then faced Kennedy. He was smiling, but there was tension bracketing his mouth. "Are you sure this is what you want?"

"To make Fi upset?" Kennedy shook her head. "But I know what this shop needs to grow, and I know that this partnership is full of exciting possibilities." Then not to sound too eager. "For both of us. Which is why I have prepared a tasting. I know that you are familiar with the HumDinger, but I wanted to take you on a journey of our four best-sellers, all of them award-winning pies made from locally grown ingredients, and let you see everything Sweetie Pies has to offer."

Cosmo lowered his head. "I have been paying Ali to sneak me pies every Sunday for the past forty years, Miss Sinclair. And I would love to sit in this shop and savor each and every item you have, but I'm not sure when

Fiona will be coming back, so I think it is best if I took those pies to-go."

More than anything, she wanted her chance to sell him on her creations, the traditional and the new items. But she had to agree, Fi had been more than upset, and Kennedy didn't want to make matters worse. She knew what it felt like to be uncomfortable in one's own home. "Of course. Let me box these up."

Kennedy took the pies behind the counter and carefully boxed each one, even adding a comfort pie to the mix. After today he'd need one. She could hear Cosmo and Paula quietly conversing. She couldn't make out the words, but the heartache and frustration were deafening. As if he really wanted today to have gone differently.

Kennedy wished for that, too. Sure, Cosmo was more than interested in doing a deal, and she was pretty sure that once he tasted the pies, he'd make an offer, but this wasn't how she'd envisioned things going down. This wasn't how she wanted to repay Fi and Paula for their trust and kindness. But she knew in the end, it would all work out.

It had to, she told herself, ignoring the little voice inside her heart that kept whispering, "How?" Because saving her shop was imperative, but doing it without changing her relationship with Luke seemed impossible.

Telling herself that this was a good deal, she tied a bright red bow on the last box, and brought them over to Cosmo. The chatter between the two died.

"Enjoy," Kennedy said. "If I don't hear from you by Monday, I will give you a call. And maybe next time we can meet in a more neutral place."

Cosmo looked at Paula and they shared a secret smile.

"I have already seen enough." He took a piece of paper out of his pocket and handed it to Kennedy.

"What's this?"

"A lovely offer," Paula said. "Cosmo had his team write it up last night."

A warm bubble of hopefulness and pride overcame her. Cosmo was so excited about this deal, he'd decided to make an offer before even arriving, and still go forward with it after Fi's threats. Kennedy knew that, for Cosmo, it was about much more than Fi's pies.

She unfolded the memo, glanced at the highlights, and gasped. "It says here you want two hundred pies a day."

"A hundred and fifty HumDingers and fifty of your choosing."

"Two hundred pies," she said, mentally doing the math in her head, her stomach spinning at the volume. She'd need to hire on another baker full time!

Two hundred pies in addition to her current customers were going to double her workload. At the price he was willing to pay, it would also double her profits, and offer a solution to her delicate problem. While creating new ones.

At that level of production, she wouldn't have any apples left over to sell. To anyone. Not that Luke was interested in part of her apples. He made it clear he was an all-or-nothing kind of guy. How would he react when he discovered that he wasn't getting any?

Especially after last night?

Not a big deal, she reminded herself. He wouldn't walk away from his distillery for her shop, so why did she feel slightly confused over news that should have her celebrating?

"I'd like the weekend to look over the contract, if that's

okay." She'd signed in haste once, and no matter how perfect this deal seemed, she'd learned her lesson. She was going to understand this contract inside and out before she signed.

She also wanted to talk to Paula. In the end, this was Kennedy's business, but she valued the woman's opinion.

"Take your time." Cosmo took the pies from Kennedy. "But not too much time. I don't want to miss the season."

Kennedy couldn't afford to miss it either. "I'll let you know by Monday."

Cosmo put his hat on his head. "Make sure you think this through, because it takes a strong woman to stand up to Fi, and although I am excited about this deal, I don't want to cause any more upset." With a slight bow, Cosmo made his way toward the door.

"I truly didn't mean to upset Fi," Kennedy said when the door closed. "Or go behind your back. I just needed to know if I secured or lost the deal, that it was all me. No history, no outside influences. Me and my idea."

Paula grabbed a comfort pie and set it in the middle of the table, then sat down. "Oh, I know that, dear, and Fi will, too, once she gets over not being in the loop. She always was sensitive about being left out. It comes with being the only girl working in her family's orchard."

Kennedy grabbed two forks and sat beside her. "And I would never want her to think that I wasn't taking her feelings into account. You both helped me out so much, I appreciate what you have done for me and how welcoming you've been."

Paula laughed. "We both know that I am the more welcoming of the two. The best baker as well, so trust me when I say your recipes are inspired."

"Fi doesn't agree." Kennedy looked at the Pie of the Day rack, and opened the contract. "And maybe she's right. My 'vegetable pies' aren't selling as well, and if I don't make this deal with Cosmo, there is a very real chance I would have to forfeit."

She was already nervous about making her monthly payments if Philip flaked. Which was a very real possibility.

"You've got to give it time, people will come around. As for the deal with Cosmo, it is a smart one. And you are a smart woman," Paula said with infinite confidence, and Kennedy found herself blushing. "Once Fi gets over the shock, and being stubborn, she'll see reason."

Paula took a bite of pie and gave Kennedy the baker-to-baker seal of approval, which consisted of licking the fork and groaning. Kennedy felt as giddy as a schoolgirl getting a gold star on her weekly test.

"Let's just hope that she doesn't take as long to come around as Luke with his veggies," Paula said, and Kennedy laughed.

"I guess stubbornness runs in the family."

"This is Destiny Bay," Paula said, handing Kennedy a fork. "It runs in the water."

Chapter 12

Luke sat in his office at the back of the barn and went over the bullet points in the proposal he'd drawn up for his meeting with Jason Stark. He'd already gone over his presentation, had cemented the points he wanted to highlight in his memory. The numbers came out on the high side for his taste, but it was an attractive enough offer to get the family to agree to a conversation.

And that's what this meeting tomorrow was about—getting Jason on board so he could run it past his siblings.

Normally, this was the point in a project when Luke would go over the offered terms again, try to streamline what he could to give both parties what they wanted. Only he was too busy staring out the window, checking to see what his sexy neighbor was doing, to focus on work.

It was all kinds of ridiculous. It wasn't like he could really see her all that well. The cottage was too far off in the distance to make out much. But he knew she was home, had watched her little car pull down the road about an hour ago and seen her flick on the kitchen light. It was the exact moment his mind gave up on work and started thinking about her mouth.

She had a great mouth. Full and sexy and always throwing off some serious attitude. He liked attitude in a woman. Especially this woman. There was something about her that got to him.

She hadn't called to say if she saw the note, not that he was expecting her to call, but it would have been nice to know how she was feeling. Between harvesting apples and catching up with her ex, Luke was surprised she'd managed to get out of bed—let alone make it to the bakery and put in a full day.

She was tough—another thing he liked about her.

The sound of crunching leaves outside caught his attention. It was late and the crew was long gone, but when he went to the window, he saw a beam of light flicker in the orchard, moving through the trees, and toward the barn.

Clicking off his office lights, Luke gave up the pretense of working, because the soft glow of the moon outlined a figure with a flashlight and red shoes. It was a female with a sweet body, silky blond hair, and a world-class ass that had kept him up all night.

Only Kennedy didn't come inside the barn, didn't even come near the barn to either thank him or bust his nuts for touching her apples without her permission. With her it could go either way. Instead, the most unpredictable woman he'd ever met pressed her face to the truck window and peered in.

She looked good and long before rounding the back of the pickup, and dropping a paper bag into the truck bed—then she followed. It took her a few tries to get up there, since the cute khaki skirt she wore wouldn't allow for much range of motion and his truck had mud tires.

But miracle of miracles, she managed to crawl in without falling, then she glanced around looking for—who the hell knew? But once she was satisfied they weren't around, she bent over and her skirt slid high enough to give him an inspiring view of her legs and—*look at that*... the hem was about one inch from giving him the best view he'd had in weeks. He was so busy staring that he almost missed the screwdriver in her hand.

Shop Girl was looking to attempt a little grand theft auto. With his truck.

Five minutes in, Luke determined that this was her first tangle with the law. She hadn't managed to do much more than scratch the paint around the back window and put her hair in a ponytail.

Luke considered going outside to lend a hand—she was working way too hard on breaking in. He had no idea why she was breaking in, but it was clear that, given enough time, she would—even if it meant breaking out the back window.

He fished his phone out of his pocket, dialed her number—and watched her jerk up and bang her head on the top rack of his truck.

"Shoot," her voice traveled through the window. Rubbing the offending mark, her head tipped down toward the glowing screen of her cell, then immediately popped back up. Darting around like a chicken caught in the sight of a predator.

Her gaze locked on the barn window, and even though he knew that she couldn't see him in the darkened room, he still felt the need to move. But then she looked at the screen again and he smiled. She'd programmed his number in. Women only programmed in men's numbers who they hope would call.

She was hoping he'd call all right. She did the smoothing of the hair down and straightening her shoulders, typical chick language for "I'm into you." So Luke crossed his arms and, with a smile that was too big and stupid, waited for her voice to come through the phone.

Well, shit, she sent him to voice mail.

The least she could do, since she was breaking into his truck, was answer. So he hung up and dialed her back. Because he, too, had programmed her into his phone.

This time she answered.

"Hello, this is Kennedy Sinclair," she said, so professional, he was surprised she didn't add, "I can't come to the phone right now so please leave a message after the beep," then give off some humanized impression of a beep.

Probably knew he'd call right back.

"Hey, sweetness."

"Oh, hey, Luke," she said as if she didn't know who had been calling. "I was just about to call you. To say thanks for the early delivery."

He chuckled. "And here I thought you were going to hang up on me again."

There was a long stretch of silence, where she glanced around, looked into the truck again, then back to the darkened window. "Sorry about that. I was busy and accidentally hit the wrong button."

She was a terrible liar.

"But seriously, thanks." This time her tone was warm, soft—genuine. And man, that lit him up inside. "Showing up to have all of my apples in the shop today was...well, you gave me a little more faith that good guys really might exist. And made what could have been a really stressful day pretty amazing. So thanks."

Luke couldn't help smiling, even though Hawk was going to rip him a new one over this. Luke knew that Kennedy had to be sore and achy, just like he knew she was determined as hell to get her apples to the shop. He told himself he did it because a few bushels of apples weren't going to solve her problems, or inflate his. The truth was, Luke did it because he didn't want to be another disappointment.

Not to her.

Her business was going to fail; he just didn't want to be the reason it did. Plus, if the Starks agreed to his proposal, he wouldn't need her apples.

Knowing that he'd brought a smile to that pretty face made it all worth it.

"Glad I could help, and I am happy you found the apples. For a moment there I wondered if you'd overlooked them somehow." Which would explain why she was trying to steal his truck.

"Why would you think I overlooked them?"

He chuckled. "No reason." And then because he wanted to feel like he was that good guy, he added, "Oh, and Kennedy, try the handle, it's unlocked."

She froze, her baby blues so big with surprise, he could see the moon reflecting off them. "I have no idea what you're taking about."

"The driver's door. To my truck. It's unlocked. And if you were planning on taking it for a spin, the keys are on the floorboard. Night now." By the time he ended the call, his prowler had abandoned her job and was hustling that sweet ass through the orchard and back to the cottage.

Luke gave it two minutes, to make sure she wasn't coming back for her supplies, before he headed down. He checked the back window—thankfully not a scratch.

Then he checked the paper bag she'd left behind. Inside was a box with a single slice of pie, a tractor-shaped cookie that was topped with green and yellow icing, and a note.

> *The pie is for helping me out. The cookie is to make you smile... K*
> *PS. In case you like what you taste.*

And taped right below the PS was a one of those decorative keys that Ali sold at her home and garden store. It was green with bright red apples on it. And Luke was pretty sure it went to the front door of the cottage.

* * *

Normally, when a woman gave Luke a key to her place, he didn't expect to be greeted with a rolling pin and apron. Unless that apron was accompanied by do-me pumps and nothing else. This apron, however, was his size, and the only do-me offer on the table was, "Do me a favor, and hand me the flour."

Not that he could see the table anymore, since it was covered with a dozen different kinds of mini pies, all cooling and all waiting for his approval. He'd tasted three so far, apple and blackberry, apple and pear, and apple and mango. The first two were fantastic; the mango was a little too out of the box to like.

So Kennedy had cut it off the list. Her feelings hadn't been wounded; there had been not a single tear, just a shrug and a big X through the idea. For someone who made his life difficult, being around her was surprisingly easy.

And fun.

"I have to come up with a catchy name that lets people know the apples are the star." Eyes twinkling with excitement, she set another mystery pie on the counter. "Ready for the next one?"

Luke would do just about anything to keep that smile of hers going, because damn, she was beautiful, but he hesitated. Bad move, he knew, but he couldn't help it.

Kennedy was clearly eager for him to taste this one, too eager for his comfort. He'd seen her going into stealth mode on the last pie, making a big deal to block his view so he couldn't see what she was making.

Not that he'd minded. Her version of blocking his view was to shield the mixing bowl with her body. And since she was still in that cute khaki skirt, and a fuzzy blue sweater that matched her eyes, Luke supported her right to surprise him.

Until he saw her cutting green leaves off this freaky red plant, which had roots. Roots indicated it was a vegetable and no way in hell was he eating a vegetable for dessert. Even if her sweater was slipping off her right shoulder, exposing a black, silky strap.

"I like the other ones better. I say cut it."

"Cut it?" Her pretty eye went wide with mock surprise. "You haven't even tried it."

"Don't need to. I already know I won't like it." And to be clear that the freaky roots would not pass his lips, he pushed the fork back.

"But you don't even know what it is," she said, pitching her voice so it sounded like pure sex.

"Then tell me." He leaned back, flashing a little sexy her way. "What's in it?"

"That's against the rules," she reminded him, padding barefoot around the counter until she was standing right next to him, her scent wrapping around him and engulfing him.

Slowly, he spun his chair to the side until they were facing each other, and she was standing between his parted thighs. "You have too many rules."

"I need an unbiased opinion, and you knowing what's in the pies can skew the results." When he looked ready to argue, she said, "I told you what was in the mango one and you wrinkled your nose and said it was weird."

"Mango and apples are weird."

"Well, this one is amazing." She picked up the fork and offered it to him by moving it back and forth in a hypnotic gesture. "I promise you'll love it. It's a crowd favorite."

He ignored the fork, instead taking in what she was saying to figure out what he was missing. "You've made this before?"

A small smile crossed her lips and she scooted closer. "I made it for a state fair when I was twelve. It was the first award I ever won for baking."

He looked at the pie on the plate, the golden crust, the crystallized sugar on top. Weird alien vegetable aside, it looked like a pie out of a baking magazine. "Did it look like this when you were twelve?"

She nodded. "I spent all summer perfecting it. My grandma was a grocery clerk and she pulled a lot of double shifts, so after she'd leave for work, I would go in the kitchen and bake. It kept me out of trouble."

Luke had a hard time imagining a young Kennedy getting into trouble. She might have spunk, but she was also a pleaser by nature. She liked rules because they made her feel safe. Gave her boundaries so she wouldn't get hurt.

"Does each pie here have a story?" he asked.

"Not all of them, but most. The ones that don't are just waiting for theirs."

"That's a lot of pies," he said.

"I had a lot of free time growing up."

Luke didn't know a lot about raising kids, but it sounded like Kennedy had had a lonely childhood. She never talked about friends or family, outside of her grandmother, and rarely brought up home. And as far as he knew, no one had come to visit or help her move.

He wanted to ask where her family was, but could tell that wouldn't be a fun topic for her. And tonight he wanted her to have fun. She was excited about her new line of mixed fruit pies, excited about her idea to tempt locals to expand their taste buds.

Luke picked up another pie. One from the back of the counter. "Tell me about this one."

"I can't without telling you what's in it. And it's against the—"

"Rules, got it." He took another pie. The apple and mango. "How about this one. I already know what's in it."

"That one reminds me of the time my grandma and I were in Atlanta," she began and he could see the warmth of the memory wash over her, feel the connection fill the space between them, and shift into something much more intimate. Vulnerable. "It was July, so it was hot and muggy.

We passed this fancy French pâtisserie. I'd never seen a pastry shop with starched tablecloths and wineglasses before. My grandma knew that I loved desserts and suggested we go inside and get something to cool off."

She broke off and cleared her throat. "Even though I was only eight, I knew we were poor, but my grandma took me inside and told me to pick anything I wanted. We shared a butterscotch and apple crepe with mango ice on top. She said it was the most memorable thing she'd ever tasted."

"And that inspired this pie?" he asked.

She nodded.

Letting go of all his expectations and preconceived ideas about the odd pairing, Luke took another bite. This time letting it melt on his tongue. After he got past the initial intense explosion of flavor, it mellowed out to a smooth sweetness, with a fresh hint of citrus at the end.

He decided it wasn't so weird after all. Just unexpected, kind of like its creator.

An unexpected bite of sweet freshness.

"And this one started it all?" he asked, pulling the root vegetable pie closer. "Which probably makes it high on your list of hopefuls."

"It's the top of my list." Her eyes went bright, and she nibbled her lip. She wasn't just excited for him to try it, she was nervous about his reaction, as if he had the power to hurt her. A position he'd never wanted to be in. "It's my favorite."

"If it's your favorite, then why do you care what I think?"

Averting her face, she concentrated on straightening the pie so that the designs she'd cut out of the top were lined up with the fork. "I know what I like, but I'm not all that great at figuring out what everyone else likes," she said with a pain so raw he felt it in his chest. "I don't want to put it out there with high hopes, only to fall short of reaching expectations."

This was about more than pies and pleasing customers—he could see it in her posture, in the way she was fidgeting with the silverware. Part of the problem with letting people in was giving them the tools to hurt you. And Kennedy had been hurt, maybe by her ex, maybe by her parents, but she'd had more than her fair share of letdowns. It was why she worked so hard not to disappoint others.

Problem was, by pleasing others, she opened herself up to disappointment.

"Whoever told you that you fell short was wrong."

Kennedy slowly lifted her gaze, her lashes fluttering up last showing him an expression that wasn't defiant, but uncertain. "How do you know?"

Didn't that break his heart. She didn't understand what he could have seen in her that others had easily dismissed. Even more, he could see that she needed to believe he saw something more. Which he did, and anyone who couldn't see what an amazing woman she was didn't deserve her trust.

You don't either, he told himself.

"My mom always said nothing that comes from the heart can ever fall short." Luke gently ran the pad of his finger over her cheek. "And you, sweetness, are all heart."

"Sometimes my heart feels so big with everyone else, there isn't room left for me," she admitted, sharing a part of herself with him that didn't come lightly.

"You're a nurturer. You have this amazing capacity to

care for others and for what you do. It's why you love baking. It's your way of acknowledging their value, making their day a little brighter."

She looked as touched by the compliment as she did uncomfortable. "Do you know why I invited you here tonight?"

"To make me eat weird root vegetables?"

She laughed and it was a sweet sound. "No, I wanted to say thank you. Not just for bringing me the apples, but for making *my* day brighter. You made me feel special on a day that was tiring and frustrating. Your thoughtfulness allowed for a reprieve, gave me enough pause to see the possibilities, and solidify things." With a soft smile she stepped off the stool and between his legs and gave him a kiss on the cheek. "You are one of the good ones, Luke."

He wasn't sure how he felt about the last half, but he wasn't complaining seeing how good she felt pressed against his thighs. "Sounds like you packed a lot into eight hours."

"I've packed a lot into my whole life." She looked at the pies on the counter, as if checking off each memory, then to the one he'd rejected. "And today, I decided I was tired of packing, I want to enjoy, *make* my life special, and go after what I want. To wake up every day and feel how I felt when I saw the bushels of apples, which, by the way, did I say thank you?"

"You did. Three times." Didn't stop her from going in for a fourth, which consisted of a sweet brush of the lips that was meant to soothe.

Luke closed his eyes at the rush of emotions that complicated something they needed to keep simple. Only the more time he spent with her, the more he respected her—

and the more he wanted her. She had a big heart and an even bigger capacity to nurture, and being on the receiving end of that kind of intense warmth was addicting.

Made him crave things he couldn't have. Do things he shouldn't do, like slip his hands around her waist and draw her near. Rub his thumb over the soft curve of her hip, and under her sweater to the even softer skin beneath, until her eyes heated with pleasure.

Only she'd invited him here to explore her new menu, not the *Kama Sutra*. Otherwise she would have answered that door in fuck-me pumps and a LET'S GET COOKING apron, instead of that skirt, a fuzzy sweater, and her dreams on her sleeve.

No matter how careful they were, they were destined to burn hot and crash hard. While Luke was a giver by nature, with her he feared he'd do nothing but take. And Kennedy had lost enough in her life.

"Do you know why I came here?" he asked.

"Free pie?"

He smiled. "That, and to apologize for putting you in an impossible situation. I knew you needed the apples, and I was pissed that you changed the locks."

"I get it." She shrugged. "I locked you out of the cottage and stole your men."

One smile and those men abandoned their post, almost costing him an embarrassing conversation with one of his largest clients. But tonight wasn't about tallying points; he'd come to prove that he was the kind of guy who followed through on his commitments. The kind of man his father would have been proud of.

"Yes, but I could have found a better solution than sending you up a tree alone," he admitted.

"I wasn't alone. Not yesterday and not today. And it was nice." Very gently, she placed her hands flat against his chest, and he was sure she could feel his heart pounding with need. "Beneath that MBA starch, you're nice, too."

Luke put his hand over hers. "Sweetness, I think you're mistaking a good day for a good decision."

"No more mistakes, I'm reinventing."

He wasn't sure if she meant her menu or herself; either way that didn't settle right. "I would hate to see you reinvent something that's already perfect."

"You can't say something is perfect if you haven't tried it," she said as if she were back to talking about the pie, but he knew better.

"Every once in a while you come across something so memorable, you only need one taste to know." And he already knew that, with her, one taste would never be enough. And no way in hell did he deserve another, but that didn't stop him from wanting it.

From wanting her.

Not when she was looking at him like she wanted it, too. Like he was the answer to all her problems, the guy who could take her day from ho-hum to Christmas-fucking-morning in one brush of the lips.

"Funny, I've always been a second helping kind of girl," she said, and before he could point out that he liked a healthy appetite in his women, she pulled his mouth to hers, proving he also found decisiveness an admirable quality.

In fact, there was a lot about her to admire, her mouth for one. Full and soft, sliding over his lips as if he were the tasting, and she was savoring each second. Seconds that turned to minutes, taking it from gentle welcoming brushes to come-and-get-me nips that blew his mind.

Which brought him to her directness. A quality that, until this very moment, he'd vastly underestimated. Kennedy
didn't play coy like other women; she was exacting and
a world-class communicator. When his hands slid south,
over his hips and lower, she moaned, groaned really, in that
breathy way that told him under no circumstances was he
to stop.

And Luke knew better than to deny a lady, especially
when she made it clear by the way she was climbing up his
body that she would like to use his lap as a seat—an order
he could get behind. And he did, lifting her until she was
straddling him and bringing his attention to her choice in
attire.

It was so admirable, it had him retracting his earlier
statement about the impartial nature of her skirt. Because
all it took was a little shimmy on her part, not that he
wasn't contributing to the cause, and suddenly her skirt
was inching around her waist—and his hands were on her
ass. A place he'd spent every waking moment dreaming
they could be, only to realize that her imagination was far
superior to his.

Betty Crocker didn't wear matching black lace panties,
or even a black thong. His pie girl was a purist, skipping all
the topping and going au naturel.

"I thought you invited me here to say thank you," he
said, knowing that even though this was the best fucking
thank-you he'd ever receive, he couldn't do it.

"I did." She pulled back; her eyes were heated and her
lips wet. "But I also invited you here because I want to
know what it's like to be with a good guy."

"Kennedy, I'm not—"

"The right good guy for me, I know." She rocked her

hips in this sexy little move that caused her to press against his erection, and his eyes rolled to the back of his head. "But you make me feel good, and this feels too right to stop. You get to me," she said, and she didn't even sound mad about admitting that he was right. "Even better, you get me."

He cupped her cheek gently, loving how soft she felt under his touch. How perfectly she fit in his arms. "Which is why this could get complicated."

"It doesn't have to be. Not tonight."

He sure as hell hoped she was right, because she reached down and tugged at the hem of that sweater, and it went up, up, and off, falling to the floor and leaving her in nothing but a black bra.

"Tonight is just a tasting," she said.

And since Like was taught that it was always ladies first, he forked off a piece of her favorite pie and held it out to her lips. "Well, then I guess we should start with your favorite."

Instead of taking the fork, she gave a wicked little smile that nearly knocked him off the chair, and ran her lips across the pie, coating the lower one with just enough filling to make it shine. "You'll love it, I promise."

Luke figured, what the hell, if apple and freaky red vegetable pie was ever going to rock his world, it would be licking it off the hottest lips in town.

Suddenly, all for new experiences, he leaned in for a taste, then a little nibble, and *holy shit!* "It's incredible."

She blushed a pretty shade of pink. "It's not a Gold Tin winner, but I think it's pretty good."

"It's perfect," he said honestly and went in for another taste.

"Wait," she whispered, leaning back to grab her phone off the counter. One minute she was straddling him, the next she was aiming her phone at them as if to take a selfie.

"What are you doing?"

"Capturing a moment," she explained. "Every recipe in my *Life's Icing Cookbook* has a picture to remind me of the perfect moment, to help me remember."

He smiled. "And you want to remember me kissing you in your kitchen?"

"No." She pressed her lips against his. "I want to remember the moment you went back for seconds when a vegetable was present."

He heard the faint *click* of the camera, tasted the tart filling on her lips, and knew he wouldn't need a picture to remember this. The image of her straddling him in nothing but filling and lace would forever be tattooed behind his eyelids.

Because it was perfect. The kiss. The pie. The way Kennedy was making these little sighs, letting him know that, yeah, she was feeling it, too. It was like a sweet treat and a wet dream all wrapped up in one addictive, hot experience.

Second helping? He went in for a third, and a fourth, and by the fifth nip he was a goner. So gone, he didn't care if this blew up in his face. He wanted Kennedy, and he wanted her for more than a night. Most important, he wanted her naked on his lap.

Trying a little nonverbal communication of his own, he slid his palms up to cup her breasts, rubbing his thumbs over the puckered tips, then beneath the lacy cups. In a move that was all kinds of awesome, he dipped the fabric down, her breasts spilling right out over the top.

With a growl, he bent to appreciate them, taste them, listening for what she liked—and what she loved, running his tongue across her nipples and not stopping until she was arching against him and releasing these sexy little sighs.

And that's when things got interesting, because Kennedy was as much a team player as she was a master with her hands. Reaching under his T-shirt, she skimmed her hands up his chest, touching every inch, until she tugged it over his head and tossed it to the floor. With a wicked little smile, she trailed her nails down his stomach, the muscles bunching in anticipation as she went over the waistband of his pants and lower. Running along the line of his zipper with enough finesse to have him bucking into her hand.

"Jesus, Kennedy," he gasped, resting his forehead against hers.

She held him there, delivering gentle kisses, nothing more than a whisper, while making short work of his belt and zipper. By the time he bucked again, which was about a second later, those fingers he loved so much were around the length of him, cool and sure, gently stroking and caressing him from base to tip and back down.

Taking him right out of his head, and his world, crash-landing into hers. A week ago this would have been mind-blowing foreplay, but after sharing stories, exposing parts they both normally kept hidden, this felt like more.

One stroke from losing it, Luke took her hands and placed them around his neck, pulling her until there wasn't enough space between them to breathe. Then he slid his palms down her back to her ass, lifting her just enough that when he set her back down, it created a friction that had her head tilting back in pleasure.

"Tighten your legs, sweetness," he said, lifting her again, and when she did as told, he slid her back down faster, barely letting her rest before she was on the move back up.

"Please, Luke, I want you now," she begged.

Grabbing a condom out of his back pocket and pushing his jeans down to his hips, he was covered and ready, lifting her up and ready to slide home, when he paused. "Say it again."

She bent forward until her hair spilled over her shoulder, and her breasts brushed his chest, then she gave him the sexiest smile he'd ever seen. "I want you, Luke."

He wanted her, too, but he wanted something else first. "The other part, sweetness. I want to hear the other part."

Her face held the cutest expression of confusion. "Please?"

"Such manners," he whispered and then gave them what they both wanted, until all there was to do was enjoy the sensation of finally connecting.

They both sighed, and he could actually hear her heart, thumping wildly, and matching his own.

"Are you calling me a good girl, Luke?" she asked against his lips. "Because right now I feel the best kind of bad."

Snagging his mouth with hers, she kissed him deep and long, making it one of those all-night kind of events that made breathing impossible. Good thing he didn't need air, not as much as he needed to feel her move.

Taking her hips, he started a slow rhythm, letting her find her balance on his lap, until they were both moving as one. As he pushed up, she pressed down, meeting him thrust for thrust, creating enough friction that he could feel her body tighten and coil around him.

Watching her take pleasure was driving him crazy, but the way she was curling her hips was quickly driving him over the edge. He tightened his grip, trying to slow down before it was over way too soon, but either his communication skills were lacking or she was done listening.

He'd put good money on the latter, since every time she'd rise up, she'd get those perfect tens just out of sucking range before sliding back down with a smile.

Shop Girl was teasing him.

So the next time she rose, Luke grabbed her waist, holding her there, then pulled her into his mouth, sucking until she was quivering against him. And when she was right there, on the brink of exploding, he reared up and slid all the way to the hilt.

"Oh God!" she screamed out.

Her body began to tremble with the beginnings of an orgasm. But Luke didn't let up, he slid his hand between them, finding that sweet spot and applying enough pressure that her breathing became choppy and her eyes slid shut in pleasure.

"Look at me," he said. "I want to watch you as you come apart in my hands."

Her lashes lifted, and the second his gaze locked on hers, he felt her body shake and then break loose and fly. With that pretty word *please* on her lips, followed by his name. And that was enough to break what little control he'd managed to hold on to, and Luke followed her over the edge—

And into a world he wasn't sure he'd want to leave come morning. A world that was as simple as it was complicated.

* * *

"That's about the sexiest thing I've ever seen," Kennedy said, sliding onto a stool at the counter, sighing at the delicious soreness.

The early morning sun peered through the blinds, warming the tiles beneath her feet while the view in front of her was hot enough to melt the polar ice caps.

Luke stood at the sink in nothing but bedhead, scruff, and yesterday's jeans, which were zipped but not buttoned, and ready to give at the simplest tug. The man knew how to pull off the morning after with as much swagger as the night before.

He glanced over his shoulder and delivered a dimple that had her good parts sighing. "And you haven't seen my best side, sweetness."

She'd seen all of his sides last night and couldn't say which was her favorite, although looking at his backside ranked pretty high. Right between his funny side and his sweet side. "I was actually talking about a man doing dishes in my kitchen."

"Then get ready to swoon, because breakfast is almost ready." Which explained the skillets on the stove and the heavenly aroma in the kitchen.

Kennedy rested her elbows on the counter and leaned forward. "You cook, clean, and make house calls? Be still, my heart."

"I aim to please." He dried off his hands and brought two steaming mugs of coffee to the counter. "Which is why I was trying to be quiet, so you could get another few minutes of sleep, before I surprised you in bed." He grinned. It was a wicked grin. "Again."

Luke had done more than surprise her last night; he'd spoiled her for other men. Sure, he was an incredible lover, but it was the tender moments in between that made her nervous.

This thing between them couldn't last. She knew that. She also understood that if he was looking for something more permanent, she wouldn't be the kind of woman to inspire that kind of commitment. She was unable to do it with her perfect match, or even her own mother. The one person who was supposed to love her unconditionally. Which left Kennedy painfully afraid that she was missing that elusive quality that led to forever.

Finding out that she was right, that she was unlovable, from a man who obviously had an incredible capacity to love, as she'd seen with his friends and family, would be too painful to survive. So she took the moment for what it was, committing to memory the warm aroma of the coffee, the way the sun cast a glassy haze over the kitchen, and the sleepy expression on his face that made him look softer. More relaxed. Like this was where he was supposed to be.

In this kitchen—with her.

Kennedy was becoming more attached—she could feel it. The way he treated her, the way he made her feel, even the way he looked at her, like right now, as if she were special. Which made her feel special.

She didn't know how to slow down what was happening between them. Being with him last night, sharing stories about her childhood, waking up to him in her space—it all felt so good.

"I hope you like peppers," he said, sliding a fluffy omelet out of the skillet and onto a plate. Grabbing two forks, he set breakfast between them, the heavenly scent making her stomach grumble. Her mouth was watering, too, but that had more to do with the wide shoulders and rippling abs on display.

"You do know peppers are a vegetable, right?"

He took a bite and washed it down with coffee. "You've been talking to my mom."

"A little." She paused. "A lot actually. I really like your mom."

"She's nosy, doesn't understand limits, and drives me crazy, but she's always there, cheering me on no matter what. And there were a lot of *no matter what*'s when I was growing up, so now it's my turn to be there for her, make sure she's happy and taken care of." He chuckled. "Not that she makes it easy." He studied her for a moment. "How are things going at the shop?"

Kennedy was caught off guard by the question, flustered to the point that she wasn't sure how to respond. They'd both purposefully kept the conversation away from business, because that seemed to be their trigger. But maybe after last night, it didn't have to be.

"Is Mom still lifting trays and working long hours?" he asked.

"Oh," Kennedy said, feeling equal parts relief and disappointment. His concern was for Paula. "I told her no more lifting the trays, and after about an hour in the kitchen, I send her out to run the front of the shop, which usually turns into her sitting down and gossiping with one of the customers."

"Thank you. She would have kept pushing and..." Luke gave a long, tired sigh. "I worry about her and my aunt. A lot. I hate the thought of the two of them in that big house alone."

Kennedy wanted to point out that he needn't waste his

concern. Those women could not only keep that big farm-house running, but run the entire country if they put their minds to it.

"If she pushes too hard, she has a flare-up and..." He shook his head. "She hates it when she's stuck in the house, and I hate it when she's in pain and there is nothing I can do to help."

There was a protective quality to his tone that made Kennedy gush. Wonder what it would be like to have someone in her life who cared for her with the same fierce devotion.

Kennedy looked at the thoughtful breakfast, then at the beautiful man who'd made her last two days magical, and a little tingle raced down her spine.

"The mornings will get colder and colder," he said, mistaking her shivers for a chill. "Nothing but my shirt isn't the warmest choice."

"You weren't complaining last night," she teased.

His eyes went hot, running the length of her. Stepping around the counter, he came up behind her, running his hands down her arms, warming them as he went. His front pressed into her back as he leaned over to whisper, "I'm not complaining now. I just don't like seeing you cold."

Cold? Kennedy was on fire, a result of being wrapped in a warm cocoon of sexy, yummy man.

"Thank you for breakfast." Kennedy turned her head to give him a languid gentle kiss on the lips. "This is sweet."

"Thanks for dessert." Luke kissed her back, and when he was done, Kennedy was breathing heavily and sitting on his lap, her feet dangling off the side. "It was hot."

One arm was around her, pulling her against him, the other resting on her thigh, his fingers gently massaging the muscles and melting her bones. He couldn't seem to stop touching her, which was fine since she was doing a little touching of her own.

"Tomorrow night Hawk and I are having a little get-together at the bar, to celebrate our new hard cider," Luke said. "Come with me."

The heater must have kicked on, because suddenly it was so warm in the kitchen, it was hard to think. Hard to process what he was saying versus what he meant, and she felt like she was suffocating.

This wasn't just a simple get-together at his bar. Word around town was this was an invite only, VIP party for vendors, distributors, and select guests. It was a cocktail kind of event that would probably make a few local papers, and maybe some bigger ones.

It wasn't the fanfare that had panic curling around her neck; it was that Luke had asked her to go with him. On a date. In public. To celebrate the release of a line he might not be able to continue when she signed the contract with Cosmo.

She wasn't sure how he'd react when he found out, but the uncertainty was worrisome enough that she didn't tell him about the deal when she could have. But Kennedy was still reeling from last night, trying to figure out what they were in private. Who they were without the complication of business. And who she was on her own.

"You don't have to make this more than what it is," she said, studying how small her hands looked against his chest.

Luke's hand covered hers. "It's just a date."

She looked up. "Is it?"

His gaze said it was more, and she took comfort in that.

It was scary to be in this, whatever *this* was, but terrifying to think she was in it alone.

"I'm not going to lie," he said quietly. "Tomorrow night is a big deal for Two Bad Apples, and for me. My dad and I talked about this day for what seems like ever. Hawk has gone all out and we put a lot into this launch, so it will be packed. You can meet a bunch of locals, drinks are on the house, and"—he cupped her cheek— "I'd like for you to be there."

This side was her favorite, she decided. That genuine, vulnerable part that he kept hidden. She'd seen a glimpse of it when he was with his family and even then she felt drawn in. Having him open up to her like that was too tempting to resist.

Kennedy had shared a part of herself with him last night, and now he was offering her a chance to experience an important part of his life.

"Sundays are my busiest day, so I have extra prep on Saturday night," she said. "I might be late."

Luke kissed her neck. "I'll be the sexy one with the great ass, waiting behind the bar."

Chapter 13

⌒

Luke watched as people mingled and chatted about Two Bad Apples Hard Cider. There was enough buzz to know that they had a hit on their hands. From the way Rogers kept grinning and hanging on Hawk's every word, Luke knew that even though the night was only getting started, this was their deal to lose.

"Help me out, Jason," Luke said, turning his attention back to the booth and his guest. "I know you don't want to deal with the harvest, so tell me what you need to say yes."

When Jason Stark had e-mailed saying he had news, Luke had invited him to the party, certain that he'd sold Jason on the proposal. The guy had left their meeting relieved by the possibility of someone else taking the apples off his hands. Only now that he was here, ten feet from Rogers, delivering the worst news possible, Luke regretted that decision.

He'd been riding the high of a good meeting and an even

better night before, and he'd gotten cocky. Allowed himself to get distracted.

"That's just it," Jason said. "I did say yes, and so did my sisters, but my older brother, Walter, thinks it's a bad move, and since he took a business class back in junior college, he thinks he's fucking Warren Buffett." Jason sat back and took a swallow of cider.

"You're each an equal owner, right?" Luke asked, trying to ascertain the situation the best he could, in hopes of finding a creative solution that appealed to everyone. "What if I buy a few acres of Yarlington Mill and Kingston Blacks from your quarter of the harvest?"

"If I owned a quarter of the apples, I would do it just so I wouldn't have to deal with the mess of harvesting them," Jason said. "And because I know how much this means."

"I know you would."

"But I own a quarter of the estate. So whatever affects the estate needs to have unanimous consent."

Luke felt the muscles at the base of his skull contract.

"What does Walter need to feel comfortable saying yes?" Luke asked, because he had known Jason for most of his life—they'd played hockey together in high school. Jason knew that Luke's word was good. Just like Luke knew that Jason had tried his best.

But Luke didn't know a lot about Jason's brother, Walter. Other than he was a decade older, had moved to Chicago the day he graduated high school, and hadn't been back. Not even for their dad's funeral.

"I don't know, I could ask him, but Walter is a tough sell," Jason said. "He thinks that if we sell you the apples, and you decide to pass on the property, then we've sold off the estate's most valuable asset."

Walter might be a prick, but he wasn't stupid. If the roles were reversed, Luke would be worried about the same thing. But the roles weren't reversed, and if he couldn't figure this out, he'd be in a bad way.

"I am going to buy the property," Luke assured him. "I just need more time to come up with the down payment. But did Walt think what will happen if I don't? The harvest will be ending and you guys will have zero time to pick and sell the apples."

"Don't remind me." Jason took a deep breath and ran a hand down his face, because he knew what Luke knew—harvesting that many acres was a full-time job. And every one of Old Man Stark's kids already had jobs—none of them here in Destiny Bay. "Walter says he already has another buyer lined up. He's hoping you pass."

At his statement, a forty-eight-thousand-pound weight settled on Luke's chest. "What are they offering?"

"A half million more, all cash, and a five-day escrow," Jason said, and Luke had a hard time breathing. "I guess the buyer is ready to close the deal the second your option runs out."

Luke gripped his forehead, hoping to relieve some of the growing pressure. "I need to talk to Walter, see if there is any way to sway him."

"The only thing that will sway my brother is money."

That's what Luke was afraid of.

"Want to go see a Blackhawks' game with me? Owner's box?" Luke asked, remembering one more thing about Walter—he was a die-hard hockey fan.

"I didn't know the Blackhawks were coming to Vancouver."

"They're not," Luke said, knowing he was going to owe

Hawk big time. "We're going to Chicago to see Walt. And catch a game. You in?"

* * *

Hours later and Luke was still reeling from the news of another buyer when he walked into the Penalty Box.

"Ah shit. I know that look," Hawk said from behind the bar and cracked open a cold cider. "It's the same look you gave me right before you told me Bridget was screwing the pool guy."

Hawk had traded in his usual uniform of a black tee and dark jeans for slacks and a button-up, transforming himself from hockey bad boy and bar owner, to VP of Business Development of one of the fastest-growing ciders on the market. Hawk hated slacks almost as much as he hated reliving his hockey days—that he'd done it tonight to impress Rogers showed just how invested in the business he was.

"He was named the Sharks' MVP last year," Luke pointed out quietly, sliding behind the bar with a big smile so that everyone could see that things were going great. Just great. He lowered his voice even more. "And this isn't that look."

"They had sex in my pool, so he will forever be the fucking pool guy." Hawk leaned in close, lowering his voice. "And that's the same look, man. Women like her suck you in, you don't see it coming, but one kiss and suddenly you're thinking with the wrong head, making shit decisions, and everything falls to hell."

"Kennedy isn't Bridget," Luke said, referring to Hawk's ex-wife.

"I wasn't talking about Bridget." And since his friend

was as puckered as a baboon when it came to talking about his love life, he added, "In fact, we aren't talking about women at all, according to you."

Luke scanned the area. Noticing that Rogers was chatting up a stacked brunette with a hockey puck tattooed on her cleavage, he lowered his voice. "It's nothing I can't handle."

"Thank God." Hawk made a big deal over wiping the nonexistent sweat off his brow. "Because from here, it looked like you bet everything on the wrong horse, then blew the backup plan to shit. Which, by the way, the backup was supposed to be the deal with Stark."

"Stark isn't my backup, just another possibility." Luke reached in the fridge, bypassed the cider, and went straight for the Jack. "And nothing is blown, just a little setback. We need to go meet with Jason's bother, give him a little nudge in the right direction."

"How much of a nudge are we talking?"

"Enough to show him we're serious about the property."

Hawk grabbed two tumblers and set them on the counter. "Or I know, what if I gave him enough for the down payment on the property? We close the deal by the end of the month. Problem solved."

Luke shook his head. "That isn't your problem to solve, man. We go fifty-fifty, that was the deal from the beginning." Because Luke would never again slacken on his responsibilities. Not when it came to family—and Hawk might not be related, but he was family.

"Then let me loan you the money."

"I don't need a loan." And he didn't want his friend to bail him out. "I need this deal to close."

It wasn't like he was asking for Hawk to front him the

money for a few acres of woodlands. Fifty prime acres of apples on Destiny Bay's bluff were going to cost a solid seven figures. Heirlooms had skyrocketed since Luke originally sold the property, but as long as the demand for cider continued to increase, so would the value of mature, producing trees.

Hawk poured two fingers in each glass and slid one to Luke. "And if you can't convince Walter?"

"I can convince him." Luke took the glass and smiled. "One night hanging with the legendary bad boy of the ice, throwing back a few while watching some hockey, and he'll be ready to talk."

Hawk groaned. "So you won't use my money, but you'll use my fame?" Luke held up his glass. "Fine, but if the Sharks are playing and the pool boy steps out on the ice, shit will go down."

"No Sharks," Luke promised. "Oh, and can you get us in the owner's box?"

"What happened to Bay View Orchards being our backup, your way of showing Shop Girl that she wasn't the only game in town?" When Luke said not a word, Hawk laughed. "Wouldn't want a little thing like our business to get in the way of you getting laid."

Luke choked. "Who says I'm getting laid?"

"You just did." Hawk shook his head with disgust. "Come on, man, didn't they teach you in that fancy business school you went to that sleeping with the competition is a conflict of interest?" Hawk lifted a brow. "No? Then how about sleeping with a girl your mom already loves is the fast track to some pretty complicated shit."

"We were both clear on how things stand," Luke assured him.

At least he hoped they were. He'd been careful to keep all talk off business, then he'd caught sight of her in his shirt, sans the bra, and asked her how things were going. He saw her confused look, which quickly morphed into the hope that he'd given up on running her out of town. And he had. Until Stark shut that possibility down. Leaving only Kennedy and her apples.

"Then why are we meeting with a guy who you know is going to bend us over on the prices of apples, because he knows he can't on the price of the property?"

Luke took a swig and let the Scotch burn all the way down. "I like having options."

"So this is just about options, and not admitting you have a problem?" he asked.

"No problem," Luke said, wondering who he was trying to convince, since neither one of them believed a word he was spewing. "I've got this handled."

Luke knew how to separate his personal life from his professional one. Understood what was on the line, for everyone involved. He'd been doing it for the past decade. But asking Kennedy for her apples now, after he knew what Sweetie Pies meant to her, felt like a dick move. Leaving Hawk hanging to dry, after all that he'd put into this company, felt even worse.

God, this was a mess.

"Good," Hawk said, grabbing his tumbler and tipping back. "Because Shop Girl just walked in here in a pair of thigh-highs and enough cleavage to be a problem."

Luke turned around and nearly choked on his shot. *Problem* wasn't the word he'd use when talking about those boots. Or that woman.

Kennedy was dressed to be seen, and every man in the

bar was looking. Including him. He couldn't stop. She had on these ridiculous leather boots, black and high, and a slinky blue top that matched her eyes and slipped off one shoulder, exposing skin that he knew to be softer than silk. And that skirt, don't even get him started—it was black, fitted, and made her khaki one look like a habit.

She glanced around, worrying that lower lip and giving herself away. She was nervous and felt out of place, he could tell. But she'd come anyway.

She'd come for him.

Her eyes locked on his, and with a sweet smile that nearly knocked him off his stool, she made her way through the crowd, not stopping until she was by his side.

"Sorry I'm late," she said. "Lauren had a study group and I got an order from Destiny Bay Presbyterian Church for a dozen HumDingers, and..." She shrugged. "I'm here."

She was. And suddenly he didn't see a single problem. How could he, when she was smiling up at him like that? Big blue eyes all wide and nervous, and that smile. Man, that smile was contagious.

"Hey, Hawk," she said. "Good turnout. People love the new cider."

"Make sure you grab a few bottles to go, they might be a limited run." Hawk lifted a single brow in Luke's direction then headed to the end of the bar. "I'll be back."

"Why do I feel like we were just warned?"

"He's just being moody," Luke said, leaning closer. "You look amazing." His lips brushed her hair. "And smell incredible. Like Christmas morning and slow kisses."

"I took a quick shower before I came." She lowered her voice, "And used pumpkin spice–scented body wash."

Luke groaned at *that* image.

"How is the party going?" she asked.

"Better now," he said, and Kennedy licked her lips, smoothing her hands down her waist and thighs. Luke's gaze locked on the target, taking his time to absorb every inch of her. She didn't seem to mind because she was doing a little perusing of her own. Maybe she was thinking back to last night, too. Or this morning.

When the challenge was gone, Luke usually lost interest. He'd never made much of a habit of seeing where things led with women. With this woman, Luke not only knew exactly how it would turn out—a disaster of epic proportions—but couldn't seem to walk away. Getting his hands, and his mouth, on her had been a mistake.

A mistake he wanted to make over and over until they both passed out from the pleasure.

She cocked her head, and a frown marred her face. Before he could ask what she was up to, she went up on her toes and checked his arms, his neck, behind his ears. Her soft fingers traced as she examined.

"What are you doing?" he asked, not that he minded her hands on him; he just had some other, more creative places she could put them to use.

"Checking for marks." She laughed. "You had vegetables last night, so I wanted to make sure you didn't have a reaction."

"Ha ha. Any more touching and I will have a reaction right here that wouldn't be conducive to working the room." He lowered his voice. "And I do have marks, but we'd have to go in the back office for me to show you."

Two high spots of color dusted her cheeks. "Which wouldn't be conducive to you working the room. Well, maybe this will help." She reached into her purse, and

Luke's head spun with all the possibilities. Last time she'd given him a key, then the best sex of his life. Maybe tonight she'd give him her panties. Or maybe it was one of those IOU sex cards.

She handed him a small to-go box. "Pie?"

"It's a mini pie. I figured you'd be nervous about tonight."

Luke found himself laughing. "Do you think pie fixes everything?"

"Of course not. Cake and strudel work just as well, and tarts are my personal favorite, but I only had pumpkin and I didn't want to push my luck." She handed him the box. "No veggies, I promise. It's my Everything's Better with Chocolate chocolate cream pie."

That it was sans apples meant she'd made it especially for him. On a day that he knew was already crammed full of responsibility, Kennedy had taken the time to bake him something special. "Thank you."

"I used to make it for my grandma whenever she pulled a double shift or had a hard day. A little sweet to get her though the night, and I know tonight is big for you."

She was smiling when she said it, but her gaze was filled with a seriousness that forced Luke to clear his throat before he spoke. "What's the other pie for?"

She looked into her purse and pulled out a second bag. "These are cookies for Ali. She had a big day with a client, too, so I am bringing her double chocolate chunk cookies. Her favorite. Nothing says celebration quite like chocolate." Before Luke could respond, Hawk was back—all frustrated and pissy.

"Can you get security to throw Ali out?" Hawk asked.

Luke scanned the room until he found Ali, leaning

against the pool table with a stick in her hand. "You're security," he reminded the guy who was six-five, two-twenty, and known on the ice as the Bone Crusher.

Hawk crossed his arms. "Yeah, well, she's fleecing Rogers, and tends to do the exact opposite of everything I say, so I'm probably not the best solution."

Luke sent Hawk a smart-ass smug look. "Is Ali too big of a *problem* for you?"

"Yes," Hawk said, dead serious.

Luke wasn't one to talk, because Kennedy touched his arm, and something stirred within him. She was a problem, all right, but she was the most appealing problem he'd had in years. Sweet, smart, and a breath of fresh air. "I'll go distract her with cookies."

He wanted to say he wanted his cookies, too, but Hawk was watching him closely, and Luke didn't want to waste more of the night convincing the guy that he had this under control.

Because when it came to Kennedy, control was impossible.

"Oh, we're not fucked at all, are we, bro?" Hawk deadpanned then rolled his eyes like a girl.

Luke poured himself another Scotch. He should be drinking cider. Then again there was a lot he should be doing as of late.

"Hey, Cosmo," Hawk said as someone slid onto the stool next to Luke. "Glad you could make it."

"And miss the chance to taste your new line?" Cosmo said, setting his hat, then a bouquet of flowers, on the bar. "Been telling customers for months about your cider, had to try it for myself to see if it was as good as you say."

"You won't be disappointed." Hawk grabbed a frosted

mug out of the freezer and poured Cosmo a glass of their reserve. "What's with the daisies? Are you here to meet a lady, Cosmo?"

"Got my eyes on someone," Cosmo said with a sheepish grin. "But you know what they say? Patience and persistence are the keys to happiness."

Hawk laughed. "And here I thought it was hot women and good cider."

"This is about a woman," Cosmo said. "After all these years, I am finally going to get my hands on Fiona's pies."

Luke choked. "Aunt Fi is selling you her pies?" This was news. Fiona would rather walk into a burning building coated with gasoline than see her pies in a retail shop.

"Well, not Fiona, but the new owner. Miss Sinclair."

Luke felt the statement hit, his lungs struggling to work through the confusion. "You made a deal with Kennedy?"

"Yup." Cosmo took a long drink, even smacking his lips when he was done.

One *yup* and Hawk looked ready to punch a wall, or Luke. "When did this happen?"

"Last week," he said, and a strange knot formed in Luke's chest. Which was all kinds of ridiculous.

So what if he'd opened up about how important tonight was, and Kennedy had had this incredible offer on the table and she didn't share? So what? It wasn't like they were dating. Or that this deal could ruin *everything* for him.

Jesus. It could ruin everything. Every fucking thing that Luke and Hawk had planned, and she didn't bother to mention it.

To be fair, they didn't talk business. Sure, he'd told her a few stories about his dad and the party, but it wasn't as if he got down on one knee.

"Miss Sinclair and I are talking about licensing the rights to sell her Gold Tin HumDingers in all of my stores." Cosmo raised his glass. "I have high hopes for this one, boys. Fi's pies deserve to be recognized. Hell, they deserve to be in stores everywhere."

Hawk was sending Luke all kinds of glares, including *What the fuck, bro?* and *Did you hear that?*

To which Luke responded, *I'm not deaf* and *Let me handle this*.

And like everyone else in Luke's family, Hawk didn't listen to a damn thing.

"Well, it isn't the real Gold Tin winner, though," Hawk said. "I mean Fi hasn't been baking for weeks now, has she, Luke?"

"Don't know, I haven't been keeping tabs on my aunt."

"I know she cooked the pie I had the other day." Cosmo's grimace said the meeting hadn't gone well.

"Well, that's good then, since Kennedy isn't Fi," Hawk added.

"The girl seems to be doing well," Cosmo said, his tone clear that he was defending Kennedy, which had Luke wondering who the older man felt he needed to defend her from. "Can't keep pies on the shelf."

Hawk grimaced. "That sounds more like a supply and demand issue to me. If I ran out of inventory, I'd be out of business in a week."

Pausing as if to consider Hawk's words, Cosmo set his glass down. "I guess I never thought of it that way. She and I were talking about a long-term deal." He looked at Luke, who was shooting Hawk every *What the fuck* look known to man—and a few he made up on the spot. "What do you think, son?"

Luke knew what the deal could mean to Kennedy. To Two Bad Apples. And to his family.

Hawk knew it as well, which was why he was returning Luke's *What the fuck* look with a *This isn't a problem, remember?* glare.

Luke didn't need the reminder. He remembered all right. Remembered the smile on Kennedy's face when he finally admitted that freaky red vegetable pie was perfect. The way she felt wrapped around him like a blanket when they'd slept. He also remembered the look on his mom's face when she lost the house. And knew that the next two seconds would decide if the only possibility he'd have left to make his dreams come true was in Chicago, sitting in his McMansion, smoking a cigar, and counting all his coins.

"Kennedy is an amazing baker, but she isn't a Gold Tin winner," Luke heard himself saying over his pounding heart, which was beating a hard rhythm of guilt and shame. "Hawk's right, you might want to talk with legal before you claim that on the boxes."

"I hadn't thought of that."

Neither had Luke until Kennedy brought it up last night, in a private and vulnerable moment. And now it was out there, floating around in everyone's head, while Luke stood there holding a piece of chocolate pie that was supposed to make everything better.

Chapter 14

O nce the rush for the Monday morning pickups and the breakfast crowd had passed, Kennedy lined her staff up in the prep area of the kitchen. After she'd decided to sign Cosmo's agreement, she'd spent the rest of the weekend and all morning focusing on her new line of pies. It was a better use of her time than thinking about Luke in her bed.

And why he hadn't been back since.

She'd been hesitant to go to his party Saturday night, afraid that taking it public would be like telling her heart it was okay to open up. At the last minute she'd convinced herself that he wanted her there. Something he'd made clear when she'd walked in and he'd looked at her as if he wanted to pull her into a dark corner and pick up where they'd left off that morning.

Then something shifted. There was no one thing she could point to, except to say he was the *perfect* gentleman.

He catered to her ever need, introduced her to his friends, even gave her a sweet kiss when he'd walked her to her car and explained that he had to take a last-minute trip to Chicago to talk to a potential client and he would be back Monday at the latest.

She wasn't surprised that he'd jump on a plane to go see a client. Luke took his responsibility to the company and his clients seriously. It was why Callahan Orchards had been so successful over the past few years. She was surprised that she'd missed him so much.

And that could become a problem.

"The apple and cranberry pie is delicious," Paula said, going in for her third bite. "The tartness of the cranberries makes the apples even sweeter. What kind of apple is this?"

"Honeycrisp," Kennedy said, unable to hide her pleasure in impressing the most impressive baker she'd ever met. "I used Callahan Honeycrisp apples, locally grown cranberries, and this amazing lemon honey that a chef I know back home makes."

Saying *home* when referring to Atlanta felt oddly wrong.

Kennedy remembered what Edna had told her when she'd stayed with her that first summer. *Home is where the heart is, child, and your heart knows where it belongs. Even when it's hurting something painful, it knows.*

At the time Kennedy hadn't understood, because her heart was too afraid to hope. Every time she thought she'd found home, it had been taken from her. But here, in Destiny Bay, the reality of finding home had somehow snuck into her heart when she hadn't been looking.

"Perfection," Paula said, and Kennedy noticed that Fi was

going in for her first bite of the tasting. Not that she was actually putting the forkful in her mouth, but she sniffed it and licked a bit of the filling.

"So this is a part of the new...How do you say it again?" Paula asked sweetly.

"Mélange—*May-lanje*—line," Kennedy said, speaking slowly and phonetically.

"May-lang line," Paula said sweetly. Kennedy was about to say close enough when Paula elbowed Fi.

"Meh-lang?" Fi repeated, not an ounce of sweet to her voice. There hadn't been any sweetness to her since she'd come back yesterday stating that, while she would never walk off the job, her coming back didn't mean she was in support of the current management. Even though Paula pointed out several times that Kennedy wasn't the new manager, but the new owner.

That Fi was willing not only to try but also to sell the new multifruit pies was enough for now.

"No, the E is accented so it sounds like an A, mélange." Kennedy extended a hand, as if she were one of the models on those infomercials. "Would you like to sample our new Apple Mélange pies?"

One hand on her meaty hip, Paula mimicked Kennedy and said, "'Would you like to sample one of our Apple May-lange pies?'"

"Close enough," Kennedy said brightly, moving on to the next part of the day's lesson. "If people ask what's in them, remember that *mélange* means 'medley.' I really listened to what you were saying, Paula, about easing people into new things." It took everything she had not to glance at the person who needed the most easing. "And I came up with the idea of making Washington apples the star in every bite, while using other fruits to elevate and showcase each type of apple's unique attributes."

"That is a lovely idea. Inventive, fresh, and very considerate of the town and Sweetie Pies' traditions." Paula turned her attention to the town's tradition police. "Don't you think so, Fi?"

Fi's face puckered like she'd eaten a spoonful of the lemon honey. "Why don't you just call them Apple Medley pies then, if they're made from a medley of fruit?"

"Good question." Kennedy clasped her hands, excited to explain her reasoning. She worked so hard to come up with pies that pleased her customers and her bottom line, while remaining true to Sweetie Pies, and what Kennedy had set out to accomplish. "I thought it was important to use the word *apple*, since that will resonate best with the locals. And *mélange*, well, it adds that little *Je ne sais quoi* that appeals to dessert connoisseurs."

And people willing to spend twenty-plus dollars on a pie.

"Connoisseurs?" Fi sent Paula a strange look. "We have any connoisseurs here in town?"

"Saul, down at the Gas and Go, eats pie for dinner," Paula offered, being helpful. "And we sell lots of pies in the morning."

"I was thinking of customers outside of Destiny Bay." A little bubble of excitement jumped in her belly. "I was actually thinking of customers outside of the Pacific Northwest. I did some research last night on shops that sell their pies on the Internet. Did you know people right here, in Washington state, pay upwards of thirty-eight dollars for an authentic Georgia peach pie? Think about what people would be willing to pay for an authentic Washington apple and cranberry pie, or one of your famous HumDingers?"

Paula clasped her hands beneath her chin. "More than twelve dollars."

The bell dinged, signaling they had a customer.

"While you two talk about feeding the world, I'm going to go feed the people right here in Destiny Bay, who don't need a fancy name to know good pie. Because Sweetie Pies has all the *gene se qua* it needs," Fi said, pointing to the sixteen Gold Tins lining the shop window. Grabbing her apron, the older woman pushed through the kitchen door and headed out front.

Paula took Kennedy's hand and gave it an apologetic squeeze. "Don't you worry about her. Your medley pies are delicious; people are going to love them. And once Fi realizes just how hard you are working to please everyone, she'll come around. She was already tasting your pies this morning, and that was a big jump. She just needs a smidge more—"

"Time," Kennedy sighed. "I know."

"Afternoon, Bitsy," Fi's voice carried through the window. "What can I get you?"

Kennedy let out a sigh of relief. Maybe Paula was right, and Fi was coming around. She might not be sweet on Kennedy at the moment, but at least she was still working hard to please customers.

"Frank asked if I could pick up his order for tonight's Bible study class," Bitsy said. "He needed to do God's work today, so I offered to do his."

Frank was the pastor of Destiny Bay Presbyterian Church, and Bitsy was his wife. Every Monday and Thursday they had a standing order for ten pies, and if Fi did her job, maybe a few of those would be replaced with Apple Mélange pies.

Kennedy poked her head out of the pass-through window. "Hey, Bitsy, I got the pastor's order right here. Give me a minute to box them up for you." Kennedy gave Fi a parting look, then smiled as if to say, *Please.*

Fi smiled back. At least Kennedy thought it was a smile—the older woman's teeth were showing.

"While she's boxing your pies, might I interest you in something new?" Fi said, and Paula had a silent clap of excitement. "Today we're introducing the first three pies in our new *Ménage à Trois* collection," her French suddenly impeccable.

Paula choked. Kennedy stopped breathing. And Fi went right on smiling.

Bitsy cleared her throat and in the most devout voice asked, "Pardon me, but I don't think I heard you correctly. Manage a what?"

"*Ménage à Trois*, dear." Again with perfect pronunciation. "Three kinds of pies, three kinds of fruit, all living together in the same flaky crust. It's just sinful, deliciously sinful."

"Good Lord," Bitsy said, lifting the cross pendant on her necklace and kissing it as if asking for divine intervention.

Kennedy needed divine intervention, too, but asking for a blessing on her pies seemed a bit frivolous with so much going on in the world, so Kennedy decided that if anyone was going to sell the merits of these pies, it would have to be its creator.

* * *

Kennedy pulled the last batch of Sweetie Pies traditional apple deep dish out of the oven, and slid in a batch of her apple and red currant pies. Her new pies had been gaining fans every day, but today was going to be big—she could feel it. The library had special-ordered ten apple and huckleberry pies to go with tonight's book club theme, she was meeting Cosmo at seven to finalize the contract, and Kennedy had been so busy in the kitchen she'd barely had time to notice it was Thursday.

Too bad that didn't apply to Luke, or the fact that he hadn't called.

She'd considered calling him, to see if everything was all right, then figured if anything had gone wrong, Paula would have said something. Then she thought about calling to say hi, only she figured that if he'd wanted to talk while he was away on business, he would have called her. And when all of that figuring led to a headache, she focused on what was important—her own business.

She could pretend she wasn't somewhat hurt, but she'd promised herself that she would never pretend again. Not when it meant missing important facts. Like what happened between them six nights ago didn't mean that their relationship was anything more than temporary. But the way he'd held her as if he didn't want to let go, how her heart melted every time she thought of the tender way he'd looked at her, how he made her feel as if she was something to be treasured, someone who was worthy of love, Kennedy knew.

This thing with Luke might not last forever, but in her heart, she wanted it to. A dangerous want to have for a girl who didn't know what forever even looked like.

Paula hobbled into the back room, her hair in disarray and her breathing heavy. "There is a mob of people out front."

"Do they have picket signs or pitchforks?" Kennedy asked. Wiping her hands on her apron.

"Do bingo cards count?" Paula asked, and Kennedy set down her rag and walked to the kitchen door.

She cracked it open, just enough to peer into the shop unseen, and a comforting warmth filled her chest. Cards covered every inch of table space, and one of those hand-cranked bingo machines sat in the front corner of the shop—which was filled with people.

Not people, customers—talking and laughing and eating. Which made them paying customers. Some of them predated the Constitution, but all of them had gray halos. Including the woman in the lavender sweater set and pearls who was turning the handle and shuffling the bingo balls.

"Is that Bitsy Evans?" Kennedy whispered to Paula.

"I think so."

Once Bitsy had left the shop the other day, it didn't take long for word to spread that Kennedy was selling sin in a tin. Representatives from every female organization in town showed up to see how they went about getting their hands on the Triple Threat pies, as they were calling them: pies that satisfied your craving, your Washington pride, and, well, put the sweet back in Sweet Spot. Bitsy claimed she was there to stop any sinning from going down, but she ordered two pies to go.

Kennedy explained there wasn't the equivalent to Viagra for ladies crushed up in the crust, and after a series of disappointed grumbles and a single hallelujah from Bitsy, she asked the women to stay. She served coffee and tea, and pie all around, and when everyone was done tasting, she shared a piece of herself. Told the women about her grandmother, her recipe journal, and why she loved baking.

In return, they each shared stories about their own lives—
and passions. By the end, Kennedy had felt a closer kinship
with the town and its residents; she'd felt as if she was
one step closer to calling Destiny Bay her home, and these
women her people.

As the women were getting ready to head home,
Kennedy asked them what they'd like to see in their hometown pie shop. Not only were they fans of her "medley
pies"—a name a pastor's wife could get behind when rec-
ommending a great place for pie—but they were also interested in smaller pastry items.

It seemed Destiny Bay had a diner, but not a place
where friends could meet and share a sweet bite, coffee,
and the daily gossip.

Kennedy said she'd provide the coffee and sweets, if
they could help her bring in the people. Cautiously opti-
mistic, she'd hoped but didn't put much weight in it for fear
of disappointment. But they had come through.

Not for Paula or Fi, or the promise of free pie. They'd
come through for her, and as incredibly foreign as that felt,
it also felt comforting.

"What are they doing?"

"Playing bingo," Paula said with a smile. "And they're
buying pie. Lots of pie."

And not all of it just apple, Kennedy noticed.

Her part-time help was behind the counter slicing an apple and Bing cherry pie into sixths. Cool and under control,
Lauren slipped each slice onto a plate.

"How can I help?" Kennedy asked, stepping in beside
her.

"I need a hot herbal, two hot tea lattes, five coffees, one
black, one with cream, the rest the works." Lauren stacked

the plates on the tray and hoisted it up on her shoulder, surprising the hell out of Kennedy. "What? On the weekends I tend bar by campus. A bunch of old ladies got nothing on drunk frat boys and a mechanical bull."

"Only because we don't have a mechanical bull." Kennedy grabbed eight mugs and the coffeepot, then started pouring. "I thought you only wanted to work a few hours a week."

"You don't have an espresso machine either. You should get one—it will attract the younger crowd, since they have to drive to the next town for a Starbucks," she said. "And I'd love to work more, but Paula and Fi only had a few hours when they hired me on."

Kennedy paused and gave her sometimes baker sometimes cashier in the BOYS ARE FUN. BUT SORORITY SISTERS ARE 4EVER T-shirt a second look. "I thought you were a marketing major."

Lauren smiled. "Double major, marketing and restaurant management." Lauren smiled, as if she was overlooked a lot, then delivered the pies, not even missing a beat when Louise Ferndale moved her walker in the middle of the walkway—and right in Lauren's way.

"She's a go-getter," Paula said, coming up beside Kennedy and bumping her with her hip. "Reminds me of someone else I know."

With a grin, Kennedy went to fill the mugs, enjoying the loud hum of the room. "Did they all come in at once?"

"Yup, started ordering pies and coffee by the table," Paula said. "Once the pastor's wife assured me they were betting with coupons and not cash, I figured they were paying customers, and started slicing. But when they kept coming, I came and got you."

"B-16," Bitsy said into the mic. "B-16."

"I got B-16," Margret Collins hollered, waving a personalized bingo stamp in the air.

"Well, I got B-16 on two of my cards," the woman next to Margret said, and Kennedy's eyes tracked to the voice. Then she blinked. Twice.

White bun, black biker's jacket, coral lipstick.

"Is that Fi?" Kennedy whispered.

"Was the second one through the door. She ordered a slice of traditional apple, but she paid for it." Paula sent Kennedy a sideways smile. "You know what this means."

"That Fi is starting to come around?"

Paula snorted and waved a dismissive hand. "That you're popular. Somehow overnight this became the spot. And if it's the spot for the bingo team, then it could become the spot for a lot of other organizations in town."

"It could even become the breakfast spot," Kennedy said, knowing that smaller items like muffins and pastries had a low cost and high margin. It was as if, here in Destiny Bay, the possibilities were endless.

Kennedy still wasn't sure if she believed in destiny, but she couldn't help thinking that this was what coming home felt like. At least that's what her heart said.

Chapter 15

$\backsim$

At exactly three minutes to seven, Kennedy locked up her shop and stepped out into the crisp autumn night. A cool breeze filled her lungs, and sent leaves from the nearby maple trees fluttering down the brick sidewalks, painting Main Street in a fire-colored snowfall.

Kennedy listened to them crunch under her boots as she crossed the street, feeling a deep sense of pride when she saw the banner advertising the Gold Tin Apple Pie Competition. Fi and Paula had made the HumDinger a national champ, and Kennedy was going to make it a household name.

Smoothing her hair, Kennedy tugged her skirt down and pushed through the massive wooden door of the Penalty Box, not looking for its co-owner, not thinking about him, and not stopping until she reached her awaiting party in the back.

Tonight was about her business, her success.

Holding up two unmistakable red boxes, she smiled. "I brought pie."

Cosmo, hat already hanging on the hook over the booth, stood. "Miss. Sinclair," he said in greeting, gesturing for her to take a seat, which she did.

He was dressed in a soft gray suit with a yellow bow tie and suspenders. His hat was a straw boat hat, and he was drinking a cold cider. Kennedy had always wanted to meet with a dashing silver fox who did business deals in back booths of bars.

"This is a mix of pies." She set one box on the table, and then the other. "And I even saved you a HumDinger, just don't tell anyone since we technically sold out before lunch."

Kennedy smiled at that news, selling out in such a short amount of time. But Cosmo shifted in his seat at the information.

"Would you like a drink?" he asked, lifting his hands to wave over the bartender—which could or could not be Luke. Not wanting to see him right then, she said, "I'm fine." And in case he persisted, which a silver fox like Cosmo would, she added, "I'm too excited about our meeting to drink. Maybe after the contract is finalized, we can celebrate with something fun."

Cosmo rested his hands on the table, his serious nature making something ping deep in Kennedy's chest. She knew the feeling well, but refused to acknowledge it. Even when Cosmo released a sigh that always preceded bad news.

Kennedy had had enough bad news in her life to know the signs. But this was Destiny Bay, a town swimming in possibilities, so his look of discomfort must be brought on by heartburn.

"As soon as I received your signed contract, I sent it straightaway to my legal team," Cosmo said, and Kennedy sat up straighter.

"Your legal team," she beamed. It sounded so professional. And final.

"There were some concerns about advertising the pies as a Gold Tin winner," he said.

"Oh," Kennedy said, knowing that was a real concern with a simple answer. "I can assure you that Fi has licensed the exclusive rights to use her pie recipes, but Paula agreed to sell me the exact apple varieties they used when creating the pies. It is the same pie you and everyone here in Destiny Bay fell in love with."

"But you're not Fi," Cosmo said, and Kennedy laughed.

"Nope, just Kennedy Sinclair, newest owner of Sweetie Pies."

"And that's where the concern comes," Cosmo said softly. "In order to sell your pies at the price point we agreed upon, they need that extra something, which is where the title came in. But you have never personally made one of the Gold Tin winners, so unless Fi agrees to bake the pies every day, legal is concerned that we can't truthfully say they are the same Gold Tin–winning pies."

"But the HumDinger is entered in the contest," she said. "So by next week it will be my pie."

Cosmo seemed relieved by this. "I didn't know you had entered. If you win, that solves everything." Kennedy felt the same relief and almost told him she'd take that drink now, when he added, "When I saw the HumDinger entered under Fi's name, I assumed she was going it alone again."

Kennedy swallowed. "Fi usually enters on her own? I thought she entered for the shop."

It was the whole reason Kennedy didn't enter. She didn't want to put one of her pies up against their biggest seller. No sense in competing with yourself.

Cosmo shook his head. "No, Fi has always entered on her own. Does she have the rights still to enter that pie since you bought the recipe?"

Kennedy grimaced. "I actually bought the commercial rights to all of the recipes, so Fi can't sell the pies, but she can make them for her family and personal use."

"Since she's not selling the pie, but entering it in a hometown competition, she isn't in breach of contract," Cosmo said.

"But if she entered it before, then how was legal going to handle it if she'd ever agreed?"

"It was her pie and her shop, so it didn't matter. But if she is no longer part owner of the shop, then Sweetie Pies technically won't be the winner. And this contract would be between Kline Fine Foods and Sweetie Pies."

"Which means you couldn't claim the title even if she wins."

"I am afraid not," Cosmo said, and Kennedy felt those words hit her squarely in the chest. "And the only way my team would feel comfortable moving forward is if the contract is made with the actual title holder, which would be Fi."

A contract they both knew would never happen.

* * *

Luke was as adept at reading nonverbal cues as he was at knowing when a company was out of options. It was what made him such an effective corporate developer.

And this deal was out of options. No question about it.

Even though it wasn't his deal, Luke felt the same burning frustration in his chest that followed a devastating loss. But this time it was accompanied by guilt and a tractor-trailer full of shame.

Not that his deal was out of the woods, not by a long shot. In fact, the look of devastation on Kennedy's face said that his option pool had doubled. But the expected rush that came with knowing the last piece had fallen into place never came.

Luke wanted this deal with Rogers to pan out, needed to buy back Bay View Orchards for his mom, but getting it like this didn't feel right.

Because everything in Kennedy's world was going incredibly wrong. And even though she had more than enough reasons to give up, she held strong, even comforting Cosmo as he delivered the fatal blow. She wasn't pointing blame, demanding to know what happened, she just nodded compassionately—understandingly—and gave Cosmo a hug good-bye. Then waited until she was alone in the booth to absorb the hit.

Like she'd been expecting it all along.

And why not? He'd told her exactly what would happen. Was pretty sure his offhand remark had been part of the force that took her down.

Only it hadn't been offhand, which he could maybe forgive. Luke had made a strategic play that was fueled by emotion when he'd opened his mouth. He was hurt that Kennedy hadn't said a word about Cosmo, especially after he'd opened up to her that morning. He was also determined to prove to Hawk that he wasn't going to let him down. So he said the one thing that would give Cosmo pause, force him to reconsider.

Now Kennedy, who had moments ago looked ready for the biggest moment of her professional life, was staring at the table, looking so damn tired and small, he knew he should turn back around and walk away. The last person she'd want to see was him.

Not to mention, Hawk was going over the offer Walter had given them, which was too pricey to make sense, and Luke needed to focus. Not that he doubted Hawk would offer up the money, but it was a bad deal all around, and the one thing Walter had been right about was that there was a lot riding on how the next few weeks played out. For everyone involved.

The smart thing would be to keep his mind on the goal and eyes off the composed way Kennedy held herself even though he knew she was falling apart inside.

Which was why Luke found himself walking toward the table, ready to absorb her anger and find a way to fix everything. Because that's what good guys did, and Kennedy deserved to see that side of him as much as anyone else in his life.

"Hey there," he said softly, sliding into the booth next to her. "You look like you could use a drink."

She glanced his way, and the second those baby blues locked on his, all the drama about apples, Bay View Orchards, and the deal with Rogers faded into the background until there was just the two of them. And the reality of what he'd done.

To her.

"I finished Cosmo's cider." She touched the rim of the empty glass. "I'm good."

She was so far from good, it broke his heart. "How about a friend then?"

"Are you? My friend?" she asked.

He didn't know what they were and *friends* didn't seem the right word, but it was a safe place to start. "I'd like to be."

His words seemed to hit a sore spot. Probably the one that had just been ripped open when he sold her out to Cosmo. He wouldn't be surprised if she told him to fuck off, and wasn't that a damn shame. Kennedy was one of the most giving people he'd ever met, but people always just seemed to take from her. Including him.

She studied him, long and thorough, as if looking for something that could make her change her mind. And God, he hoped she found it because he didn't want to be just her friend; he wanted to be the one guy who didn't let her down, leaving her stranded and alone in the middle of the shit storm he'd brought on.

With a sad smile, she whispered, "I missed you this week," then rested her head on his shoulder and cuddled close.

That was it. No yelling, no blame, just five sweet words and a gesture that changed everything. Had every protective instinct rearing up to save her from the disappointments of the world—including him.

It was clear that she had not a clue as to his role in her current situation and, as Luke slid his arm around her, that he'd missed the hell out of her, too. Which left him with two options: Fix this mess, or she'd lose her shop—and he'd lose a friend.

"I thought about calling," he admitted. "But once I landed in Chicago, things didn't go as expected, and well..." He stopped, mid-bitch. Because when had he become an excuse guy? "I should have called. To say I had a great time last weekend, which I did, then to apologize for disappearing."

"That's okay, life happens." She gave a little shrug, then pulled the sleeves of her sweater over her hands. "It was kind of crazy here, too, as you saw." She nodded at the empty glass. "Cosmo wanted to sell Sweetie Pies in his supermarkets."

Truth time. Luke tilted her face until she was looking up at him. "Cosmo told me the other night. Said he was excited about the possibility of working with you."

"Oh." Her gaze dropped to her lap. "Well, the excitement was short lived."

"I was surprised when he told me, because I had just seen you that morning."

"I know, I'm sorry," she said as if he shouldn't be on his knees begging her for forgiveness. "I didn't tell anyone. I thought if I did, it would make it real, and then if it fell through, it would hurt so much more." She looked up and the tears lining her lashes made his chest constrict until it burned. "It doesn't, though. Make it worse. I don't think it could hurt worse than this. I was so close and everything just fell apart."

She shrugged and sat back, and Luke wanted to pull her into his lap. Tell her he'd fix everything and she didn't have to worry, but she straightened and cleared her throat.

"Your mom and Aunt Fi found out," she added. "I guess I'll have to explain that Cosmo wants to work with the Gold Tin winner, and that although he loves the pies, he needs a winner to command the higher price point."

Luke wanted to punch himself, because what she was really saying was that she wasn't a winner. That Cosmo didn't need her, because on her own she wasn't enough.

"I am so sorry, Kennedy." Luke tucked a stray hair behind her ear. All Kennedy wanted was to start over, share her recipes and a piece of herself with people, and make a life here in Destiny Bay. And he had complicated that for her. "Is there anything I can do to help?"

"Not unless you know of someone who wants to give up their spot in the competition to an outsider," she said to the floor. He heard a little sniffle and *shit*. She was crying.

And Luke found himself in a place he'd promised himself never to be again, standing between two things he cared for, and having to choose. Last time it was between his family and his freedom—and he'd chosen wrong.

Maybe this was his chance to get it right. Walter hadn't refused their offer; he'd just countered it with a ridiculous one. So Luke still had options. Kennedy had none, and how he chose to move forward from here would determine the kind of man he truly was.

He looked at Kennedy, really looked at her, and that ache in his chest, the one that started the day his dad died and expanded when he lost the house, disappeared the moment those baby blue eyes locked with his. He knew the kind of man he wanted to be.

"I can do you one better." He fished his cell out of his pocket and scrolled though his contacts, found who he was looking for, and hit Call.

"What are you doing?" she asked.

He held up a finger while it rang. Then the phone picked up. "Hey, Sally, this is Luke Callahan from Two Bad Apples. Sorry to call so late, but I was wondering if you could make room for one more entrant. She is the new owner of Sweetie Pies, and new to the area."

He listened to Sally on the other end, then said, "That's

great. I owe you." He disconnected and pocketed his phone.

"Who was that?" Kennedy asked, and the cautious hope he saw swimming in her expression tugged something deep down. "Sally Miller is the Gold Tin coordinator and a good friend of my mom's," he said. "Her husband owns a sports bar in Tacoma, and was Two Bad Apples' first customer."

There went the misty eyes he was trying so hard to avoid. "You didn't have to do that."

"I wanted to. And she said that even though the entry period has passed, she could make room for one more. Especially a local."

Something about that last word had her sliding her arms around his neck, and holding on. He held her back, and damn, it was the first time in a week that he'd felt whole.

They sat just like that, holding each other in the back booth of a sports bar, with the game on the big screen and Johnny Cash coming through the speakers, for a good while.

"Thank you," she finally whispered.

"Now, all you have to do is win," he said to lighten the mood, but it had the opposite effect.

She sat back, her hands coming to cover her mouth, which was gaping open. "Oh my God. I have to win."

"You've got this," he said truthfully. She was an amazing baker, and if she played to her talents, instead of trying to play to everyone else, she could win this thing. And he would never see those apples again.

A problem he'd worry about later.

"I have to *win*, Luke. With a recipe of my own. While going up against the sixteen-time champion."

"Sixteen times means she comfortable, secure," he said, cupping her face. "When people get comfortable, they make room for someone with the determination and drive to move right in."

"How am I supposed to sneak past Fi Callahan?" Kennedy asked. "The woman has eyes in the back of her head. The second she sees me coming, she'll take me out at the knees with her rolling pin. She might be old as dirt, but she's got a good swing, fast and accurate."

"People with talent don't sneak, they put it out there." He took her hand. "Put yourself in that pie, Kennedy, and people will love it."

"Thank you. I needed to hear that," she said. "Especially when she's got access to the same apples as I do."

"Lucky for you, I know this guy, and he's kind of a local expert on all the varieties of apples."

She flashed a smile that lit him up. "Yeah?"

"Yeah." He took her hand and threaded their fingers. "Heard he's a real badass, too. Sexy and charming. I could give him a call if you want."

"I want."

He could only hope that in the end she was still saying the same thing.

Chapter 16

Kennedy stood at the top of the bluff at Bay View Orchards, staring down at the crashing waves below. A chill blew off the rough waters, chapping her face and sending a little shiver over her skin. "I can see clear across the bay to the little islands out there."

"It's actually just a few rocks that the harbor seals use as a playground," Luke said, coming up behind her. She could feel the heat of his body seep through her clothes.

She turned her head to look at him, caught by the beauty of the dozens of acres of gently rolling orchards covered in a kaleidoscope of apples and bright green leaves. The scent of fresh-cut grass and ripened fruit permeated the sea air as gulls caught the wind in the early evening breeze.

"On a clear day you can see the whales off the coastline heading north." While her gaze tracked, he slid an arm around her waist, effortlessly pulling her back to his front, and warming her from the inside out.

She'd been dying to touch him since he'd walked over to her table, like some kind of good guy for hire, looking charming and sexy in a pair of butt-loving jeans and a blue flannel.

"Last one, ready?" His other hand came around her, holding an apple. It was on the smaller side, light green, and russetted around the stem.

She shifted so she faced him. "Is that a pippin?"

"Nope. And no more questions, it's against the rules." He pulled a small knife out of his pocket and sliced off a sliver. "I want an unbiased tasting."

He held the piece against her lips, just like he had with the other varieties, only when she took a bite, she let her lips graze his fingers, lingering long enough to let him know she liked his rules.

"Wow," she said, surprised by how firm the texture was, yet it was incredibly plump and juicy. He ran his thumb along her lower lip, catching the juice as it ran over, only to bring it to his mouth and suck.

"So sweet."

"Wait for it," he whispered.

She didn't have to ask what *it* was, because as soon as the first note hit, it was followed by a tartness that was complex and sharp, and her taste buds came alive wanting more.

"It has a piny aftertaste," she said. "And it's not a pippin?"

"Close, it's a pippin and a Honeycrisp. We call it a crispin," he said, putting his knife in his pocket. "My dad spent twenty years cross-breeding different varieties to finally get this. He wanted an apple that was firm and kept well, but had several levels to it, not just tart or sweet, but a complexity that would carry over through the fermenting process."

"It's incredible."

Luke smiled. "He would have loved to hear that. It's even more developed after a few weeks in storage. And when fermented?" Luke closed his eyes. "Incomparable."

"It would make the perfect base for a pie," she said. "But you already knew that—it's why you brought me here."

He shrugged. "It needs some acid to cut through the sweet notes, but I hoped that it might be the something different you were looking for."

She went up on her toes and kissed him lightly, lingering long enough to taste all the levels that made up this man. He was firm but sweet, and so much more. With her arms still around his neck, she pulled back. "I like the sweet notes."

"Me, too." His hands slid down to settle on the curve of her lower back.

"And I like that you brought me to your home."

Kennedy couldn't put her finger on what happened, but something shifted ever so slightly. With a tired smile, he kissed her nose, then pointed over her shoulder.

"Speaking of the house, it's over there."

She turned and Kennedy's breath caught. It wasn't just a house; it was the centerpiece of the property.

Perched beneath an oak tree with an aged tire swing sat a beautiful farmhouse with white clapboard siding, a bright blue door, and enough charm to be on the cover of a magazine. It wasn't big by any means, but it had amazing floor-to-ceiling windows that spanned the back of the house, looking out onto the orchard and distant waters.

"This place is enchanting." It was made for a family, she decided. A single story of history and memories held together by love and a wraparound porch.

She felt him smile against her hair. "My mom used the same word. Unless she was talking about the barn." He pointed to a sad-looking bundle of boards and siding, which appeared to be some kind of faded red structure that was sagging with age.

"That's a barn?"

He chuckled. "It was my dad's distillery. He'd disappear in there for days at a time, tinkering with his cider. Come out looking like a mad scientist or some kind of mountain man." He looked down at her. "It drove my mom crazy. But she loved him."

"Your family owns this place?"

"It was our summer home," Luke said, a soft reverence to his voice that gave her pause. "And we spent nearly every weekend here. My mom stood right there, where that sunroom is now, and said she could happily spend the rest of eternity looking at the ocean and those trees. So my dad bought her the land as a wedding present, and built the sunroom for their tenth wedding anniversary."

Sunroom was an understatement. The structure was more like a cathedral observatory with wrought-iron-encased leaded-glass walls and ceiling. Inside was a green oasis of plants and ferns, surrounding a charming sitting area that was perfect for reading, or whale watching on a clear day.

"Now I know where you get your romantic side from." She pressed back into him teasingly and he tightened his arms. "Did Little Luke swing on that big tire over there?"

"All the time," he said like a boy retelling his greatest

tale. "Until Hawk dared me to swing off the bluff and plunge into the ocean. Mom caught us and threatened to cut it down if she ever saw us doing that again. Then she made enough casseroles to last through winter."

"Stress baking. It's a dangerous habit."

"Well, tonight you won't be stress baking; you'll be baking up new recipes, right?" He sounded so concerned, as if the thought of her being stressed out brought him pain.

"No stress baking," she promised. "After you taught me all of the different kinds of apples, and let me taste them, I think I have an idea that will blow away the judges' taste buds and put me in the running. Thank you for that, by the way."

He shrugged like it was no big deal, but to her it had been everything. He'd taken the time to listen to her problem, then help her find a solution. Never once did he tell her what to do or how to feel, just let her experience what she needed then took her to one of the most beautiful orchards in the state. Where he hand-picked a dozen different apples, all heirloom and all holding so many possibilities, explaining the benefits and the drawbacks of using each one.

Kennedy hadn't a clue as to how close baking and cider were when it came to acidity, sweetness, and overall balance. Luke's experience with the apples and his thoughtful suggestions sparked so many ideas, she couldn't wait to get in the kitchen and try them. But since every time she'd thanked him, he seemed to get uncomfortable, she decided to change the topic.

"Is that why your mom sold the shop, because she wanted to move out here full time?" she asked, figuring that if she owned this place, she'd retire tomorrow.

Luke exhaled, then he leaned back against a tree, pulling

her with him until all she felt was him. A big, warm, protective man wrapping himself around her. It was a feeling she could get used to.

"I think she sold the shop because her body is tired," he said. "But she wouldn't think to come here, since we don't own it anymore."

She remembered the real estate sign at the top of the dirt road where they pulled in, and suddenly felt like she was trespassing. "Then whose apples were we eating?"

"By the end of the week they'll be mine," he said, looking over the endless view of apples. "Tomorrow, Hawk and I will accept the owners' offer and buy back the apples."

Luke didn't seem thrilled over the idea; in fact, he seemed a little overwhelmed. "You don't sound happy."

Luke let out a humorless laugh. "One of the owners won't piece out the harvest. So if we buy, we buy all fifty acres' worth."

Kennedy had no idea how much fifty acres of heirlooms at wholesale would cost, but she knew it would have been a heck of a lot cheaper to buy her three acres. But instead of running her out of business, like he'd originally set out to do, Luke found a different path. One that allowed her a chance to live out her dream, a realization that was as foreign as it was touching.

"Why did your mom sell the property to start with?"

"She didn't," Luke said so quietly, she barely heard it over the ocean breeze. "I did."

"You sold it?"

He laced their fingers and led her along the jagged bluff. Maybe she should have thought to change out of her skirt and big city shoes, she told herself as she stumbled while navigating the rocky surface in sky-high heels.

Always the gentleman, Luke slowed his pace and wrapped her hand around his forearm for balance. "After my dad died, I discovered they were drowning in debt. A few bad harvests, followed by never-ending medical bills, my college tuition, grad school, it had all piled up."

"Oh, Luke." She squeezed his hand. "That must have been so hard."

"I was off making a life for myself, so I had no clue about their debt."

The pain and guilt in his voice were hard to hear. Luke didn't just love his family, he felt responsible for them. It was as if he believed that it was his job to ensure their happiness and health. A steep job, even for one of the good guys.

"I had the choice of selling off this place or leveraging Callahan Orchards, both of which would break my dad's heart, but I did what I thought was best at the time." She could only imagine how hard choosing between giving his mom her dream home and saving his family's legacy could have been. "If I had just stayed, I would have seen the problems and could have stepped in and avoided this entire situation."

Kennedy looked at the property again, and instead of thinking about the romantic views and charming porch, she thought about what it must have looked like to a teenage Luke. It would have been daunting, confining, even para-lyzing.

"You grew up knowing that this would all be yours. That Callahan Orchards and everything that came with it would fall to you." She squeezed his hand. "You were born into a future that family responsibility dictated and planned. It left no room for possibility. That's a lot for anyone to take, especially a kid who had dreams of his own."

And Luke would have had big dreams; it was the kind of person he was.

"In the end, the only thing I wanted was more time with my dad. More time here." As if he needed to distance himself from the memories, he started walking, this time leading her through the orchard and toward the sunroom, her heart aching for the man who'd lost so much. "When I sold the property, I put in a first right of refusal clause, which means I have until the end of October to make a fair bid."

The only reason he would wait was if he was short on capital.

Kennedy thought back to their talk in her bakery when he offered to buy her out, then she remembered what Paula had said about Luke needing the apples to be happy. And that was when the severity of the situation hit her. "You needed my apples to buy this place."

"In a roundabout way, yeah." He opened the ornate glass door and sunlight-heated air soaked into her bones, warding off the last of the chill. The raised ceiling gave the illusion of being outside, while the lush green of the plants and a hint of citrus from the potted orange trees brought about serenity that went soul deep.

The room was warm and cozy, made for playing games and watching the stars. It was the kind of place that encouraged memories, and instilled their longevity.

Luke led her to a chaise lounge in the center of the room, where he tucked a soft blanket tightly around her. "Better?" he whispered.

"Much," she said, moved by how naturally he cared for others. "Thank you."

With a nod, he turned, staring quietly out onto the bay.

"Hawk and I signed a deal to be the exclusive hard cider supplier for a large chain of sports bars. The payment for our first delivery would give us enough money to put down on this property."

"Luke, that's incredible."

He glanced over his shoulder, and his smile said it was anything but. "We're short on cider."

Kennedy felt sick. "Let me guess, three acres short?"

He didn't have to answer; his expression said it all. He wasn't trying to chase her out of town or even secure his own happiness. He was trying to secure his mom's, and that more than anything called out to her.

"Why did you help me tonight?" she asked. "I wouldn't have been able to get in the contest myself, and I would have had to sell you the apples." Which she'd bet would be half the price of what he was going to pay.

"I lost my mom's property because I was too busy playing big businessman. I don't want you to lose your shop because I wasn't smart enough to think my way out of a problem."

She thought back to a moment ago, standing on the bluff, realizing how sweet he'd been for not standing in the way of her dream. What she hadn't known was that he'd put his own dream in jeopardy for hers. "But what if you lose this house again because of me?"

"I won't." He turned toward her and, squatting down to get at eye level with her, rested his hands on her knees. Even through the thickness of the blanket, she could feel his heat. "And it's more than this house. I helped you because I don't want you to go."

Kennedy swallowed through the emotion. "You don't want me to go?"

"No, sweetness, I don't." Luke sat down next to her. Leaning back, he rested his arms on the curved back of the chaise, bringing him in close, so his thigh was flush with her bare legs and his arm pressed against her shoulder.

She wasn't sure if it was the easy contact, or the idea that he didn't want her to go, but the panicky feeling that set in after her talk with Cosmo was back. Not sharp enough to make every breath a struggle, but her chest tightened in a way that had her heart straining. "Why not? Me going would make your life easier."

"But it would make everything else harder," he said.

"So you want me to stay because you'd feel guilty if I left? Responsible for me losing my place?"

If that were the case, she'd rather know now. The last thing she wanted to be was one more person he felt responsible for. If he wanted her to stay, she didn't want it to be because of some superhero complex or doing the right thing. She wanted it to be because he saw the possibilities in them.

In her.

"I want to you to stay because of this."

One minute his lips weren't anywhere near her mouth, the next they were caressing hers, languidly exploring one corner, then the other, and finally coaxing open the seam. With a moan that came from so far inside, it might have been her toes, she opened her mouth to deepen the connection when something vibrated between them.

This kiss was different. Sure it was sexy and succulent, but it was also emotional and unexpectedly tender.

All of the earlier lust and primal desperation that had driven them from the start was gone, replaced with an understanding that took her by surprise, and a gentleness that made her feel as though she was precious.

Maybe it was the expected crash of an emotionally charged night, or the fact that she was sitting in the middle of Luke's childhood, kissing in the sunroom that he might end up losing because he chose to help her, but suddenly she felt unsure. Nervous like the scared girl whose mom had finally come to visit, but no matter how hard Kennedy tried, she would never be enough to stay, to keep.

To love.

Kennedy pulled back. "What is *this*, Luke?"

"*This*," he said, and the only contact they had was his hands on her cheeks and the faintest pressure of their thighs brushing. "Is perfection."

He tilted her head to the side and his lips brushed hers again. It was sweet and erotic and perfection indeed. A small burst of hope welled up, almost making her believe that, maybe for him, she was perfect.

Then that little voice in her head nagged that she was far from perfect. She focused on the sounds of the crashing waves, the gentle sway of the swing, and the fantasy that maybe she belonged here—in this family-ready home with this family-loving man, but she couldn't get past the word.

Perfect was impossible. A fantasy. And she didn't want a fantasy. She wanted this to be real. Opening her eyes, she knew she wanted this to be the truth.

"I don't need perfection, because I'll never be perfect," she said as he kissed down her neck. "I just need to know that I'm enough."

Luke lifted his head to meet her gaze, staring for what seemed like an eternity. With a single fingertip, he traced the lower curve of her lip. "You are more than most people will ever be."

"I'm also more stubborn than most," she reminded him quietly.

"I think stubborn is sexy, and when I said *this*, I meant you, sweetness. I want you to stay because you're simply you," he said, and the conviction behind his words rocked her.

Her breath caught and her heart stopped to absorb the words, to analyze what he really meant. Only there was nothing to understand beyond the fact that she could easily fall in love with him. She was already in love with his family, his town, the way he made her feel.

And she was one kiss from falling completely.

Holding her gaze prisoner, Luke moved in slowly, sliding the blanket down her shoulder, her lap, to the floor, giving her time to back away. But Kennedy was tired of backing away, so she met him halfway, and when their mouths brushed, she knew.

Knew she'd fallen a long time ago. The first time she'd seen him with his family. Seen what a loyal and loving man he was—knew she'd give anything to have a chance at that kind of connection. To be on the receiving end of an unquestioning affection that left her breathless.

"I want this, too, and by *this*, I mean you." She sank her hands into his hair and pulled him back with her. Into her arms and into her heart.

"Thank Christ," he said, going up on one knee and moving her backward. She felt the arm of the lounge and, at his request, lay all the way back until his body was covering hers. "Because I've wanted you since I left your house last week."

"All you had to do was call," she whispered against his lips.

"I'm more of an in-person guy. The intimate nature of a face-to-face allows me to assess a person's unique wants and needs," he said, and she shivered from her lips to her toes.

She rested her hands above her head, on the arm of the chaise, and played coy. "And what is it that you have assessed? From me?"

"Oh, sweetness, you're an open book. I've been saying from day one that you want me to kiss you." He ran his thumb over her lips and they quivered in response. "But what you need is a hot, wet kiss. Right…" His finger trailed down her neck, between the valley of her breasts, not stopping until it was running over her center. "Here."

With a needy sigh, Kennedy arched up into his hand, wanting more of that delicious pressure.

"I don't imagine me being right this particular time is a bad thing?" To prove his point, he skimmed that sweet spot again, only this time he went under her skirt to find wet silk.

"Admitting something like that could give you a big head," she said. "Maybe you should try it again and let me see."

He pressed against her, proving how big his head had become. "That happened the second you walked in the room wearing these boots. Did I mention how much I like these boots?"

She bit her lip and shook her head.

"So much so that the rest of this is just window dressing." The zipper of her skirt gave, and Luke slowly slid it down her legs, and to the floor, leaving her in her blouse, boots, and silk.

He lifted a brow. "Red?"

"These are my power panties," she admitted. "I wear them when I need a little extra swing in my step."

"It's helping with my swing." He grinned as his fingers wrapped around the ankle part of her boot, sliding it up the inside of the couch. Her knee bent and her leg parted farther with every inch gained, until he hooked her knee over his shoulder. "And to be clear, I said you needed to be kissed, not touched."

Watching him watch her, Luke knocked her other leg to the ground, leaving her completely open for his viewing pleasure. His brow puckered and Kennedy reached for the blanket, but he stopped her hand. Then one by one, he unfastened the buttons of her blouse, his knuckles brushing her breasts, her stomach, until he reached the last one. With a wicked smile that offered her a round-trip ticket to the promised land, he carefully parted the two halves of her blouse.

"Power bra," she whispered.

"Perfection." Sliding down her body, with delicious slowness, he took his time. His lips finally making contact when he placed a languid, openmouthed kiss right above her belly button.

"Luke," she moaned and could feel him smile against her belly. "I believe that you said my need was a bit—" She gasped as he nipped her hip.

His gaze met hers though his thick lashes. "Your need is a bit what, sweetness?"

"Lower," she managed.

"Here?" His tongue licked along the waistline of her panties, delving beneath the fabric to tease.

"Lower." Her eyes slid shut with anticipation.

"That's right. I remember now." Before she knew what

was happening, his clever fingers had pulled her panties to the side, and Luke was kissing her exactly where she needed.

No wonder he'd managed to rise to a corporate developer in just a few short years, she thought as he drove her slowly out of her mind. The man was an expert at assessing needs, because before she could ask for more, he was giving everything.

Using her one leg for stability, Kennedy pushed up into his mouth. Never one to pass up an opportunity to prove her wrong, he slid his hands beneath her, bracing her weight and lifting her higher and higher until she felt her body tense, the pressure so powerful it was impossible to breathe.

"There," she screamed.

He was right. He was so damn right that he took her out of her mind and over the edge, and this time when she felt him smile against her, she didn't talk at all. Other than to cry out his name as she exploded.

Breathing heavily, trying to figure out if she was still in her body or had somehow managed to burst right out of her skin, Kennedy opened her eyes to find Luke watching her, unwavering, as he stood completely naked and ready for the à la mode.

"I wish you could see what I'm seeing right now," he said with an awe that people usually didn't use when talking about her.

"My power panties," she said, self-conscious.

"You have power, sweetness, but it has nothing to do with your panties," he said, kneeling on the couch and covering her completely. "It has to do with you."

He kissed her lips.

"Just you," he said and entered her in one hard stroke, and he felt good. So good that *perfect* didn't cut it.

"You make me feel powerful," Kennedy said and slid her hands up his chest to lock around his neck. "You make me feel special."

With a deep groan, Luke took her mouth and kissed her as his body started to move. His hands were hot and possessive, sliding down her sides, brushing the edges of her breasts, before slipping to her butt and pulling her toward him, until she felt so full, so complete.

They clung to her as if needing to touch all of her at the same time. Claim her as his.

The only person who had ever claimed Kennedy was her grandma. But Edna was getting older and wouldn't be around forever, and Kennedy was terrified to float around in the world alone. She desperately wanted to be a part of something real and deep. Something that would last forever.

And there was Luke, holding her, moving with her as if he wouldn't ever let her go. And the vast emptiness she'd carried with her since Philip—since her mom—the one in her chest that ached so bad it'd gone numb, became warm and full.

"So sweet," he whispered. "So damn sweet."

She gave herself over to the slow withdrawals, and even slower thrusts. With Luke, sex didn't feel like a physical act between two people; it was more like communicating without the pressure of words. The sharing of pleasure that led to the merging of moments where the only option was to be open to the possibility of more.

And Kennedy was more than open. She was there with him, in his childhood home, seeing for the first time what it was like to feel cherished. To be with someone who believed that she was as special to him as he was to her. And Luke was beyond special. She was pretty sure he was the one.

He pulled her closer, pressing his face into the curve of her neck, and her eyes went watery. He whispered her name, as if it was the only thing that mattered. As if she was the only thing that mattered. And that more than anything had her body tightening around him.

He pressed a kiss to her neck, then another, and before Kennedy could stop it, she was crying out his name again. The orgasm took her over, wave after wave of pleasure hit, and then she felt Luke give a final thrust and his body coiled as he followed her over.

Neither of them moved, just lay there on the chaise, surrounded by windows and the most spectacular view in town—the bay was nice, too. When she finally shifted to get up, his grip tightened.

"Stay," he whispered.

Forever? she wanted to ask.

Chapter 17

Downtown's historic district had been transformed into an autumn wonderland. Garlands made from dried maple leaves and twinkle lights were strung between the gas lamps that lined Main Street. A giant pumpkin patch filled the park in the middle of the town square, overflowing with hay bales and festive-colored decorations, while people visiting the Sixty-eighth Annual Gold Tin Apple Pie Competition made their way around the maze of booths—tasting the top apple pies in the country.

Kennedy sat behind her table, wearing a SWEETIE PIES apron and her power panties. She'd considered the NUT BUSTER apron her grandma had given her, but decided against it since the majority of the judges were in possession of a set of their own, and because her entry had not a single nut in the recipe.

Plus, Kennedy wasn't all that hung up on busting nuts anymore. Luke had more than come through for her this past week, proving that there were good guys out there. She'd just been looking in the wrong places.

The location of her booth—right in the heart of the festival—had attracted more tasters than she could have anticipated, including several retail outlets and restaurateurs who, having heard the whispers about a deal with Kline Fine Foods, had come to see what all the hype was about. She'd chatted with more industry experts in the last few hours that she had in her entire eight years at Le Cordon Bleu. And she'd impressed them.

So had her pies. Some people asked for a second tasting, while others wanted to exchange contact information or find out about special event orders. Cosmo had also stopped by to tell her that her pie was delightful, and that he was pulling for her to come out on top.

Today couldn't have gone more perfectly, and she owed a large part of that to Luke. Who was talking to a couple of suits at the Two Bad Apples table. Like several times over the past week, he glanced up at the same time she did.

Kennedy gave a little wave, and he gave back a wink that, even across the distance of the park, had the power to make her knees wobble.

He didn't look away, instead tuned out everyone around him and flashed her a secret smile, to let her know he was thinking about her.

After securing her an entry in the competition, he'd volunteered to be her focus group and offered to help prep her booth for the event. Not that she'd needed the help, since a handful of volunteers—regulars from her shop and even the pastor's wife—showed up to help the new girl out. They brought enough garland and apple blossoms to decorate the White House, passed out flyers advertising Sweetie Pies, and even walked around pre-selling pies for the shop.

Kennedy had been beyond touched. She'd felt like one of them, a part of something special.

But it was Luke's belief that gave her the boost she needed to experiment with the new apples he'd introduced her to. A tiring task since she was still baking for the shop every day, leaving her only the nights to experiment. The result was more than worth it. Kennedy's Apple Harvest Citrus Pie had all the makings of a winner.

Made from Bay View Orchards crispin apples, the pie had a heavier crust cut from more butter than shortening, and scented with a variety of seasonal citrus, adding a zest of freshness to the rich, syrupy cinnamon filling. It was a complex and delectable pairing that tasted like all the best parts of coming home.

Inspired by her time with Luke on the bluff, the pie was heavenly indulgence at its finest. Every bite would forever be a reminder of how it felt to be cherished. If even just for a moment.

"Kumquats, huh?" Fi said, taking a tentative sniff of the air. "Never heard of using kumquats in a pie."

"They're not in the pie," Kennedy said with a smile. "They're in the crust."

"Huh," Fi tutted with genuine interest. "Then what's in the pie that makes it stand up so well?"

Kennedy looked around with mock suspicion, then leaned in until Fi was leaning, too—almost toppling over the table. "It's a humdinger of a secret."

Fi lowered a single brow. "I know your secret, missy, and I hope it isn't distracting you from your work at the shop. I'd hate to see you create a *humdinger* of a problem by letting a proven product take the backseat to your new flirtations."

Kennedy knew Fi disapproved of her professional aspirations, but it hurt to think she might be against her personal ones as well. Sure, she was a three-time failure when it came to relationships, but she saw promise with Luke—and she hoped that his family did, too.

"Sweetie Pies will always be my main focus, Fi. I'm out here to put my best foot forward and see what happens, just like everyone else." When Fi didn't look convinced, Kennedy added, "In fact, I made more HumDingers than usual this morning, figuring tourists would want to grab the sixteen-time winner before they headed home."

"Seventeen-time winner, if the whispers are true."

Kennedy kept her smile in place, but that didn't mean the hope she'd worked so hard to foster these last few weeks didn't take a hit. If Fi won, then Cosmo's hands were tied—and getting legal to approve a deal at the right price point would be impossible. An outcome she had completely dismissed.

It wasn't that Fi didn't deserve the title; her HumDinger was one of the best pie recipes Kennedy had ever had the pleasure to make. The tasting experience was even better. But Kennedy had put everything into her Apple Harvest Citrus Pie—and Sweetie Pies. Her entry was good enough to go head to head with the incumbent—and even win. It just depended on where the judges' preference fell when it came to traditional versus something a bit bolder.

"You and I both know that there have been no whispers," Ali said, resting her pitchfork against the booth to grab a plate of Kennedy's pie. In between her shifts as the scarecrow of the pumpkin patch, she'd managed three complete rounds of tasting. "Judges can't say boo until they've made their final decision."

"Well, maybe *whisper* was the wrong word. Barbara Cooper does have a rather loud shrill to her voice. But she said this year's HumDinger was better than last." Fi patted her coifed hair. "I believe this entry has a *gene se qua* that has been missing in years past."

Kennedy didn't know what special thing Fi had added, but she was confident the woman spoke fluent French— when she chose.

Ali rolled her eyes. "Barbara Cooper isn't a judge."

"Well, she's the editor over at *Southern Cooking Magazine*, so the woman has clout."

"How long are they going to stay back there?" Kennedy asked, scanning the crowd for a sight of the judges. "They disappeared into the town hall over an hour ago."

"A hundred and one entries are a lot to consider," Ali said around a mouthful of pie. "They narrow it down to the top ten front runners, then hold a closed tasting in the mayor's office."

"That's why we had to submit two pies," Fi explained.

"My money's on you." Ali sent an apologetic shrug Fi's way. "Sorry, Ms. Callahan, but Kennedy's pie is a clear winner. It follows all of the requirements of the contest, but pushes the limits."

"Are you calling me a rule breaker?" Kennedy thought back to all the rules she'd broken with Luke and giggled.

"No, you just like to see how far you can bend them," Luke said, walking up behind her, his voice pitched low enough to send a warm sensation sliding through her body.

Kennedy turned around and her heart flipped. *Oh my*, did he ever look good. Dark jeans, blue sweater, and rugged man good. His hair was windblown, his cap said TWO BAD APPLES, but beneath the sexy cider guy persona was the same hungry look that he'd had last night during their tasting—in bed.

"What are you doing here?" she asked. "I thought you were working the cider booth."

With all the apple enthusiasts and media present, Hawk and Luke had set up a booth at the entry to the competition, to hand out samples and create a buzz. It was working— their booth had been busy all day.

"Hawk is taking over so I could come and sample your pie," he said, and that warm sensation headed south, stopping below her belly button.

"Great," Ali said, throwing her hands up. "I told the kids to throw pumpkins at the big bad Hawk in the pumpkin patch after they announce the winners. Now, who I am supposed to scare with my pitchfork?"

"The judges are back," Paula said, so excited her cane wasn't even touching the ground as she toddled over. "They're about to announce the winners and I overheard someone saying that it was nearly a tie."

"Nearly a tie?" Excitement and a whole lot of panic flooded Kennedy's system at the thought. She was about to get her wish—the hard truth of whether she was cut out for this place. A place she'd come to think of as home, and a shop she'd come to think of as hers. Then there was Luke and his mom, both connected to this town, her shop, and her growing sense of home.

Kennedy had always prided herself on the ability to handle the truth. But this time the truth and her happiness were all tied up into one complicated knot of emotions and possibilities—which settled painfully in her chest.

A warm hand slid around hers and gave a little squeeze. "It doesn't matter what's in the envelopes, or whose name they call," Luke said. "There was no other pie talked about as much as yours. People even asked me if I thought it was good enough to beat the Callahan HumDinger."

"You're right, son. Who cares what the judges think." Fi gave Luke's arm a pat, then tipped her SECOND PLACE IS THE FIRST LOSER visor. "Yet here we all are, standing around waiting to hear who takes first."

Kennedy ignored this. "What did you say?"

"Callahan or Sinclair, didn't matter. All of the pies are Sweetie Pies, but my personal favorite is the Apple Citrus."

"Because I used your dad's apples?" she asked, not caring that his opinion mattered so much.

"Because it reminds me of you. Of our day in the sunroom," he whispered, and if there were any doubt that she had fallen in the past few weeks, that one sentence confirmed it. Kennedy was desperately in love with Luke Callahan.

"Your daddy's apples, huh?" Fi said, eyeing Luke with suspicion.

They hadn't told anyone about their relationship, probably because they hadn't defined it with each other. But it didn't take a genius to see that there was more heat generated between the two of them than was used to bake the hundred or so pies.

A mic turned on as the mayor took the podium and all eyes went to the stage. All eyes except for Kennedy's. Hers stayed right on Luke with his handsome face, strong shoulders, and gentle spirit. He not only carried the weight of the world on those big shoulders, but he'd managed to make her world a little easier.

Brighter.

Luke didn't move, just stared at the stage. "What?"

"Nothing...everything...never mind," Kennedy said, feeling silly.

He turned just his head, his eyes lit with humor. "That really narrows it down."

She sighed. "I just wanted to say thank you."

That got his attention. "Go on," he said, his gaze zeroing in on her. And to be at the center of that kind of intense focus was unnerving—and thrilling.

"Thank you," she said to his chest. "For helping me with today and for believing in me when I didn't have the courage to believe in myself. I wasn't ready to give up, but I couldn't figure out how to stay and fight."

"Kennedy." He cupped her chin and tilted it up. "I made a call and showed you some apples; you did the rest."

She shook her head, realizing that it didn't matter if she won or lost, because right now, with him looking at her all soft and ooey-gooey, she felt as if she'd already won.

Sure, without the Gold Tin, it would be harder to make a go of Sweetie Pies, but not impossible. She'd come to Destiny Bay to take a chance on something great, make a new life for herself, and possibly find a home—and a place where she could be happy. She'd found that—and so much more.

The way her heart swelled confirmed it.

"When I got here, I wasn't sure if I'd ever fit into a place like this, where people care for their neighbors. It was so different from where I grew up." She placed her hand on his chest. "How I grew up, but now I can't imagine ever going back to that kind of life."

"Kennedy—"

"No, wait," she said and felt his heart pick up beneath her hand. "I know you're going to say you were just being neighborly, but you gave me something to fight for, Luke. Made me realize that it doesn't matter if I win or not, I will get that contract with Cosmo, or maybe one of the other venders I met today. Bottom line is, you made me feel like I belonged even when I made your job harder. You showed me I can build a life here, make relationships, and find my happiness. You make me happy, Luke, and for that I wanted to say thank you."

She watched as Luke's face softened, his posture curled in around hers as if wanting to be right there with her, but his smile never came. "Kennedy—"

"Good afternoon, ladies and gentleman," the mayor's voice boomed through the microphone. "Welcome to the Sixty-eighth Annual Gold Tin Apple Pie Competition. A hundred and one pies were baked and tasted, and our seven esteemed judges have carefully cast their votes." The mayor held up three envelopes, each leafed in a different color metal, and the crowd cheered. "There are three winners in my hand, and I have to say the margin between Gold and Silver was the closest it's ever been. Now on to the winners.

"On behalf of the National Apple Council, I'd like to congratulate our Bronze Tin winner." The mayor opened the first envelope. "Entry number 71, Sara-Lynn of Pie in the Sky, from Aberdeen, Texas, for her Poached Apple Pie with Moonshine and Caramel Glaze."

"You got this," Ali said over the cheering crowd.

"I hope so," Kennedy said, because even though she'd just said it didn't matter if she won or lost—she totally wanted to win. She wanted to prove her pie had what it took to stand out. That she had that *gene se qua*, even if people like her mom and Philip overlooked it.

Luke hadn't and he knew what special was. Just look at his family, his friends, his hometown. He was surrounded by amazing and wonderful people every day, and yet he saw something in her that was impressive and worthy. And it was time she started seeing that for herself.

"And the Silver Tin goes to..." The mayor took his time opening the envelope. "Entry number 101, Kennedy Sinclair of Sweetie Pies, from Destiny Bay, for her Apple Harvest Citrus Pie."

Kennedy strained to hear over the blood pounding through her ears, but she was pretty sure that her name had been called—but not for the Gold Tin. A hard concept to take in because she'd given it everything she had, but it somehow wasn't enough. Which was strange, because she felt as if it were. Believed deep down that her pie was a winner.

She turned to Luke and heard herself say, "I'm sorry."

His expression was concern and something that made her stomach queasy. "Why are you apologizing? You just won second place in the biggest apple pie competition in the country."

"I know, but..." So much was riding on this. So many people were counting on her. Cosmo, Paula, her bingo team. Luke. They'd all helped her, invested time and belief into her. And she couldn't help thinking that she'd somehow let them down.

"No *but*s, sweetness," Luke said, so much affection in his voice she felt it hard to swallow. "It was the closest margin in the contest's history, and you took on a sixteen-time champion with a pie you created a week ago. That is nothing to apologize about."

She managed a watery smile. "You're right, I took a risk, and I shouldn't regret it."

"Whoa." He stilled. "But do you? Regret it?"

Pushing through the disappointment, she thought back to her journey. How she got here, how the recipe and this day had come about, and suddenly Silver felt pretty damn good. "No. I don't."

"Well, good to hear," Cosmo said, joining them. "Because it was a solid pie, a true contender." He sounded as proud as if she'd just won the Gold.

"I'm sorry, Cosmo, I know this wasn't what we were hoping for."

"Maybe not, but that pie impressed the hell out of me." He took off his hat. "You, Miss Sinclair, impress the hell out of me."

"You're impressed by premade crust, Mo," Fi said, and Kennedy turned back around, surprised to find the older woman had come back over and was standing by her side.

"Fiona, if you're here to gloat, now is not the time," Cosmo said sternly.

Fi's face fell at his words. "I wouldn't gloat at a time like this. Even though the girl and I differ in opinion some of the time, she's a part of this family now. And when family is in need, we rally." She looked at Kennedy and pursed her lips. "This is my rally face."

Kennedy laughed, and the weight of the disappointment that came with competing like a warrior and walking away with the consolation prize lightened. She knew Fi wasn't just referring to the Sweetie Pies family, but the greater family that made up this incredible town of Destiny Bay.

"Thank you, Fi." Kennedy hugged her. "And congratulations, your HumDinger is amazing."

Fi waved her off. "Don't thank me just yet. That Gold Tin could belong to anyone here. Celebrating would be premature." She eyed Cosmo. "Real women don't go for the premature stuff."

Kennedy wanted to point out that it could go to almost anyone there, anyone except her and Sara-Lynn, but the mayor was talking again.

"And this year's Gold Tin winner is a surprising mix of old and new." The crowd held its breath as the mayor opened the third, and final, envelope. Paula and Fi exchanged a look that Kennedy couldn't decipher, and Cosmo squeezed the rim of his hat. "Entry number 9, Kennedy Sinclair from Sweetie Pies, for her Deep Dish HumDinger."

"Oh my God," Ali screamed. "You won!" She hugged Kennedy then grabbed her shoulders. "You! Won!"

The breath rushed out of Kennedy's lungs. People turned to stare, a round of congratulations exploded around her, but she found it hard to understand what was happening. Felt the familiar embarrassment creep up, knowing she'd have to explain to everyone that her pie wasn't chosen. She wasn't picked.

"I'm not the one," she said, looking at Luke, everything blurring around her. "I don't know what happened, but they got it wrong. I'm not the one."

"They got it right, child," Fi said.

"I don't understand." She felt the first sting of tears behind her eyes.

"You're the one," Fi said with a smile. "I was getting ready to enter my pie this morning and someone told me that the true test of a pie was in the recipe." By the way Cosmo and Paula were grinning, she knew they were the two someones.

"I snuck into the shop when you were busy loading the car and stole two of the HumDingers you'd baked this morning," Paula said, giddy at the idea of stealing something.

"Then I entered your pies," Fi finished.

"Why would you all do that?" Kennedy asked the collection of people whom she'd come to consider family.

"That pie belongs to Sweetie Pies," Fi explained. "I had my time, and now it's your time."

"But I didn't win," she said to Cosmo, knowing that the truth was the only way she'd feel comfortable moving forward—even if it meant moving forward without a corporate client. "It was Fi's recipe that won."

"I wasn't making up that part about Barbara Cooper saying this year's entry was better," Fi said, taking Kennedy's hands in her frailer ones. "Those pies had a *gene se qua* that is unique to you and your baking style. And the judges tasted it."

"A *gene se qua* that Kline Fine Foods would love to sell in our stores," Cosmo added, and Kennedy felt like laughing and crying all at the same time.

"Before I can agree . . . " Kennedy turned to her mentors, that burning sensation getting worse by the minute. "I want to make sure that Fiona and Paula are at every meeting we have, so that they are aware of what is going on, and can extend their wisdom when I need it."

"You don't have to do that," Paula said, her face beaming with pride—pride for Kennedy. "We sold you the shop because we believed you were the perfect person to take over. So wherever you decide to take Sweetie Pies will be the right direction."

"Fi?" Kennedy asked.

"As long as my picture is on every box that goes out, I'm good."

"Then we're good?" Kennedy asked, her chest so full of hope she was sure it would explode.

"We're better than good." Cosmo put his hat back on.

"You know what this means?" Luke asked.

Kennedy's heart sank at the realization. She'd been so busy thinking about her own problems, she'd forgotten about Luke's. "That you have to find new apples?"

Kennedy felt warm hands settle on her shoulders. "That your stubborn streak is powerful enough to enter one pie and walk away with two awards. And you know how I feel about your stubborn streak."

Kennedy looked up and saw him smiling down, with an expression that spoke volumes. He was showing her that he was there, he had her back, even though this meant he had to pay top dollar to make his goal.

Last week, Luke had faced a difficult choice, and yet he'd chosen her. And he was choosing her now, stubborn streak and all.

"This is how I feel about you."

Kennedy rolled up on the tips of her toes, not stopping until her lips met his in a kiss that was soft and giving. A thank-you that couldn't be said with words, and a promise that she was too scared to say. She heard Paula clap and Fi chuckle. Ali, well, she was bemoaning the fall of a good woman. But Kennedy didn't care—she was too happy to think about anything but Luke. And this perfect moment.

Happy that she could stay. Here in Destiny Bay.

"You are one of the good guys, Luke." His smile faltered and Kennedy kissed his cheek. "You are."

Cosmo cleared his throat and Kennedy stepped out of Luke's arms. "I'd like to drop by the shop next week with the final contract." He paused. "As long as that's okay with you, Fiona."

Fi considered that for a long moment, where everyone was holding their breath. "Bring me flowers and maybe this time I won't hit you with the car."

Cosmo laughed, then patted Luke on the back. "I never would have thought to check in with legal about this Gold Tin title business so I'm so glad you mentioned it, Luke. It worked out better than we could have hoped."

Everything stilled, slowing to a painful stop. Kennedy's smile died, and Paula clutched her heart. Ali, she was back to clutching her pitchfork. And Luke, *oh God*, Luke was frozen. It took Cosmo a moment to realize that the air had shifted, and the celebratory joy vanished.

"You told Cosmo that it would be a legal problem to sign with me?" Kennedy asked, her throat so tight, the words cut on the way out.

"Lucas? What did you do?" Paula said, and that simple question, combined with the panicked and apologetic expression Luke wore, was like a knife to the chest.

"I guess you do love being right," Kennedy said, hating the vulnerability in her voice. She stepped back from the force of the truth, and wrapped her arms around her stomach while the shock of it all reverberated through her. "And here I thought that maybe you'd actually loved me."

He stood there silent for a moment, heartbreakingly horrified, as if he could see the pain pierce right through her chest. Her heart. Her soul. Until she was sure there was no layer left unmarked.

"Kennedy," Luke said, but this time the sound of her

name on his lips made the sick feeling in her stomach come back.

"Why don't you buy us ladies a drink," Fi said to Cosmo. "And let's let these two talk."

Kennedy didn't want to talk, she wanted to run—all the way back to her grandma's and hide. But no matter how hard she wished it, her feet refused to move.

So did her heart.

Then she remembered wishes weren't real, and apparently neither were good men.

"How could you do that?" she demanded. "You knew what it could mean for me."

"Let me explain." A statement she knew well, which was only necessary when trying to lessen the blow.

"When people get comfortable, they make room for someone with the determination and drive to move right in," she repeated, her hand covering her heart, holding it there as if the action alone would keep it from breaking.

"It wasn't like that."

"Of course it was, and I am the stupid one for letting you make me feel comfortable, because you moved right in and I didn't even wonder why."

"You weren't stupid, I was," he said, but she wasn't listening; she was too busy seeing everything for what it was.

She drew in a shaky breath, pleaded with her heart to hold it together until she was alone. But it didn't work; she felt the frayed edges pull until she was certain they would all unravel, right there. Become nothing more than discarded threads of who she was.

"The surprise dinner, the unexpected delivery, taking me to your childhood home." Her voice broke on the last word. "That was doing your due diligence, studying me to figure out what I needed from you so you could close the deal, right? You wanted your apples. Told me from the start that you would do anything to get them, and the rest of it was strategy, a play from your game book. And I fell for it."

"No." He stepped forward and her feet finally got the message and moved back. "Okay, at first it was, but then something changed, and I got to know you."

This time when the tears threatened, she couldn't stop them from flowing. Didn't want to. Because it wasn't her heart that was weeping; this time it was her soul. "What changed was you slept with me, tactical error on your part, because then your conscience kicked in and that good guy complex you are so proud of wouldn't let you screw me over. Well, guess what? You did anyway. And this. *This*"— she clutched her chest—"hurts so much worse than losing some stupid apples."

"I don't want the fucking apples," he said. "I want you, I want more of this feeling that I can't explain, but can't ever imagine losing."

Kennedy knew what it felt like to be overlooked or forgotten, but that gut-wrenching pain was nothing compared to what it felt like to be a second thought. Fi was right— second place was the first loser.

She bit her lower lip to keep it from shaking, and when she was sure she could talk without completely losing it, she said, "Well, guess what? This *feeling* you don't want to lose was never there to begin with. That's the problem with lies, Luke. Once you see them for what they are, everything that was special before suddenly seems empty." She wiped angrily at her cheeks. "And I don't want to feel empty. Not anymore. I want what everyone else seems to find so easily."

"Nothing is easy," he said. "You have to fight for what you want, give me a second chance to fight." He took her hands in his and she wanted to say yes, wanted to give him the chance, but her words stuck in her throat, creating a silence that lingered and grew until speaking became impossible.

It wasn't the comfortable silence they'd shared in the sunroom or at the cottage; this was strained and awkward. Painful. The kind of barrier that happens when one finally sees the truth through the trees. "I've fought my whole life, Luke. I guess I was looking for love this time around."

Unable to hold his gaze, Kennedy glanced around at the town square, at the people laughing and celebrating—sharing a history and a lifetime of memories that could bond as easily as they could isolate. Then she looked back at Luke and knew that she could never have what she wanted here. "The funny thing about good guys is that saying good-bye hurts so much more."

She brushed his cheek with her lips then stepped back—all the way back. And even though the words burned so hot they'd leave a mark, she said, "Good-bye, Luke."

Chapter 18

Luke worked from home all day Sunday and straight through the next few days, even pulling an all-nighter on Wednesday. When he wasn't in the orchard, he managed to find enough paperwork to keep him busy, and when that ran out, he double-checked the work orders. But now the sun was rising and he needed to head home and shower before he came back to the harvest once more.

And since he'd blown it with Kennedy, he headed across town, instead of to the cottage, where he imagined sliding into bed next to her warm body, and rousing her awake with the promise of hot coffee and an even hotter shower.

For a woman who chose a career that started with the sun, she sure loved to sleep in. So he'd have to get creative. Wouldn't be a problem since he loved getting creative with her.

Too bad his creativity was only good for dreaming, because the reality was he'd screwed up. In true Luke fashion, he'd been so focused on the big picture, he'd missed all the little signs along the way. Like the fact that he was pretty sure he loved her.

Shutting off the engine, he checked his phone. He had a dozen texts; a few from his mom, one from a customer, the rest from Hawk. None from Kennedy.

He thought about calling her again, but knew today was her big day with Cosmo. And he hadn't managed to get over ruining her last big moment.

There was a lot he couldn't seem to get over these days. He was about to take his dad's cider national, get back his mom's property, and set things right. Yet all he could think about was that haunted look on Kennedy's face, the way she'd held it together long enough to assure everyone that she knew she hadn't been chosen—that she knew this moment had been coming all along.

And Luke, always living up to expectations, had delivered. He'd delivered a blow that took her out at the knees.

God, he was a bastard. Kennedy had come here looking for a fresh start, to make the shop a success and Destiny Bay her home. She clung to the good memories because there hadn't been a lot of them in her life. And Luke had managed to taint the few positive ones she'd created here. And for what? A business deal.

It was like his dad all over again, he thought, walking into his house and slamming the door shut behind him.

"Careful, or you'll shake the air out of my meringue."

Luke rounded the kitchen corner and found his mom standing behind the counter, and Hawk manning the juicer. "What are you doing here?"

Paula lifted the wooden spoon and smiled. "Making my son breakfast."

"Don't fall for it, man," Hawk said, squeezing oranges. "She lured me out of bed with the promise of a home-cooked meal. Flapjacks, bacon, sticky buns, the works. When I showed up, she handed me an apron and a bag of oranges. That was three gallons ago. Haven't seen a single sticky bun."

"You can't celebrate without mimosas, and that cartoned juice doesn't cut it."

Hawk looked over his shoulder. "This is the first I'm hearing of mimosas, man. I say run while you can."

"He'll do no such thing," Paula said, pulling a third apron out of the top drawer, when Luke didn't even know he owned one. "Now suit up. You're in charge of the pancakes. The Stark family should be arriving in a few minutes and they'll be hungry."

"Stark family?"

"Ah, shit," Hawk grumbled.

"Why are they coming here?" Luke asked Paula, his eyes squarely on Hawk, who went back to juicing as if the end of world hunger depended on it.

"They're coming to get the papers signed for Bay View Orchards," she said. "Now can you get the pancakes going? The ham is almost ready to come out and I'll need the griddle for the hash browns. Nobody likes mushy hash browns."

"Nobody likes a snitch either," Luke said, looking at Hawk. "And I'm not ready to make the offer."

"And I'm not ready to admit having a numskull for a son either, but life moves forward and here we are." She set down the spoon. "Did you think I wouldn't find out?"

Luke let out a breath. "I didn't want to get your hopes up in case the deal fell through. I know how much that house meant to you; I couldn't stomach the thought of you losing it twice."

"I'm not going to lose the house," Paula said, exasperated. "And I was talking about how you misled that poor girl, then broke her heart."

"I didn't mislead her," he said honestly. He'd been a straight asshole from the start. And she'd still accepted him as he was. "I needed the apples to close a deal with..." He sighed. "Long story short, I thought I was saving Bay View Orchards, doing what dad would have wanted."

"Your dad would have wanted to you act with compassion," she said, and Luke felt all of the shame and disappointment ball up. But then his mom lowered her voice and took his hand. "And, son, your dad would have taken one look at how that girl made you smile, brought the life back to your eyes, and he would have wanted you to go with your heart."

"Even if it meant not getting you your house back," Luke said.

"How about you guys take this in the family room and I'll finish up here," Hawk offered.

Paula put her hands on her hips. "Just because I'm not looking your way, don't think that means I'm not talking to you, too, Bradley."

"Yes, ma'am," Hawk said, sounding thoroughly scolded.

"The deal with the Starks is between me and them," Luke said, making it clear that he wasn't backing down. He'd given up a lot for this to happen, and he'd be dammed if his mom stepped in and messed it up. "And I think Dad would have done whatever it took to make sure you were able to sit in your sunroom and watch the waves, just like he promised."

Paula's eyes glazed over. "Is that why you're doing this, to fix the mess your dad left behind?"

Luke shrugged. He didn't know why he was doing it anymore. Maybe it had started out as him trying to fulfill his dad's last wish, but somewhere along the way, he was ashamed to say, he did it to prove that he wasn't the kind of guy who bailed on family when they needed him the most.

Even though that was exactly what he'd done to Kennedy.

"Oh, Luke." Paula walked around the counter and cupped his cheek. "No house can give me back what I lost. It was never about that sunroom; it was about sitting by your dad's side, sharing the beauty of the world with the one person who I wouldn't have to explain it to."

Paula's eyes filled with sadness and a quiet understanding. "Your dad read me better than I read myself, and vice versa. That's what love does. So I know that he wouldn't want this. He wouldn't want you living your life to make up for something you didn't do. I knew the company was in trouble; I could have called you at any moment to ask for help."

"I would have come," Luke said past the emotion in his throat.

"I know you would have, but your dad and I wanted to go through this alone, just the two of us. Maybe that was selfish, but we didn't want to spend our last months together fixing things; we just wanted to be together. And we got that time, and it was perfect, but now it's your time."

The same words Fi had said to Kennedy.

Luke thought about the past few years, how every thought and action he'd made was through the filter of how it would affect his family. Then he wondered what it would be like to start a day without expectations. Start every day waking up next to someone who read him better than he read himself.

And that, *that*, would make him happy. Get rid of this emptiness Kennedy had warned him about that felt like it was eating him whole. Only she'd said good-bye, made her stance on a second chance clear, and the best thing he could do for her was to give her space. So that she didn't feel like she had to leave to find her home.

"I don't want to make it worse," he said, running a hand down his face. "For her."

"The only way you can make this worse is to let her think you don't care," Paula said quietly. "You've got a girl down there about ready to make the biggest deal of her life and she wants nothing more than to have somebody stand by her side and share her beautiful moment."

"She's not leaving?" he asked, because last weekend she'd said good-bye, and it had seemed so final.

"The girl's got more pluck than that," his mom said, and a huge wave of relief rolled over him. Of course she wouldn't leave—Kennedy was one of the strongest people he knew. She'd picked herself up and pushed forward. He loved that about her.

"She's staying," he said almost to himself.

"She's staying, delivered her first payment yesterday," Paula said as if she'd never doubted Kennedy. Something Luke would never do again. "Only Cosmo's coming in today and she's all alone, her apples are still hanging from the trees, and come tomorrow she'd going to have to find someone to help her deliver." Paula leveled him with a look. "Do you want her calling someone else, asking them to be a part of that moment?"

"No," Luke said without hesitation. In fact, he wanted to spend all the beautiful moments with Kennedy, the rough ones, too. He wanted to spend every single moment he could with her. No expectations and no expiration.

Paula smiled and pulled him in for a hug, and every muscle melted into her. She might be a foot smaller, but she gave hugs that could make a grown man weep. And Luke nearly did.

With a pat to the back, she looked him in the eye. "That's what I thought. Now, I suggest you shower, then get yourself down there before she forgets all of your good qualities, and only remembers the bad ones."

"What bad ones?" Luke asked.

"I have a list," Hawk offered. "It's on the wall in the women's room at the bar. Want me to call the cleaning guy and have him read it off to you?"

"No." He already knew, could write that list himself. Hell, he'd shown every one of them to Kennedy. Regret and a nasty collection of bad decisions coiled in his stomach. "I doubt she'll even want to see me."

"Of course she will," Paula said gently. "That girl might not like you very much right now, but I know she loves you. And there's always a second chance when it comes to love." At this point, the only way he stood a chance was if love came with nine lives.

"What about the Starks?" he asked, knowing that was a problem he could fix.

"Hawk and I will handle them," Paula said, walking back to pick up her spoon. "Since he's buying Bay View Orchards."

"What? No way," Luke said.

Hawk rolled his eyes. "Told you he'd freak."

Luke walked around the counter to get in his face. "Yeah, because *we* already talked about this, and decided that *you* have sunk enough money into this—"

Paula inserted herself between the two boys and raised her spoon with intent. Even though she came up to their chests, they both backed down. "That contract said that our family had the first right of refusal on the property, and last I checked, Hawk is family. Is he not?"

Luke sighed. "Yes."

"Then are you going to stand there and tell me which son is allowed to buy that property?"

"No, ma'am," Luke said, and Hawk smirked behind her back at Luke.

"Good, because Bradley is as much mine as you are, and if he's going to be a partner in this company, then he needs to bring some apples to the table."

"A partner?" Hawk said, and this time Luke smirked. "In Callahan Orchards?"

"Yes, dear, catch up," Paula said. "It was what Orin wanted, we just didn't trust your wife, but now that she's gone, it's time to bring the family back together. Not to mention, you're a grown man. You were a son to us, and you need a home of your own."

"I have a home." Hawk blanched. "I'm buying the apples for the business and the house for you."

It was Hawk's cheeks that Paula patted this time. "Nonsense, you have a place above the bar. You're never going to catch a wife living there."

Luke heard Hawk ramble off a list of reasons why living above the bar worked for him, but Luke wasn't listening; he was too busy grabbing his coat. Kennedy's shop opened in less than an hour and he had a lot to get done if he was going to prove that he deserved a chance at being her partner.

A chance at earning her love back.

* * *

Wednesday came surprisingly quick. Once word spread that Destiny Bay's own Shop Girl had taken two titles, the store was a never-ending hive of activity, which helped distract her from the pain. Kennedy hurt more than she'd thought possible. The loss went deeper than anything she'd ever experienced—even with Philip and her mom.

This kind of loss was the kind one never got over. The past few days were proof of that. She was trying to move on, only she found herself going back and replaying every moment, desperate to figure out what had been real—and what had been a lie.

No matter how many times she told herself it was all a lie, she couldn't get past how real it had felt to her. Then she would remind herself that if it had been real, he would have come by to check on her at least. He'd left a few messages that first day, but she hadn't been ready to talk, didn't know if she'd ever be ready. A nonissue really, since she hadn't heard a word from him in three days.

So yesterday, after a much-needed cry—and a caramel pumpkin pie—she dried her face off and reminded herself that she'd been through worse. That this, too, would pass, and she might be a Sinclair, but she wasn't a quitter. So she'd called Cosmo, told him she was ready to sign those papers, but she'd need an advance—which she used to make her first payment to Paula and Fi.

Then she focused on all the good things happening in her life. Possibilities that she'd never imagined, right there, just waiting for her. All she had to do was sign on the line and embrace her new life.

But when the bell above the door jingled, all the oxygen vacated her lungs, and she decided that she didn't want a new life. She wanted the one she'd spent the past few weeks building with Luke.

"Hey, sweetness," he said, standing at the door, the morning sun casting a silhouette over half of his face. She squinted to see if it wasn't a lack of sleep playing tricks on her.

Nope, it was Luke. Standing in her shop, looking dirty and tired and so handsome she ached to run into his arms. Only to remember that the embrace she'd once thought of as safe had shattered her world, to a point that it still ached to breathe. So she held the counter instead, reeled it in, and reminded herself she had no idea why he was here. "Can I help you?"

He took off his ball cap and walked toward the counter, her heart pounding with every step he took. "I have a delivery for the owner of the shop."

"Deliveries come through the back door."

"This delivery needed to be done face-to-face." His eyes were calm and locked on hers. "Through the front door." He slid a delivery slip across the counter.

With a shaky hand, Kennedy took it. It was a purchase order for the remaining three acres of apples, with a bold red DELIVERED stamped across the top. She handed it back. "You don't have to do this. I made a few calls to other companies."

"Well, call them back because it's done."

"Done?" Her face went slack and she looked out the window. What the hell was she going to do with three acres of apples at once?

"Well, I have the truck loaded and just need to know how much you want delivered and how much you want stored. Free of charge, of course."

"Of course." She forced herself to smile through the tears. He hadn't come out of love, he'd come out of moral obligation, because she was another person he was afraid to disappoint. Not because he realized he didn't want to be without her. "I can e-mail you about the delivery size and times."

"I estimated how many you'd need. Based on past orders and the expected increase due to Kline Fine Foods." He rattled off some amounts and days as if every word wasn't breaking her heart.

"Thank you," she managed, hoping he'd just leave. It was taking everything she had not to lose it, and she was holding on by a thread, but if he kept talking to her like another customer, she'd break—and wouldn't that be humiliating.

He took the slip from her hand, then walked around the counter and cupped her hips. "I also came to tell you that I'm sorry. I'm sorry about the apples, and the games, and ruining your day Saturday." He pulled her closer. "But most of all I'm sorry that I let you walk away thinking that I hadn't chosen you."

"Where are you going with this, Luke?" she whispered, because more than anything she wanted to be chosen. She wanted Luke to choose her, because her heart had chosen him and he was there to stay.

"When I said I didn't know what this was, I lied," he

said. "I knew what it was, almost from the start, but I was too scared of losing you to admit it."

"And now?" she asked, afraid to hope.

"Now, I'm scared that I've lost my chance. Lost my shot at something beautiful and special." He ran his thumb over her cheek. "I'm terrified that I lost the woman I love."

She sucked in a breath. "You love me?"

"Every single part of you." He put a finger to her lips. "And before you give me a disclaimer of the parts I don't know, know this. You are the most incredible, sweet, amazing, and stubborn woman I have ever met. When I am with you, I see the world differently, because I see it through your eyes. The more I see, the more I love you."

"Luke," she breathed.

"I don't need to land some big deal or buy my mom that house to prove I'm a good guy; being around you is all the proof I need." He gave her a gentle kiss. "Being with you is all the proof I need, because you are as good as they come, sweetness. And if you'll let me, I will spend the rest of my days by your side, proving that you are so special to me, I'd choose you every time."

Barely able to speak through the tears, she wrapped her arms around his neck. "I choose you back."

"Thank Christ." Luke wrapped his arms around her and pulled her against him in a kiss that seemed to span eternity. "You're my view, Kennedy. You're what I want to look at forever."

And in that moment, Kennedy knew what forever felt like, and when she kissed him back, she knew what it tasted like, too. Forever was the same as coming home.

Romance blooms again in Destiny Bay...

Look for *Feels Like the First Time*, the next
book in Marina Adair's Destiny Bay series,
available in April 2017.

A special preview follows.

Chapter 1

Nothing pissed off Bradley Hawk quite like being played. Except, being played while wearing nothing but boxers and an epic case of bedhead.

For a guy whose front door faced Main Street, to grab his hockey stick, forgoing jeans, and rush out the door was a bonehead move. But he'd heard the alarm sound, the one rigged to let him know if someone was tampering with his inventory, and acted without thinking.

A trait he'd worked hard to overcome, with little success.

Over the past few weeks, several empty kegs had disappeared from his bar. Not enough to call the cops, but enough to make him think one of his employees was selling them on Craig's List.

It wasn't about the money. For Hawk, it came down to getting screwed over by someone he trusted. Because the Penalty Box wasn't just his sports bar and grill, it was his home. The employees his family. And he refused to let his home be torn apart from the inside.

Not this time.

So pants be damned, Hawk raced down the steps of his apartment, which sat above the bar. The wood planks were cold beneath his bare feet, slick from the fog that had rolled in off the Pacific Ocean.

It was late spring in Destiny Bay and Mother Nature was acting as if she were menopausal, her mood fluctuating from hot-flashes to freeze your nuts off. This morning's mood was the later.

The sun was beginning to rise over the lush peaks of the Cascade Range, painting the sky a hazy mosaic of purples and blues. It was barely past dawn.

Meaning, it was too early for this shit.

Unfortunately, it wasn't too early for the Senior Steppers to be out. Dressed in their matching velour sweat suits, white walking shoes, and knit caps, the group was hitting their stride and passing Steel Magnolia, the garden art shop next door, when Hawk hit the sidewalk.

A collection of shocked gasps filled the air. Two of the ladies even clasped their chests in a way that had Hawk skidding to a stop.

"Sorry, if I scared you, ladies," Hawk apologized, dropping his hockey stick to a nonthreatening pose by his side. "Did you see anyone suspicious walking around the parking lot?"

"We were too busy staring at your stick to notice," Fiona Callahan, his best friend's aunt said, her eyes dipping embarrassingly low. "About time too. We started to feel left out, seeing as all of the other girls in town had their peek."

"Can I get a picture with me holding it?" Margret Collin, the senior center's Sunshine Girl, said pulling out her phone. "For Instagram. I'm trying to build my following. And me holding a Stanley Cup winner's stick would gain a lot of likes."

It would gain Hawk a never-ending supply of shit from his friends.

"Maybe later, I gotta go," he said, ignoring the giggles, and a catcall from the pastor's wife that would make even the most confident man blush. The flash that lit up the parking lot as he raced toward the loading dock behind the bar, *that* was hard to ignore.

Hawk reached the dock, saw the stack of empty kegs that he'd left out as bait, and nothing else. No prowler, no group of employees plotting how to take down the bar one keg at a time. He spun around looking in all directions, his eyes expertly scanning the shadows for movement. Nope, Hawk was completely alone—and missing three kegs.

Crap.

He lowered his stick once again and considered accepting the loss. That way he could go back to bed and pass out until next week. A decent night's sleep would bring some perspective to the situation.

Ever since he and his best friend's company, Two Bad Apples Hard Cider, had taken off, Hawk was busting his ass to fulfill cider orders by day, and running his bar at night.

Today marked his first day off in three months, and he'd be damned if he was going to spend it in a dark parking lot, contemplating who was screwing with his stuff.

Determined not to waste another second, Hawk headed for his apartment. He'd made it as far as the middle of the parking lot when a loud noise came from the back of the garden art shop next door.

Normally this wouldn't set off red flags, since the owner

tended to work at the most infuriating hours—namely the five hours Hawk actually got to sleep.

But this wasn't the normal power-saw cutting through steel grating he'd come to know and loathe. This was more of a scraping of metal across the concrete.

Like someone dragging a keg through Steel Magnolia's back room.

Hawk closed his eyes and let out a slow breath, for the first time feeling sorry for the poor SOB who had the misfortune of trying to hide stolen property in Ali Marshal's work space. Ali didn't like people invading her space, and she might be small enough to pass for Tinkerbell, but she packed one hell of an attitude.

Not to mention she was lethal with the blowtorch.

"You might want to come out," Hawk said crossing the parking lot and walking up to the back door of the repurposed machine shop. "You're safer facing the music and turning yourself in, trust me."

When he got no response in return, Hawk accepted his fate and pushed through the unlocked door. Only instead of finding one of his night staff huddled in the corner with his kegs, he found his thief standing over his missing metal canisters in a pair of combat boots, a welder's mask pulled low, and a blowtorch in hand.

A lit blowtorch.

"What the hell are you doing?" he hollered as the red flame closed in on one of the kegs.

Ali's head lifted in his direction, and from behind the mask he could feel the narrowing of those intense green eyes. The blowtorch flickered twice in warning.

Hawk jumped back right before the heat would have singed his chest hairs—and other, more crucial, parts. But that wasn't what had him stepping back. Ali had spent the better part of the past decade threatening to roast his nuts, so that was nothing new. What was new, was the light blue, strapless number that hugged her curves and showed off those toned legs.

Ali either wore coveralls or denim, always black and always with a *Bite me* attitude that left men panting or praying for their lives. Men who weren't named Hawk.

Not only had he known Ali when she was a pierced nosed teen, she was also his sister-in-law. Well, she had been before Hawk's wife, Bridget, traded him in for a shinier model. He'd lost the ball when Bridget kept yanking his chain, but kept the kid sister.

Although, she didn't look like a kid in that dress. Which in no way excused the sharp jolt of awareness that was anything but brotherly. Something else he'd been trying to overcome as of late.

"One mark on my keg and I'll post a photo of you in that dress on my timeline," Hawk said, folding his arms across his chest—making damn sure his eyes didn't stray below the chin.

The blowtorch flickered out and she flipped her mask up—and yup, those emerald eyes were skewering him. "*Your* kegs. Huh?" She set the blowtorch on the table and took off her work gloves. "Funny, since they were sitting on *my* side of the easement."

"The easement is on *my* property, giving you and your customers access to your side of the parking lot."

"My latest customer wanted a garden fountain made from kegs. How was I to know that those weren't for me?"

"I don't know, maybe by the Two Bad Apples logo on the side of each and every keg," he said taking in the nearly finished fountain, confirming, first off, that Ali was one hell of a talented artist. And secondly, exactly where his other kegs had disappeared to. "If that wasn't clear enough, then the other ninety-seven sitting in my loading dock should have been a clue."

She smiled, all smug and attitude. "Right. I guess I can see that now. Next time you might consider keeping them on your side of the easement to avoid any confusion. Or perhaps post a sign there for folks to see. Kind of like the Parking for Steel Magnolias Customers Only signs your bar patrons continue to ignore."

Ali took off her mask and set it on the work bench, leaving her in just her boots and that dress. Those chocolate brown curls of hers, once released, tumbled down to brush her bare shoulders and frame that expressive face.

God, she was stunning.

"Hawk?" she asked in that self-conscious tone that always got to him. So when she crossed her arms in front of her, a clear sign she was picking up on vibes he'd tried to keep in check, he locked his focus on her face, even though he knew her current stance must be doing incredible things for her cleavage. "What are you staring at?"

"You're soldering in a dress." He waved his hand as if all put out over having to explain the obvious. "I was just checking to make sure you hadn't burned yourself."

"It's just a dress," she said acting as if it was nothing out of the ordinary. But for whatever reason her in that dress was extraordinary. It was also a sign that something was up. And unlike his patrons, it was a sign he refused to ignore.

"It's not just a dress, and you know it."

"Says the man breaking and entering in his skivvies,"

she snapped, confirming something was up. "And really, do you have to wave your stick around all the time? As your friend, it's my duty to tell you it's getting a little embarrassing. I mean, most of the town has already seen it."

She punctuated the word friend, yet, strangely enough, she was looking at him as if he were a sculpture she couldn't wait to get her hands on. Or rip out his throat.

Either way it overrode the F-word he was coming to hate.

Hawk casually swung his hockey stick in his trademark *winning goal* motion, tightening his abs and flexing his biceps. "Some ladies out front were begging to hold it."

Ali rolled her eyes, but not before Hawk noticed her breath quicken. "Tell Fi she can buy a bigger one online for twenty bucks. Now if you don't mind, I have work to do."

"Have at it," Hawk said, and then, he had no idea what came over him. Maybe it was the uncertainty in her gaze, or maybe it was that sexy as hell dress. But he snatched her cell off the workbench and, flipping it to camera mode, snapped a picture.

Ali's face went slack, she looked down at the light blue silk that would be the talk of the town, and launched around the workbench, grabbing for her phone. Which Hawk held over her head and out of reach.

"Give it back, Bradley." she said jumping up to snatch it out of his hands. But her five-feet-nothing was no match for his six-feet-five-inches of bad ass hockey player moves. Her elbows though, those had some serious force behind them.

"Not until you tell me what the dress is about, Aliana." When she didn't elaborate, just locked eyes with him, he added, "One swipe and it goes viral."

"Fine." She poked him in the peck. Hard. "One of my sculptures is going to be in a magazine."

"You've had a dozen of your sculptures in magazines. None of them inspired Tiffany blue silk."

"It's the cover, and what kind of guy uses the word Tiffany blue? Oh, wait the same kind of guy who doesn't think selling hard cider is a pussy job."

"Cider is the next working man's beer. The dress?" He lifted a brow.

"Of *Architectural Digest*."

Hawk almost believed her. She'd been talking about that magazine since high school. Except there was that slight waver in her tone, one that she hadn't ever been able to hide from him. "And you were so elated, you decided to celebrate by wearing a dress at six in the morning?"

"There's a party. Now give it back." She jumped up to snatch it back, but if there was one thing that playing in the NHL for over a decade had taught Hawk, it was how to spot a deke. And Ali was using the magazine's prestige to fake him out, distract him from the real issue.

"A party?" he asked, sliding an arm around her to keep her from ramming him in the shins with her steeled toes, which only managed to press her body flush with his. Noticing her gaze went right to his mouth, he let loose a grin. "A party that requires a dress like this, is a party I'd hate to miss. So tell me, Sunshine, who's the lucky guy?"

He didn't mention that whoever the guy was he didn't deserve a woman like Ali. Or that his plan to mess with her somehow backfired, because he couldn't seem to stop looking at her lips.

"Are you offering to be my date?" A totally cool, almost bored expression crossed her face as she casually rested a hand on his chest—her fingers gliding down is abs. "Because I'm sure my mom would love to see you." She looked up at him through her long, thick lashes. "So would Bridget."

It was as if a Washington winter snow had blown through the shop. "Bridget?"

"Oh, didn't I mention?" Ali said, snatching her phone back. "Bridget's in town. Just in time for my big night. You think she'll want to hold your stick?"

About the Author

Marina Adair is a No. 1 national best-selling author of romance novels and holds a master of fine arts degree in creative writing. Along with the Sugar, Georgia series, she is also the author of the St. Helena series, The Eastons, and her upcoming Sequoia Lake series. She currently lives with her husband, her daughter, and two neurotic cats in Northern California.

As a writer, Marina is devoted to giving her readers contemporary romance where the towns are small, the personalities large, and the romance explosive. She also loves to interact with readers, and you can catch her on Twitter at @MarinaEAdair or visit her at www.MarinaAdair.com. Keep up with Marina by signing up for her newsletter at www.MarinaAdair.com/newsletter.

Fall in Love with Forever Romance

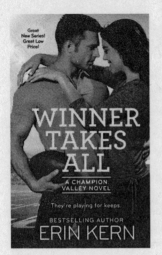

WINNER TAKES ALL
By Erin Kern

The first book in Erin Kern's brand-new Champion Valley series, perfect for fans of *Friday Night Lights*! Former football player Blake Carpenter is determined to rebuild his life as the new coach of his Colorado hometown's high school team. Annabelle Turner, the team's physical therapist, will be damned if the scandal that cost Blake his NFL career hurts *her* team. But what she doesn't count on is their intense attraction that turns every heated run-in into wildly erotic competition...

LAST KISS OF SUMMER
By Marina Adair

Kennedy Sinclair, pie shop and orchard owner extraordinaire, is all that stands between Luke Callahan and the success of his hard cider business. But when the negotiations start heating up, will they lose their hearts? Or seal the deal? Fans of Rachel Gibson, Kristan Higgins, and Jill Shalvis will gobble up the latest sexy contemporary from Marina Adair.

Fall in Love with Forever Romance

MEANT TO BE MINE
By Lisa Marie Perry

In the tradition of Jessica Lemmon and Marie Force, comes a contemporary romance about a former bad boy seeking redemption. After years apart, Sofia Mercer and Burke Wolf reunite in Cape Cod. Their wounds may be deep, but their sizzling attraction is as hot as ever.

RUN TO YOU
By Rachel Lacey

The first book in Rachel Lacey's new contemporary romance series will appeal to fans of Kristan Higgins, Rachel Gibson, and Jill Shalvis! Ethan Hunter's grandmother, Haven, North Carolina's resident matchmaker, is convinced Gabby Winter and her grandson are meant to be together. Rather than break her heart, Ethan and Gabby fake a relationship, but if they continue, they won't just fool the town—they might fool themselves, too...

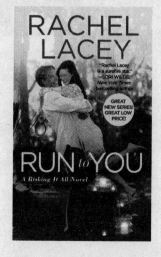

Fall in Love with Forever Romance

AN INDECENT PROPOSAL
By Katee Robert

New York Times and *USA Today* bestselling author Katee Robert continues her smoking-hot series about the O'Malleys—wealthy, powerful, and full of scandalous family secrets. Olivia Rashidi left behind her Russian mob family for the sake of her daughter. When she meets Cillian O'Malley, she recognizes his family name, but can't help falling for the smoldering, tortured man. Cillian knows that there is no escape from the life, but Olivia is worth trying—and dying—for...